Wylder Promises

by

Sarita Leone

Wylder West Series

Wylder Promises

Cover Art by *Tina Lynn Stout*

The Wild Rose Press, Inc.
PO Box 708
Adams Basin, NY 14410-0708
Visit us at www.thewildrosepress.com

Publishing History
First Edition, 2023
Trade Paperback ISBN 978-1-5092-4820-9
Digital ISBN 978-1-5092-4821-6

Wylder West Series
Published in the United States of America

Even trail dusted, Lane Hutchins made a woman's heart quicken. He had always turned heads when he'd been a young man. Time did well by him, turning his fresh, handsome features rugged and the spry step to a confident swagger.

If she had a free hand, she would use it to pat her hair, but the fabric kept her at a disadvantage. She arranged her features into what she hoped was a neutral expression as he stepped up onto the wooden planking.

"Trudy." His voice, so deep and with its southern resonance, sent butterflies spiraling low in her gut.

No one had called her that in over a decade. Her mouth went dry, and it took a moment to find her voice.

"Lane." A small jut of her chin toward her chest, but no smile. It wouldn't come. "No one calls me that anymore."

His brow furrowed as he shifted the saddlebags on his shoulder. When he reached for the bolt of fabric, she didn't resist handing it over. It had been a long time since a man carried her burdens.

"Are you married again? If so, I apologize...I wasn't aware that you'd taken on the 'missus' again."

She shook her head. "I'm not married but folks around town call me Gertie. I haven't heard the other in so long, it took me by surprise." Tilting her head to one side, she added, "Seeing you did the same. What are you doing in Wylder?"

His smile set off a new round of fluttering in her midsection. "A happy coincidence?"

Praise for Sarita Leone

"Again, author Leone treats the reader to a story filled with non-stop action as well as a deep and touching romance as it develops between two people who, while brutalized in the past, come to find in each other a balm for more than just a broken heart. Well done!"

~Wild Women Reviews on Christmas in Wylder

"This was a great Christmas story. It keeps the reader interested all the way through to the end. I thoroughly enjoyed reading this book. If you love Christmas and romantic westerns, then you will definitely want to read this book."

~ Sherrie Lea Morgan on A Wylder Christmas

Dedication

For Vito
Sempre per sempre

Chapter 1

September 1, 1880

The promise of forever swam in the depths of his eyes. The deep caramel color of good whiskey, they held her captive, offering everything she ever dreamed of—and so much more. The only place she felt truly at home, in his gaze.

"My sweet Trudy, you know I've got to leave."

Her heart stuttered in her chest. Their time together had been too brief. She wasn't ready to let him go. Not yet. Good Lord, not ever.

Her arms tightened around his shoulders, and her fingers wove into the thick, dark-brown waves that touched his jacket collar. She twined her fingertips in the curls, spiraling them around her ring finger above the gold band that shimmered in the candlelight.

A gentle fingertip to trace the two stars on the collar of his gray uniform jacket. Lieutenant Colonel. Pride swept through her. He had to return to his men. Yet she hated moments like this.

"Can a wife help it if she wants to keep her handsome husband in her arms?" She mustered a smile. Tears were for later, after he'd gone. Now, something to keep him hopeful on the battlefield, the thought of a loving wife awaiting his return. She had taken extra care this morning, wearing the blue floral

1

dress he liked so much. Hopefully the memory would bring him joy in the days ahead. "I'll never like this part, but I'm so grateful you were able to slip away for a night. Such a blessing that your regiment is nearby." She brushed a hand over his chin, sealing the feel of his warm skin in her memory so she would be able to hold it with her. A woman needed memories, too, so she let her skin linger on his. "Your men won't hardly recognize you without that scruffy beard."

He chuckled and pulled her even closer. "I'll be back home with you soon. Until then, remember to always keep the six-shooter near you. And don't worry your pretty head about me. As soon as we get those Union troops taken care of, we'll all get back to good southern living, I promise."

A final kiss, then he took his arms from her.

As he turned to walk out the door, she reached out a hand.

He couldn't go—not when she still needed him.

Not when they had a baby on the way.

Not when—

"No!" The darkness absorbed her scream as Gertie tore at the bedclothes. Her head thrashed from side to side on the pillow as horrible images flashed through her mind. "No—no, don't leave—"

"Missus Jackson, I'm very sorry but your husband—"

"No!" The word sliced the air and filled her head as she gasped for breath.

She pushed up, then jumped from the bed. Her nightdress caught on one heel, and she tumbled forward onto the hard wooden floor. On her knees, she scoured the darkness for any sign of her beloved Will, but he wasn't there.

Not anymore.

Gertie sat back on her heels and scrubbed a shaky hand over her cheeks. In her sleep she'd cried so hard the neckline of her cotton nightdress had grown damp and her skin turned clammy. The hair beside her temples escaped its braid and stuck to the tears drying on her skin.

The nightmares were so vivid. No amount of time dimmed their clarity.

She never saw Will after he left that morning to rejoin his men with the Army of Northern Virginia. Not even a corpse to bury. The moment he walked out the front door of their red-brick house in Richmond was the very last glimpse she had of her husband.

Had she known, she never would have stood on the front steps and waved as he left. No, she would have grabbed him back and forced him to abandon his command.

She would have told him about the child she carried, the precious miracle that would grow their family and make their future bright. Yes, she would have done that, had she known.

But she hadn't, and she still kicked herself for having been such a good soldier's wife, sending her man off to be killed with a smile. What a fool she'd been. What fools they'd all been, thinking the South could beat the damn Yankees.

Lord, but she hated the way her life turned out.

It had been over a decade since Will's passing, but the nightmares persisted. They came less often now, but she still could not count on getting a full night's sleep because she never knew when the terror would strike.

Or how hard it would shake her from her bed and the life she'd managed to pull together for herself.

"I'm fine." The whisper was loud in the silent house. Her heartbeat and breathing slowed to near normal, but the familiar veil of sadness fell across her shoulders. The widows' vestments were heavy, but she had grown accustomed to them and wore the invisible shroud like a shield. "He's fine."

That Will was all right, in Heaven or wherever dead Confederate soldiers went, came as her biggest wish. If only there were some way to know that he'd made it to the hereafter without incident, she might be able to drop the shroud—at least for a while. It plagued her that he'd died alone on the battlefield. Had he been scared? Did he suffer? Had he thought of her at the end? Called for her, even?

And where had he gone? Heaven, she supposed. But what did the place look like? Was he happy? Please, Lord, let him be happy. Let him not be suffering. Let him know she still loved him—and that she would love him forever.

The widows' burden, to move forward with a chunk of her heart missing while she carried the memory of her beloved so closely that nothing else mattered. Nothing else, not any of it. And not in this world, or whatever followed.

Will's passing had left her a shadow of her former self. The Trudy he loved died with him in northern Georgia. She would never live again and that proved to be a heavy cross to bear. But bear it she did—year after year and nightmare after nightmare.

She sighed. A glance out the window behind her gave no indication of time, but it didn't look as if daybreak loomed nearby. The purple-black sky dotted with shining points of light seemed primed to stay.

She knew better than to attempt to get more rest. Sleep was an elusive bedfellow who would not return, so she pushed to her feet and reached for her night jacket. Sewn from the same lightweight cotton as her nightgown, the wrapper reached to her hips and fastened down the front with a row of white buttons. A line of fancy, dark-green embroidery adorned the space beside the buttons, a decoration she'd added herself after picking up the set at Lowery's Dress Shop.

A widow, yes. Dead and buried, no. As a living, breathing woman, she deserved a nice touch here and there, so she made sure to care for herself the way she knew Will would want. It didn't come easy, that attention to her own needs, but with years of practice, she accomplished it. Most of the time.

She lit the candle on the bedside table. Then, she took a minute and arranged the bedclothes. There were rules she lived by, and one included making her bed every morning. It didn't matter that the sun wouldn't rise for hours. The bed must be fixed as soon as she left it.

She had learned there were things in life she could not control. War and the toll it exacted. The price of love and the messy aftermath of losing that blessing. What others believed or the way they treated her. Those, and so much more, were out of her hands.

Others, like the bed and her house, were under her domain, so she managed them well. One had to assert control whenever possible. The notion had gotten her through more harrowing moments than she cared to remember, so she stuck to her routine.

When the pillow had been fluffed and propped against the plain pine headboard, she picked up the candleholder, put a hand near the flickering light to keep a stray breeze from snuffing it out, and headed for the door. She pulled it wide and stepped out into the hallway. Her bare toes skimmed the hardwood floor before they made it to the rag rug runner going down the center of the space. She'd saved fabric scraps for two years to make a rug long enough to accommodate the hallway. Every time her toes sunk into its softness, a burst of pride shot through her.

Yes, she might be alone. Damaged from loss. Breathing past a shattered heart. Left adrift with no one to count on save herself. And saving herself? She'd done a lot of that in the years since Will's death.

But she was doing it. All of it. Making her way in the world. Staring down her demons, even those that came during the night—especially those that brought her back to the horrible days following her sweet man's death.

She'd made a new life for herself. Despite the heartache, pain, and loss she'd done it. And that, the knowledge that she wasn't defeated, was enough company during the long, dark hours before dawn.

That, and a cup of strong coffee, would take her through to the morning.

And whatever followed.

****

Early on a Wednesday in September and the sun hung high in the western sky. Gertie held a hand over her eyes, shading them and wondering how much time she had before noon. Not long, by the looks of it. Not a cloud to be seen, only deep blue with that big, fat sun.

6

She sighed. It amazed her how there were days like this, when she rose before the sun and got right to her chores and errands but still found herself scrambling to get everything done. Not yet midday and her bones were weary.

No rest for the wicked. A smile came upon her, from the inside out. As a child back in Richmond, the statement had scared the bloomers off her when the good, but loud, Reverend Marks made frequent use of it in his sermons. It had been punctuated by a fist slamming on the scarred wooden pulpit.

Times had hardened her. Neither the sound of a man's fist nor loud threats frightened her now. She'd endured too much to scare that easily.

She pushed the reverend from her mind and surveyed her surroundings.

This quick trip out on Bone Orchard Road to the Wylder Cemetery confirmed that the spot didn't look overly unkempt. Anyone with a family member interred might put the extra effort in when visiting to clear a weed or two at a neighboring grave. Standard kindness in the town to do so, and it kept the gravesites of even those without buried kin cleared and tidy.

The cemetery should be presentable for the Founder's Day celebrations. Granted, they were a few weeks away, but Gertie liked to have all her ducks in a row, especially since she headed the planning committee. Her third time as chair of the group, she didn't ordinarily give in to prideful views but being asked to lead it again this year made her chest puff out as far as a male grouse in heat. Unlike a bird, she didn't need to win any suitors, only give the town another event that would keep them talking for the rest of the year.

Violet Bloom, their pretty schoolteacher, did that with their Christmas party. The young woman had been in town a bit over two years and had done well by Wylder with both of her holiday events. Granted, the first year there had been a fire at the schoolhouse, and nefarious men tried to assault the teacher and her nice Chinese friend, but that couldn't be held against the woman. Besides, Violet managed to shoot one of the assailants dead, and the townsmen put the fire out before it claimed the schoolhouse.

A little excitement didn't dull a Wylder event, not even when gunshots and flames were added to the mistletoe and caroling. Violet's parties counted toward keeping the town's spirits high.

Gertie would never again be as young or beautiful as Miss Bloom, but she hoped her hard work and the fun to be had at the Founder's Day festivities helped make her contribution to Wylder's annual event calendar as appealing as the schoolteacher's. Last year had gone well, and she was determined that this year's would be even more memorable.

This close to noon, Wylder bustled. Wednesdays were considered a good day to come to town to run errands. No drunken weekend shenanigans to contend with, especially this early. But although she'd never been inside, she assumed the Five Star Saloon did a brisk business any time of day. Still, midweek attracted ranch and homestead families to town, so she wasn't surprised when she turned left onto Wylder Street and saw a line of buckboards in front of the mercantile.

She nodded to Addison Merriweather, the attorney, as she came abreast of him. A big, muscular man with a smile as wide as Medicine Bow River, it still amazed her that he spent his days upholding the law. By the size of his biceps, the man looked ready to build the town on his own, rather than keep it as lawful as possible.

He smiled and dipped his chin. "Ma'am. Pleasure to see you this morning."

Daisy Bloom, one of Violet's sisters, laid claim to the man. They were a good couple, both well-educated and kind, so she ignored the butterflies fluttering low in her belly. She had no right to be affected by another woman's man. Besides, he smiled at everyone, which proved she didn't get special treatment.

"Nice to see you, too." She nodded to where he leaned a shoulder against the doorframe. "Are you keeping clients in or out?"

A deep chuckle as he stood upright. "I would love nothing more than to be put out of business because the great citizens of Wylder became completely law-abiding." He ran a hand over his chin and raised one eyebrow. It made him look like a pirate, and in that instant, she saw that the man's charms ran deep. "However, I am not foolish enough to believe that will ever be the case. No, I'm merely between visits to the jailhouse and heading home for lunch with my lovely wife. A good time to pause and catch a bit of air, is all."

She wondered if his wife realized her good fortune. Men were plentiful in the Wyoming Territory, but they were not all nearly as upstanding as the one before her.

A breeze swept across the wooden walkway, sending the spicy scent of the man up between them. Or as fine smelling, she thought.

"Yes, I imagine anytime a fellow as busy as you can find a few minutes to relax is a good time." A line of perspiration trailed down her spine. She wished she hadn't worn the heavy chambray dress, but it had pockets, and her trip to the cemetery made it necessary to carry a few small gardening tools. Funny how the shears and spade felt heavier now than they had an hour earlier. "Well, it's been nice to see you. Please give my regards to the missus."

The attorney tipped his head. "Will do. Now, don't stay out in this heat too long." He cast a glance toward the sky. "Might be September, but the sun isn't putting away her fire just yet."

She nodded her thanks. How considerate, to worry about her becoming affected by the heat.

"Why, I will take care. I must go to the mercantile but then I'll head home."

"Sounds good."

She gave one final smile before she turned and walked away. His kindness lightened her step and, not for the first time, she felt a pang of longing. Not for Mister Merriweather—she certainly was not the kind of woman to yearn for someone else's husband—but for a man who cared how she fared. The last time she had one, she'd been a married woman.

It felt like a lifetime since those days.

A lifetime and a heartbeat, all in one, since her dearest held her in his arms.

She shook aside the sadness threatening to push away her good humor. These days, thoughts of Will were, more than at any other time of year, both a blessing and a curse. They lifted her high and dropped her to her knees. Best to keep her mind off the man, and all she'd lost, if possible.

Gertie put her hand on the door leading to the

mercantile. At least it would be cooler inside the building.

Hopefully Finn Wylder would have what she needed in stock, and she could shop without having to special order. Those orders were not guaranteed to arrive, but the celebrations were a given so she couldn't take a chance on not getting what she needed.

A deep breath of cooler air settled her tired nerves a bit. Sleepless nights, terrifying dreams, weeding the graves of the town's dead…almost too much for one soul to bear. She looked around at the shelves piled high with goods and, not for the first time, had a fleeting idea that it would be lovely if Finn had a section marked "Potential Husbands" for women like her to peruse the goods.

If wishes came true, they'd all have a kind man to cuddle up with.

But Gertie's heart knew better. Her thoughts were fanciful, not meant to become reality.

She'd had her perfect man. A once-in-a-lifetime love—and once in a lifetime didn't ever happen twice.

Chapter 2

It had been a long time since Lane Hutchins sat astride a horse such a long stretch without a break. When he had last done so he'd been a much younger man. A dozen years past, at least.

His back ached during the first week out before he crossed the Mississippi River. His legs, too. And the shoulder that plagued him during the long months while he lay in a hospital bed cried for mercy.

Then, he had almost been sure he would have to give in to his traitorous body and catch a stagecoach out west. But that would mean selling Belle, and he and the mare were practically kin. He couldn't leave the beautiful bay with anyone else, so he soldiered on. Eventually he either grew accustomed to the aches and pains the trip inflicted or his muscles strengthened along with his will, because now the discomfort didn't hardly bother him.

There'd be a period of stiffness and maybe even a bit of pain for a few days once he stopped riding, but it would be well worth it. A man only had a certain number of opportunities to serve his friends and family, so when one arose, he had to be ready to take on the challenge, even when it meant he'd pay a price for doing so.

Belle quickened her step as they rode into Wylder, almost as if she knew they were near a livery with soft bedding and sweet hay. He leaned forward and placed a palm against her neck. He couldn't ask for a better animal. She'd gotten them both clear into the Wyoming Territory without any trouble at all.

They both deserved a rest.

He found the livery without difficulty. The town's layout proved more organized than most places he had passed through. More than a jumble of listing, rotting shacks, or a row of unpainted wood buildings, Wylder had some order to it.

He passed a couple of saloons. The Five Star, with its wide wooden boardwalk and bat-wing doors, caught his eye. He'd belly up to the bar before the day faded into night.

A large building with a sign proclaiming it the Social Club brought a grin. He'd seen inside his share of "social clubs" in his lifetime. He much preferred to not pay to satisfy his needs, but every now and then the itch grew too strong to ignore so he handed over some cash to a woman willing to accommodate him. Good chance the Wylder County Social Club's doors would see him pass through them, too.

A gemstone store with a Chinese shopkeeper standing in the doorway. Back home in Virginia, that wouldn't present itself. The man nodded, his black hair hanging in a long braid down his back, so Lane touched the brim of his hat in response. Imagine that. His first howdy-do with a Chinese man. The folks back home would find it interesting—that is, if he had any left to impress with his worldliness.

Which he didn't. Aside from the man whose errand sent him westward, Lane was alone. All those he knew and loved were killed in the war or died in the subsequent years. Rebuilding Richmond had gone well for some but not for all. His kin had never been from money, and when most of the men didn't return from war, farmland went untended. Bills mounted. Banks came for land and homes that had been in the family for decades.

And the women and children scattered, finding refuge with distant family and friends.

The South as they all knew it had died. And its death left many, like Lane, alone. So, no one to impress save himself with his greeting a Chinese man on the street in broad daylight. Inconceivable in Richmond but apparently commonplace out here.

Near the gemstone shop, on the other side of Wylder Street, a bank, an attorney's office, and another office. The lettering on the plaque beside its door too small to read from the back of a horse, but through the window he spotted a man at a desk poring over a stack of papers. So, the Wild West had some brain power to go along with its grit and muscle.

A boardinghouse. He'd likely look there for a room after getting Belle settled. He needed a bath something fierce. Trail riding didn't give a man many chances to freshen up, and mostly he didn't care. No one save the horse to smell him, and he felt sure she didn't mind if he reeked. But he'd have to see Trudy soon, and when he did, he didn't want her to fall over in a faint from his trail stench.

Trudy. The sister of his Virginia neighbor and widow of his best friend. The man who'd treated his entire regiment like his own brothers. The same one who died in his arms on a bloody battlefield, leaving him with regrets and memories too horrible to share with anyone.

Will had been like a brother to him, but Lane had betrayed him in his heart.

He'd loved the man's wife since the moment they'd met, all those years ago on her wedding day. One look from her and he'd lost his heart, right before he stood beside Will as the pair took their wedding vows.

Damn, but if life didn't make the road from birth to death a bumpy one. Seemed like he got over one hump before the next came upon him. It had been that way his whole life—why should it be any different now?

After he arranged for Belle's care, he headed on foot toward the boardinghouse. The saddlebags slung over his shoulder were covered in trail dust, same as him.

He caught a peek at himself reflected in a shop's wide window. A rolling ball of dust, covered in dirt and grit from the tips of his boots to the crown of his Stetson. Well, he could fix it with a good long soak, provided he didn't run out of steam before hitting that place near the end of Wylder Street.

What had the sign said? Cumberland's Boardinghouse—no, that wasn't right. Clawson's—no, not that, either.

His head felt packed with sawdust, and his gut stood as empty as a pine tree after a woodpecker went after it. Lots of room where there shouldn't be and a fuzzy feeling in between his ears that wouldn't pass until he filled his belly.

It didn't matter, whatever the name of the boardinghouse he planned to get a room, a bath, and some food. After that, to the Five Star, where he'd hopefully find out a thing or two about how Trudy fared—and where she lived.

He looked over toward the mercantile. A big place, two floors, even. Tomorrow he'd go in and replace some things that were used up on the trail. But not now. Culpepper's Boardinghouse came into view, and nothing could keep him from seeing its owner and settling in.

Except—

The door to the mercantile swung open, and Trudy stepped out. He'd recognize her anywhere. The tilt of her head and the way she lifted her face to the sky and inhaled so deeply, as if she were savoring every bit of freshness the world offered, were dead giveaways. He stopped to stare, sure she wouldn't even know he watched.

Except she did. Her head turned toward the street, and her gaze met his.

And suddenly he didn't feel nearly as worn out as he had a few minutes earlier.

****

Hell's bells. She'd been in Wylder so long her mind had gone soft.

Gertie stood on the walkway in front of the mercantile, her arms heavy with yards of blue-and-white-striped chambray. Finn promised to deliver the rest of her order to her house later in the day, if he got a break in business or, if not, after he closed for the night. A nice man, that Finn Wylder, to offer to do more than simply sell the goods. The man's kindness garnered appreciation, and she planned to bake one of her signature pumpkin breads this afternoon to thank him for his trouble.

But she'd taken a bit of the yardage with her to get a jump on the cutting and sewing. Last year's school buntings had served as a feast for mice sometime during their long storage. She couldn't have mouse-eaten fabric fluttering in the breeze above the schoolhouse door and its windows.

So, a last-minute sewing job. It could have gone to the Widow Lowery and her pleasant seamstress, Laurel, but they were probably already busy making dresses for any woman in town who could afford the extra expense. Many ladies kept a Founder's Day jar tucked away, filling it with spare change throughout the year. That way they could fancy up a dress they already owned or, if one were lucky enough to have accumulated a decent handful of change, buy something new. Sewing for the festivities probably had Lowery's Dress Shop hopping.

She clutched the chambray close as the tall man walked toward her.

Even trail-dusted, Lane Hutchins made a woman's heart quicken. He had always turned heads when he'd been a young man. Time did well by him, turning his fresh, handsome features rugged and the spry step to a confident swagger.

If she had a free hand, she would use it to pat her hair, but the fabric kept her at a disadvantage. She arranged her features into what she hoped was a neutral expression as he stepped up onto the wooden planking.

"Trudy." His voice, so deep and with its southern resonance, sent butterflies spiraling low in her gut.

No one had called her that in over a decade. Her mouth went dry, and it took a moment to find her voice.

"Lane." A small jut of her chin toward her chest, but no smile. It wouldn't come. "No one calls me that

17

anymore."

His brow furrowed as he shifted the saddlebags on his shoulder. When he reached for the bolt of fabric, she didn't resist handing it over. It had been a long time since a man carried her burdens.

"Are you married again? If so, I apologize…I wasn't aware that you'd taken on the 'missus' again."

She shook her head. "I'm not married, but folks around town call me Gertie. I haven't heard the other in so long, it took me by surprise." Tilting her head to one side, she added, "Seeing you did the same. What are you doing in Wylder?"

His smile set off a new round of fluttering in her midsection. "A happy coincidence?"

As if she'd believe that. "You can't be serious."

The schoolteacher, Violet Bloom, walked toward the mercantile door. Not in the mood to explain about the man beside her, Gertie gave a smile and murmured, "Violet." She took a few steps in the opposite direction, leaving the teacher no option but to return the fast greeting.

Lane walked along with her, so she kept moving. Better to look as if she were on the way to somewhere. By now, the man generated attention. People peered from behind shutters, curtains, and through seemingly disinterested eyes. All for pretense, for newcomers were scrutinized as soon as their boots stepped over town lines.

They passed the jailhouse. Branch Wylder stood in the doorway with the pocket watch he favored in his hand. He nodded when he caught her gaze. She felt his appraisal on her back as they walked by. She imagined the man beside her did, too.

"Are you going to tell me why you're here?" She gave him a side glance. He acted as if it were the most ordinary thing in the world to be strolling down the rough western street instead of along Virginia's cobblestoned walks. "I don't believe the coincidence bit for an instant."

The man chuckled, and it brought up a memory she'd considered long forgotten. Him, on the porch with Will, the pair discussing the price of seed or some other mundane bit of business. They shared so much that she didn't always pay attention to their after-dinner chats, but hearing their voices through the open window kept her heart warm.

Gertie took a deep breath and held it. Not all memories brought heart-stopping pain. Some, like this one, came with a brief wave of sadness, a longing for what had been but was forever lost.

"I should have known better than to try to sell you a tin horse. You never did fall into any of our silly traps, did you?"

She smiled at the memory of Will's tendency to entertain with ridiculous jokes. He loved to make people laugh, as did Lane. Together, they were the life of any party or the momentum to keep conversation light during dinners.

"I tried not to, but you two kept coming up with new riddles and jokes. You caught me a time or two, I'm sure."

"But not now?" His words teased, but she heard a wistfulness beneath them. So, he missed Will, too. "I can't catch you with my silly response, can I?"

They reached the end of the street. She hesitated, not sure how far he meant to walk with her.

"No, I'm afraid those days are past."

Silence hung between them for a moment. The sound of horses clip-clopping on the dirt lane and the rumble of wagon wheels dimmed. Funny how two people could find a cocoon in the middle of a busy street and stare at each other as if every breath they shared might tear the insulation they'd built from around their hearts. Gertie held her breath as she watched Lane consider his words. Beyond the dark-blue eyes she knew so well, a wave of emotions that he couldn't hide from her.

Hers wasn't the only heart that missed what the war stole from them.

Finally, he blinked. "Well, then I guess I'd best hand over the truth. I'm here running an errand for Grant. I've got something to deliver that he didn't trust to get here on its own."

Well, if that didn't beat all. The brother who swore he'd never speak with her again if she left Virginia sending the man who cried for forgiveness as she packed her bags to leave behind a life of luxury for one filled with hardship and uncertainty.

Well, hell...there were still moments that shocked her, even after she believed she'd seen all the world could throw her way.

Gertie took the fabric from him, tugging when he didn't surrender it easily. She took a step away from the man—and away from her house. It wouldn't do to have him trail her home. Instead, she set off for the church beside the schoolhouse and spoke over her shoulder.

"Well, you'd best get back on your horse and take yourself—and whatever Grant sent you with—right back to Richmond. Tell him I don't want anything he's got to offer. Not now. Not ever."

She took the steps to the church at a near run. The doors were open, so she pushed her way inside and sat on a bench near the back.

Her heart pounded in her chest, but she took several slow, deep breaths to steady herself. Long moments passed as she mulled over what had happened.

She never expected to see Lane Hutchins again. Never. Yet here he was, in Wylder, and looking to take up as if no time had passed.

As if her life hadn't fallen apart…and she hadn't had to rebuild it inch by painful inch.

Gertie lingered in the church so long she worried the priest might try to counsel her. He glanced her way every time he walked up or down the center aisle. She felt certain he added chores to his schedule so he could pass her time and again. But she kept her head bowed, as if deep in prayer, while she sideways glanced through the window nearest where she sat. The hard wooden bench against her bottom did not provide comfort, but the view couldn't be better.

Lane stood near the end of Wylder Street for a long time. He stared down the lane at the church, his feet spread shoulder width apart and his face hidden in the shadow of his wide-brimmed, black Stetson. Once, he took two steps toward the building but got no farther. Perhaps the sanctity of a church kept him in place. Or maybe the harsh edge to her parting words did it. She didn't know which saved her from a second encounter, but gratitude seeped into her bones when the man turned on his heel and headed back down the street.

He'd begged for forgiveness once, and she had not

been willing to grant it. Truth is, she had been unable. Too caught up in the hard glare of love, loss, and grief to give solace to another.

Today he hadn't done the same, so perhaps he'd come to terms with Will's death. She couldn't be certain, but his pleas were probably unnecessary anyway. How could one man take responsibility for another's death during war? It made no sense then and even less now. Besides, time dulled the lines between what one should have done and what had happened. She didn't care hardly at all then and not one bit now.

Good that he'd walked away. Lane should return to Richmond immediately. He wouldn't find peace in Wylder—at least, none that she felt prepared to offer.

A sigh escaped her, providing an opening for the priest. She didn't attend this church, but the Wylder gossip line gave her his name. She looked up when his quiet, kind words reached her ears.

"May I be of service, ma'am?"

His eyes were as compassionate as his voice. A fast head shake. "No, thanks, Pastor James. I'm fine." She stood and lifted the bolt of fabric off the bench. "I needed a place to rest. And pray, of course."

A nod and an understanding smile. "Of course. Well, if I can't be of use, I'll get back to my duties."

He didn't ask her to leave, but she didn't need an invitation. The man didn't run a shelter for those without business in his church. She offered a small smile and walked down the aisle toward the door, remembering to keep her spine stiff enough that he would never entertain the thought that she needed assistance.

She didn't require anything from him, or anyone

else. She'd learned years ago to depend only on herself. Whatever she needed, whether it came as a task done or a comfort from fear or illness, she gave herself.

There wasn't a priest—or man, for that matter—who could help her.

No one could return her Will to her. And any other thing they might offer did not interest her in the slightest.

Chapter 3

When a woman's husband dies, she has few choices.

She could remarry and gain a new man to fill the void left by her husband's passing. Many women chose the option, and while Gertie had no intention of taking on a second husband, she found no fault with those who did. Widowhood offered a lonely existence. Why look down on women who preferred companionship to the emptiness that came with staying alone?

A wife left behind by a husband's demise could also mourn herself to death. She'd seen that happen, back in Virginia. A friend who lost her beloved at Gettysburg grieved herself into her own grave. Not a pretty sight, a woman consumed by sorrow. It didn't serve any good purpose that she could see, aside from eliminating the long, lonely years of survival without a partner.

An alternative to either of those, choosing to live a remaining life with as much happiness, dignity, and purpose as one could muster, appealed to Gertie more than the others. She'd chosen to make the best of the hard hand life dealt her.

Her move to Wylder made that mission less difficult. She arrived knowing no one and that gave her the advantage of not having to share her history. If she kept Will's death to herself, there were no pitying glances. No awkward, but well-meaning, questions from newfound friends or complete strangers about her plans to marry again.

It eliminated the need to look sorrowful. That gave her freedom, both in her heart and her dealings with others. Part of a widow's countenance, from the points of view of those around her, often included never smiling or laughing, not going after meaningful pursuits, and certainly not showing an interest in remaining on her own. She learned many things when her husband died, and one of the first was that everyone had an opinion of how she should feel, act, and move forward. Everyone, including her brother, Grant.

When they walked in her shoes, they could formulate opinions and share them with her. Until then, she invited the world to keep their thoughts to themselves. She wore the widow's burden, and no one else had the right to poke in on her journey. Sometimes the truth of her life dropped her to her knees and filled her with doubt that she'd ever be able to draw a new breath. She struggled harder to live on her own than anyone would ever imagine possible—unless they stood in the sad shoes she now wore. Other times, though, her heart lifted enough that she almost felt as carefree as she once had been. Almost.

A widow's life became a teeter-totter. No one saw that she rode the contraption, because the smile she kept in place hid her truth. Times she soared and others she hit the ground with a painful thud—but always, she sat astride and tried to find equilibrium amidst the ups and downs.

She mused over all of it on the walk back to her house. Falling into contemplation on topics she fought to keep pressed down deep where they couldn't hurt kept her from meeting the looks of the few folks she passed.

It had been wise to not lead Lane to her home. Where she lived and what she did were of no consequence to the man. Whatever he learned, he would surely take back to Grant and the last thing she wanted was for her brother to know anything about her.

Grant. Another person who had no right to the details of her life, despite his thinking to the contrary.

A river of sweat trickled down her back and made her chemise so wet it stuck to her skin. The fabric in her arms hadn't felt heavy back in the mercantile, but by the time she walked down her street, it felt like it had been woven from river rocks. Still, she didn't regret bringing it with her. Once she got cleaned up, she would begin to cut triangles for the school's new bunting.

Her house sat right beside the Harvey home. Thomas, a mining financier from back east, lived with his teenage daughter, Alexia, on the other side of the picket fence that ran between their properties. The girl had lost her mother, and he, his wife, during childbirth a few years back.

She understood their lives. Loss translated, whether it was husband or wife, mother or daughter. Death left an imprint as final as the act itself.

When she came upon Alexia staring at the sky, the way she did now, she didn't wonder what occupied the girl's mind. It could be anything.

Alexia's gaze fell when Gertie walked past. A smile tugged the corners of the bow-shaped mouth up, although even from a distance the older woman could see a sheen on the pretty eyes.

She put an extra bit of warmth in her voice. "Well hello, dear. Isn't that a beautiful sky?"

The girl wore braids wrapped around her head, off her shoulders to provide relief from the heat. A lot of girls wore the fashion, but most had mothers or sisters to help them get hairpins in place. She suspected that Violet, who kept company with Thomas, stepped in to assist the young woman with details such as hair.

"It sure is. I'm trying to decide whether it's robin's egg blue or turquoise." She crossed her arms over her chest and tipped her head to the side. A thoughtful stance that made her seem older than her delicate years. After a glance at the sky, the girl met Gertie's gaze. "What do you think? Which blue is it?"

While all she wanted stood beyond the front door of her house which sat few feet away, she shifted the fabric bolt onto one hip and tilted her head toward the sky. The sun hung directly overhead, so she didn't need to squint or avoid looking at it. And there were no clouds to offer distraction. Just an endless expanse of lovely blue sky.

She wasn't altogether comfortable with heartily proclaiming anything turquoise. Books lent reference to the color of oceans being that shade, but she had never witnessed an ocean so she could not say. But she had seen birds' eggs. Plenty of them.

"Robin's egg blue, I think. It's soft and gentle yet vivid. Not so hard to startle one but not washed out, either." She dropped her gaze to the girl's and nodded. "It is the perfect shade, one that invites but doesn't stifle and warms without harm."

The declaration met with silence and a long look at

the sky. She waited, giving the girl a chance to consider her thoughts. The light-brown eyebrows came together in a thin line above the probing eyes, then relaxed.

"I agree." She turned to face Gertie and waved her arms wide. "Miss Bloom says we should be observant, that walking through the world without seeing it is wasted effort. We're supposed to be looking for layers in things and people and trying to understand all we can about whatever we're looking at."

"Your teacher is a wise woman. I've always figured it best to consider what lies beyond the surface of a thing. Or a person, as well."

"She says that what we see isn't always the full picture." The young girl sighed, so long and deep that it sounded pulled from the tips of her shoes. "It's lucky that you walked by because I could ask you for an opinion." Another sigh. "But sometimes I have no one to talk with and it's all so confusing."

Divine timing, she thought, that she passed at this exact moment.

No smile or girlish enthusiasm in view. One more sigh, then a gaze that dropped to the ground. Seeing Alexia this way broke Gertie's heart.

She gentled her tone. "I'm sure your father is interested in hearing your observations."

The toe of one shoe scuffed against the dirt. In a low voice, the girl said, "I have questions. I can't ask Father some things."

A motherless girl…of course, she had questions—every girl her age did. She assumed they were of a feminine nature and that's why she couldn't go to her father with them.

Well, if Thomas would stop dawdling and marry

Violet already, the child wouldn't have to go looking for women to discuss particular things with. The two had been keeping company since shortly after the schoolteacher's arrival in town. Why didn't they make it legal already?

But none of that changed the fact that Alexia needed help. She shifted the fabric so she could reach out and put a hand on the other's slender shoulder.

"It must be hard not having your mother to turn to. I'm sorry for that, honey." The girl didn't meet her gaze. Again, she stared at the ground, and a toe gave a slow scuff in the dirt at their feet. "I know I'm not your mother, but I'm here, and you can ask me anything. I'll do my best to help you."

A long moment, then the lowered gaze rose. The bright eyes showed both doubt and hope, a mix that tugged at Gertie's heartstrings.

"I mean it, Alexia. What kind of questions do you have?"

The girl inhaled so deeply that her shoulders rose. She seemed to be weighing her options as she let the air out in a long exhale. Finally, she nodded.

"Okay, then. If you don't mind, I do have a few questions."

Now they were getting somewhere. Hopefully she could put the girl's mind to ease in short order, because the fabric grew heavier by the minute, and the sun's unrelenting heat threatened to turn her to a puddle in front of her own house.

"I don't mind at all." She swallowed, thinking of the pitcher of lemonade sitting on her kitchen table. "What can I help you with?"

Alexia straightened, a hopeful smile on her face.

"What do you know about—" She lowered her voice, even though they were the only two standing on the street. "—breasts?"

****

Lane leaned back in the bath.

Heaven. Or as damn near to it as he'd come in weeks.

The tin tub wasn't long enough for him to stretch his legs out, but he didn't mind a slight bend in his knees. Water, soap, and time to relax his aching muscles proved more than enough to satisfy him. He'd be happy to leave the layers of grime coating his body in the water when he stood but while it soaked off, he lay back in quiet contentment.

Funny how a man could think better when he wasn't in a saddle.

Also amusing how his mind went straight to the woman whose presence in Wylder gave him reason to be in the tub in the first place. Had Grant not asked him to go on this errand, he would've been back in Virginia, miserable as ever and wondering what the hell to do with whatever remained of his life.

With the end of a cigar clamped between his teeth, he ran a hand over the scar stretched across his shoulder. He winced and bit down hard. Whether his body still felt pain in the spot or the memory of it brought the twinge, the blasted thing still held him captive. He'd kept the arm, thanks to the work of a skilled field surgeon, but the body remembered the event almost as if it happened last year instead of the previous decade.

War wounds. He didn't figure any man who'd served escaped without them. Some physical, others mental. For most a combination of both, probably.

He took the cigar from his mouth and spit a bit of tobacco over the side of the tub. He'd have to remember not to bite the damn things. Every time he did, he got a chunk in his mouth. He enjoyed smoking the stuff every now and again, but the idea of chewing it into a soggy clump turned his stomach. A man should know where to draw the line on such things, and he drew it with tobacco on his tongue.

But Trudy, now that line he wouldn't mind crossing. Of course, he never would. Will might be gone, but in his eyes, she still belonged to his best friend. Besides, Grant would have his head hanging from a wall in his back parlor if he touched her. And surely, he'd smile while he stuffed his head, the way he did with the pheasants and deer trophies he collected.

Just one more hunting prize. Yes, he'd stay away from the woman to keep his hair where it belonged.

But that wouldn't come easy. In the years since he saw her last, she had become even more desirable. Sure, some men might look and think her a bit old. She must be a couple years past thirty by now, if his arithmetic and memory served him right. And with the serious gaze and touch of sadness that walked with her, she might not be enticing enough to other men.

None of that mattered to him. That she managed to keep herself alive after leaving the soft life in the South she had been born into showed intelligence and strength. Determination, too. And walking through the world as if her heart hadn't been torn apart by loss revealed the depth of her love and the respect she had for her husband.

In his eyes, those traits made Gertrude Jackson a

rare find.

He'd had his share of women. Few men got to his age without some knowledge of the female sex. But none of those experiences ever made him believe in forever. Or love. None of it, the romantic nonsense he saw affecting other men, bringing them to their knees and turning strong men weak.

Trudy, though, made his knees wobble.

And if he allowed himself to react without interruption from his mind, she would make other parts of his anatomy nice and firm.

He contemplated the look she'd given him earlier. Surprise tinged with a whisper of pleasure, or at least that's what he hoped he saw in those captivating eyes. He wondered what it would feel like to see more than polite satisfaction in her gaze…

His mind strayed where it had no business going. He laid his head against the high tin tub back and closed his eyes. The water grew cool, but he didn't mind. It refreshed him but didn't keep his body from heating as he thought of delightful Gertie.

A slight shift of his hips to give his form more space. His knees dropped open, resting on the tub sides as he became aroused by the mental images dancing in his head. It had been a long time since he'd felt the touch of a woman against his skin…

A knock came at the door to the tiny room that housed the bathing tub. Minimal, without anything fancy, it served a single purpose. A wooden sign in the yard in front of the house advertised baths for a quarter, so he stopped in and so far, the warm water and private moments had been good value for his money.

The knock tightened his brows.

The door opened inward, and the young woman who showed him to the accommodation poked her head around the battered wood slab. She couldn't be more than twenty, but she already had a tough edge to her. When she smiled, it didn't reach her eyes.

Before he could open his mouth, she stepped inside and closed the door. His gaze went to his pants. Lying across a chair atop his holster, they were too far to reach. The long-handled Bowie knife he'd leaned against the side of the tub facing away from the door waited, though. He removed the cigar from his mouth and held his arm over the side of the tub. A tap to flick ashes, then he dropped the hand out of sight.

"I'm not quite finished, but if you give me a minute I'll be done."

She dropped to her knees and smiled again. A hand went to the ribbon tie at the neckline of her blouse and tugged. The fabric fell open, exposing a good expanse of creamy skin peeking above the cut of her camisole.

"I hoped you might need more than a bath." She trailed a fingertip down the slope of her neck and across her breasts before she dropped it into the water and circled it on the surface. The soap bubbles had long since gone. When she looked down, she got an eyeful. "Oh, well...I see you're very much in need of a little something extra."

He swallowed hard when she wrapped her hand around him. Her touch wasn't tender. A tug to start, then an almost disinterested slide with his length surrounded by her fist. Her gaze went from his form beneath the water to his face, then back to the job at hand.

Lane brought his knees together and placed his free

hand over hers. "That isn't necessary."

He removed her fingers from around his privates and smiled as he brought their hands out of the water. When he released hers, he flicked his finger and sent water flying through the air between them.

Her eyes turned stormy as she reached for him again. This time, he grabbed her wrist.

"But you know you want it." Her insistence did nothing for his libido.

"As I said, I'll be through in a few minutes. If you'll kindly leave, I'll towel off and dress."

She hesitated when he released her, so he stood. His excitement waned but not so much that he'd become flaccid. The evidence of his arousal bobbed inches from her face, and he wondered if he shouldn't sit back down. Who could tell if she might decide to act like an angry cat and bite when vexed?

A flush rose in the woman's cheeks as she stood and tied her blouse closed. Without a word, she turned and left the room.

He respected that some women found themselves in dire circumstances and needed to resort to any means to make a bit of spare change to help feed a child or fill their own belly. A sad, but true, fact of life. And while he'd gladly leave a tip for her, he had no intention of being groped by a strange woman.

Lane stepped out of the tepid bath water and reached for the scrap of threadbare toweling that hung on a hook beside the door. He turned and dropped what remained of the cigar in the tub before he began to dry off.

Didn't it figure that the woman in his mind, the one who occupied his dreams, wasn't the one who walked through the door? Probably better in the long run, seeing as he wanted to keep his head and all, but, damn, for once, he'd like a dream to come true.

Chapter 4

Gertie gave the chambray pieces a long look. It had been a while since she'd sewn a banner, and she'd forgotten how many triangles it took to make a length long enough to hang. And she had not one, but several, to construct for the schoolhouse.

A wave of trepidation tickled the edges of her mind, but she pushed it away. Not the time to doubt her abilities. The town counted on her to get every duck for the Founder's Day celebration in a row and she intended to do exactly that. She hadn't let them down yet, and this certainly wouldn't be the year she would do so.

Besides, she had faced a lot bigger demons than sewing up banners, for goodness' sake.

The knock on her front door came at exactly the right moment to save her from one more foray into the land of uncertainty. She stood and walked from the dining room into the hallway that led to the front of the house. A square of glass set in the center of the door gave her a peek at who stood on her porch.

She pulled the door open and smiled at Alexia. Brenda Milligan stood beside her.

"It must be your lunch hour if you're here. Oh, my, but the day has gotten away from me." A smile for the two girls and a wave to bring them inside. "I trust you've eaten your noon meal before trotting over here?"

Alexia nodded. Her handmade dress still had some crispness to it, as if the fabric had been pressed. The details on the blue-and-white outfit were a little fancier than most dresses for girls her age. She suspected the aunt who lived in Philadelphia may have sent it. If not, the Widow Lowery had outdone herself.

A ribbon held the Milligan girl's hair back off her thin face. It matched the other's dress so well it had to be part of the ensemble. Alexia's hair had been secured with a length of frayed brown grosgrain. She imagined the two must have swapped hair accessories.

A sweet gesture, especially since the Milligan family, with their many children, scuttled to make ends meet. The children were all intelligent and well-mannered, but times were hard in their house, and in a place as small as Wylder, that could not be kept secret.

"We ate." Alexia put her arm around her friend's shoulder. "I hope it's okay that I brought Brenda along to work on the garlands with us. I didn't think you'd mind. And she sews so she'll be a big help."

Gertie said a silent prayer of thanks. She'd had a need and the universe sent an answer to her dilemma in such short order that her head would have spun had she not been so eager to get to work.

"The more, the merrier." She turned and led the way to the dining room. Behind her, footsteps on the wide oak floorboards. The house wasn't huge, but it sat larger than most in town and on one of the quietest streets. Yards here were bigger than in other spots, and many were fenced in by white picket rows. "How is your mother, Brenda?"

The girl's voice, so soft and polite, came

immediately. "She's fine, ma'am."

"Well, I'm glad to hear that. Please give her my best." She turned and raised a concerned eyebrow. "And Beatie? I heard she's been feeling poorly. Has the little one rallied?"

The Milligans had a half-dozen children. Beatie, the youngest daughter, caught the spotlight a few years back at the party on Christmas Eve when she decided to add to the holiday singing program with her own rendition of "Rock-a-Bye, Jesus." It had been a hit and had made the little one a town sweetheart.

Unfortunately, the child had begun to suffer from seizures. They came on without warning, and as far as she'd heard, Doc Sullivan hadn't found a cause for them. Or, a cure.

"She's feelin' well, ma'am." Brenda wrung her hands together. So, the wee one hadn't had a seizure of late, but the family still worried. "Nothing since last week. Mama says it were only a passin' thing, that our girl will be all right now."

A nod and smile hid her thoughts, but they were what the young woman needed so she gave them. "I'm sure your mother is right, honey. Please, give her my best."

She led them into the dining room where the fabric triangles sat stacked on the table. Thread, scissors, pins, and needles were beside them. "So here we are, with the buntings. I know they don't look like much now, but we'll get them pulled together."

A hand wave toward the chairs on the far side of the table. "Sit wherever you like, girls." When they were settled, Gertie took her place across from them. It had been a long time since she'd given a sewing lesson, but a woman didn't forget how to pass on the stitches and techniques learned at her mother's knee.

Brenda needed no help to thread a needle and begin a simple hemstitch around the edges of the cut fabric pieces. Without hems, they would unravel quickly. She wanted the decoration to be useful for a few years, at least, so the attention to detail mattered.

Alexia's fingers were clumsy, and her stitches were uneven, but Gertie did not criticize. She got the girl started and then let her learn by doing. Eventually her skills would increase, if she kept at it. But if she were dogged over every missed stitch and bumpy knot, she might give up. No one gained proficiency at any skill by declaring defeat.

So, she watched from the corner of her eye and feigned complete unawareness of all her difficulties. When she heard a sharp intake of air and saw a fingertip disappear between lips, she pretended not to notice. To the girl's credit, she did not complain even though she pricked her fingertips more than once.

Miss Milligan acted wise beyond her years, demonstrating the solid upbringing her parents were obviously giving their children. She kept abreast of her friend's struggle but did not jump to interfere. The glances and small twitches of her lips as she watched but minded her business impressed Gertie. She made a mental note to comment on the girl's maturity the next time she bumped into her mother. A woman should know how her children act when out of her sight. In this case, Missus Milligan could be very proud of her daughter.

The hour allotted for their school lunch break flew by. A glance at the clock on the mantle put an end to her musing.

"I believe it's time for you girls to head back to the schoolhouse." When the pair looked up and pulled sad faces, she nodded. "Wouldn't be fair of me to keep you longer and make you tardy. I'm sure Miss Bloom has lessons for you that take precedence over sewing buntings."

She placed the triangle in her hand on the stack with the other hemmed pieces. With the girls' help, the pile had grown.

Alexia bit the end off the thread she'd knotted and placed her piece on top of the others. She raised an eyebrow and cast a glance at the table. "Would it be okay if I took a few to work on tonight?"

If she refused, the girl would lose the chance to practice her stitches. And it would help get the buntings complete in time to hang them for the celebration.

"That's a great idea. I would appreciate your doing that." Gertie picked a discarded length of thread off the table and rolled it in her fingertips until it made a soft little ball. "With the understanding that your schoolwork gets done before you pull out a sewing needle. It is important that you don't miss any of your studies, Alexia. I'm sure your father wouldn't appreciate my distracting you from your work."

The girlish smile brightened the room. "Father's grateful that you're teaching me to sew. When I asked his permission last night, he said to give you his thanks. And, he said he'll be by soon to thank you in person."

Such kindness warmed her heart. Since the Harveys moved into the house next to hers they had a neighborly relationship. The man and his daughter arrived with crushed dreams and broken hearts, and she recognized their grief. It made her more inclined to lend a hand when she could. The pair had some rocky times, and the child had even been sent back east for a while, but life had evened out for them, and she was glad for that.

To step in now and again to help raise the girl was an honor. Someday she expected Violet Bloom would take up the position, but for now, she didn't mind one bit.

"Well, you go ahead and tell your father that there's no need to thank me. It's been a pleasure spending time with you girls." She walked them to the front door. "You can stop by after school to pick up some sewing pieces for practice. I'll have it bundled up for you."

"That would be fine, ma'am. Thank you."

Both seemed reluctant to leave, but she didn't let them stay. A tug on the handle to open the door and a fast side hug for each, then she sent them on their way. "Now, back to Miss Bloom's schoolroom. And no detours, you hear?"

The girls nodded their understanding. A last smile, then they hurried down the front path to the street.

Her gaze drifted to the left. A horse and rider moved slowly in the midday heat. A residential lane, not real busy at this time of day. Tumbleweeds pressed against fenceposts, the only movement aside from the rider. As he rode closer, her blood turned cold.

Just her god-awful luck. Coming her way, the one man she didn't want to see on her doorstep. Had he not spotted her already, she may have hurried inside and slammed the door shut.

But he had seen her. The man jerked his chin

toward his chest as he pulled up at the path leading to her porch.

Lane stopped and swept his hat from his head. His hair shone, damp waves against his scalp sending a soapy clean smell into the air. The breeze carried the scent up to the porch.

"Good afternoon, Trudy." He'd shaved, scrubbed up, and changed his clothes. A glance at his feet. His boots shone. So, the first thing the man had done after she walked away was wash the trail grime off.

"Nobody calls me that anymore." She met his gaze and tried to harden hers, but it didn't come without a price. The man tugged at her heartstrings, opening the spots she believed closed long ago. He slid off the horse, dropped the reins over the hitching post at the end of her walk, and came up the path. A bit of her past and recollections of those happy times hit her like a whirlwind. Her knees wobbled, so she put a hand on the doorframe to steady herself. "I told you that already."

He took the steps in two quick moves, and when he stood on the porch in front of her, she got an even bigger whiff of the scent of him. Soap. Water. Man. All in one neat package and swirling up her nose and into her mind to dance with memories she'd tried to lock away.

"You did." His tone smooth. Soothing. So Southern, it pulled her in and wrapped her in its charm. "But I can't think of you as anything other than gentle Trudy."

"Yes, well…"

****

It took a bit of doing, but Lane finally convinced Gertie to accompany him to an early dinner at the

Wylder Hotel. He'd asked in at the boardinghouse and been assured that the best place to get a decent meal was served in the hotel restaurant.

Even if the food proved to be lousy, just stepping past the wide front door into the lobby turned the day magical. Who would have guessed that a few steps from the dust and grit sat such opulence?

Of course, it paled by comparison to what they were accustomed to in Richmond, but it certainly put most frontier structures, at least the ones he'd seen, to shame.

The hotel lobby, with its polished floorboards, plush burgundy velvet sofas, and marble-topped tables, screamed elegance. Chandeliers sparkled, their hanging prisms sending spots of golden light dancing along flocked wallpaper. Heavy draperies hung at the windows, so long their fabric pooled on the gleaming floor.

A pair of wide doors led off the lobby into the restaurant. Before they reached it, sounds of tinkling glassware and the murmur of conversation met his ears.

At the doorway, a man dressed in starched white shirt, black jacket and trousers, and a blue string tie nodded his head in greeting. Even this early in the day, he presented himself with care. For an instant, they could have been in Richmond as easily as the West.

"Welcome to the Wylder Hotel dining room. Table for two?"

He removed his Stetson and held it loosely in one hand. The other he placed on the small of Gertie's back, grateful that she didn't step away when he touched her. "That's right. And if you have a table tucked in a quiet corner, so much the better."

The man stuck two hand-lettered menus beneath his arm and swiveled to survey the dining room. The time of day may have contributed to its emptiness. Less than half the tables were occupied.

He turned back to smile at them. "You're in luck. The table in the corner should suit."

They followed the man to the spot which sat off to the far side of the room. When they were seated, he placed the menus down and went back to his post at the door.

Lane looked across to the woman seated opposite. A flickering candle in the center sent ribbons of light across Gertie's face, neckline, and the top part of her dress. The wall sconce dripped a soft golden circle onto their heads.

The perfect spot for two old friends to reconnect.

"You look lovely today." As the words left his mouth, he almost wished he could take them back. They were true, but the last thing he wanted her to think was that he'd come west to sweet talk her.

Damn, but he couldn't think of any natural or easy way to deal with his sentiments for the woman, not without wondering if she questioned his motives. Not for the first time, he wished Will had survived. If he had, they would all be back east, and he'd probably be bouncing his best friend's children on his knee instead of feeling unsteady about speaking with his widow.

"Thank you, although I'm pretty sure you complimented me when you arrived on my doorstep." She patted her hair with a hand that shook ever-so slightly.

So, she felt unnerved, too.

Time to put an end to the awkwardness between

them. He placed his forearms on the starched white tablecloth and leaned forward. He lowered his voice, although they were too far from anyone to be overheard. "Well, a beautiful woman deserves more than one compliment." When she raised a hand to protest, he went on. "No, don't try to tell me it ain't so. Look, if we were back in Richmond, where women are treated like women, you would hear fine things all the time. Every day, in fact." He swept his gaze over the dining room before bringing it back to her. "But because you're here, out in the western frontier where bits of civilized living are few and far between, you're not used to hearing the truth about yourself. But that doesn't make it any less true, Tru—ah, Gertie."

He'd have to practice getting that to fall from his lips with ease.

"I'm not the same woman who left Virginia." An air of sadness tinged the words. Had it not been completely unacceptable he would have taken her in his arms to try to soothe away some of the pain that showed when she spoke. "I've changed."

Truth hung between them, a tie that bound as well as a barrier to hold them apart.

"We all have."

Hell, he hardly recognized himself sometimes. The man who had gone off to fight a war that seemed would be won within a month had died on a battlefield. Even the man who'd returned home in defeat, along with countless others, was long gone.

Life beyond a war meant finding solid ground again. The search persisted, dogging him every day and with each step he took, a never-ending quest to find a place that felt like home in a skin that didn't seem to fit him anymore. He'd talked with other men who survived the war. Some had expressed similar feelings, so he knew he wasn't alone, but that didn't make the untethered lightness of his current existence any less disconcerting.

He longed to feel rooted in one place again, the way he had before the war that had stolen so much from so many. A square of land, and a woman to share it with...how had that become his impossible dream?

Whiskey smoothed away the rough edges. A shot or two—hell, sometimes a bottle—eased the memories that dug at him when he slept. Sometimes they crept up like one of those native scouts, quieter than a rattler against the silken desert sand but set to strike the instant his guard dropped and his mind wandered. He hated their control over him, but it took energy to endure the hard lines dug into his being, souvenirs from the battlefield.

To this day, he still caught a whiff of blood on a breeze or the whimper of a man's last breath when he didn't expect them to appear. They were stealthy and unwanted, yet they showed up. Imprinted on his mind. Invaders touching his soul.

No one could ever understand how it felt so he didn't try to explain. No one left to tell besides Grant, and he certainly didn't want to hear stories from the war.

So, he learned to protect himself as best he could. Build a wall around such things. Smile when he would have screamed. Act as if he'd forgotten the past. And drink when the pain became too much to bear.

"Lane? Lane, are you all right?"

It hit him that he'd let the memories consume him,

that he'd been pulled back into the reality of his previous life.

A quick shake of his head to chase away the demons lurking in the dark recesses of his mind. Damn them all to Hell, but couldn't they stay put for once?

His gaze met the soft eyes staring at him from across the table. She reached a hand toward him and placed it on his forearm. The touch, so light it might have been a butterfly landing on his shirtsleeve, also held strength.

She spoke softly, concern pulling her features tight. "You went off somewhere for a minute. Are you okay?" A slow slide of palm across fabric brought a scratching whisper, almost as if his emotions had their own sound. "You had a long ride out here. Do you need to see the doctor? I'm sure someone could go for him. It's no trouble."

When she raised a hand toward the man who seated them, he grabbed it and brought it down to rest on the table. Her hand fit in his grasp so well he didn't release her straight away. His touch didn't garner a protest, so he ran a slow fingertip across the tips of her fingers.

Work-worn. No stranger to menial duties, a fate that came to her after Will's passing.

Had she remained in Richmond, her slender hands would have been smooth. There would have been nothing denied her, no comfort too out of reach for the family's money. She would have lived her days with every need seen to.

Yet she chose to leave it all behind and come to this lawless territory. And, to the calloused fingertips that showed she did for herself now.

He pushed memories of days gone by from his

mind and cleared his throat. "No need for that. I'm fine."

Her gaze probed. "You weren't completely fine. This isn't one of your riddles where you cover my eyes, feed me vanilla pudding splashed with bourbon, and call it catfish." A tiny smile. "You and Will fooled me that day, but you can't do that now. No, I see you, and something happened a minute ago."

They had been so young on that day. No burdens to shoulder and no hint of what would come. Just fun, and lots of it. He missed those moments.

"I guess we've known each other too long to hide the truth, haven't we?" He sighed, then released her hand and sat back. "Sometimes my mind pulls me to places I don't want to go, shows me things that are better left lying in a corner of my head rather than right in the center." He shrugged and wondered if she could understand how this felt. After all, she was no stranger to loss. "I never know when it will come on me or what will bring certain memories crashing back, so it's a shock every time it happens. You'd think I'd be used to it by now, but I'm not sure I'll ever be."

Gertie took her hand off his arm and gave him a pat before she sat back. He couldn't tell, but maybe she thought he'd lost his mind.

"I'm so sorry. I had no idea." She looked away, toward the man who stood in the restaurant doorway. He had grabbed two menus and turned to lead a couple to a table. When she turned back and met his gaze, a sheen covered her eyes. "But I do understand. You'd think that after so much time it would stop happening, but it doesn't. It keeps coming and coming without warning…to drop you to your knees again and again."

She brushed a fingertip beneath one eye and shook her head. When she spoke, he had to lean forward to hear her. "I'm so sorry."

He had finally found someone who understood the workings of his tortured mind.

And it gutted him, knowing the beautiful woman was no stranger to wounds that festered for a decade or the pain they caused. It seemed that kind of agony should be left to men since they were the ones who created most of the misery in the world.

Chapter 5

Gertie rose before dawn but not because of the night terrors. Her sleep had been peaceful, filled with bits of dreams of a faceless man. She didn't know the identity of the one who walked beside her during the dark hours. Safety and security arrived with him, and had she been able to thank him for it, she would have. It had been a long time since she'd woken so refreshed.

Home meant a lot of things to different people. For her, it had always been about the kitchen, the heart of the house. She hummed a bit of an old lullaby now as she moved about the comfortable space.

Of course, when she and Will were first married, she learned that the heart of a marriage went well past the kitchen and that the deepening of a relationship between husband and wife happened in the bedroom. Her cheeks heated now, so many years past her wedding night, as she recalled the hours she and her man shared in their marital bed.

She waved a hand before her face and took a step away from the stove.

Those days were gone. Looking back never brought her forward.

Thanking the dead or those in dreams served no purpose. And if she knew anything, it was that every person's life should have something to give it meaning. She'd had that once and had even been offered the promise of motherhood, but it had been denied her. This new existence and the sometimes seemingly paltry reasons she gave herself to move forward couldn't hold a candle to her previous life, but it would have to do.

A pair of pumpkin bread loaves was ready to be pulled from the oven, so she grabbed two thick dishtowels and reached into the mouth of the beast. That's what she thought of the large cookstove during the summer months. But when the snow fell and cold winds blew, the cast-iron monstrosity became a beloved heat source.

Both loaves had risen nicely and were golden brown. Their split tops hinted at the spicy goodness beneath the surface. She tipped the treats out of their pans and set them aside to cool.

She couldn't thank the dead or her dream man, but the two young women who pledged their help with the celebratory buntings deserved some attention. The bundle of sewing she'd left on the front porch for Alexia had been gone when she returned home from her early dinner with Lane. She had no doubt that the enthusiastic new needlewoman would return the completed packet by day's end.

Her prized bread recipe, one of the few she still used that came with her from Virginia, would bring smiles. The Milligan family would especially enjoy the indulgence since she didn't imagine they got many small pleasures.

With a last deep inhale of the warm, buttery loaves, she turned toward the dining room. There were plenty of lists to make for the upcoming festivities and any spare minute to do so couldn't be squandered. She had no idea how she would accomplish everything. She only knew that she would. Somehow.

****

Lane went out of his way to try to forget a lot of what he'd done in his lifetime. There were enough unfortunate decisions on his conscience to send all the angels and saints in Heaven running for cover. He assumed every man must have a mental list of items he'd be ashamed to own up to. His list didn't stretch too long, just enough to remind him he'd not always done the right thing.

But hell, he didn't need an inventory to remind him of that, so he kept the memories pushed down and focused on making it through a day without adding to the sins he'd already committed.

Most times, he managed to keep that door shut and locked. Other days, like this one, memories seeped past the cracks above and below the mental barrier and plagued him.

He tried to concentrate on this moment, rather than those that niggled at him.

He stood in the Wyoming Territory. A destination of sorts, if he kept his mission for Grant as his sole reason for being in the West. But it wasn't, no matter how many times he told himself that he'd only traveled this far to make a delivery for a friend.

A look up at the sky. This western sky looked higher than when he'd stood below it in the South. Along with so much else, it made him conscious of the vastness of this land—and the inconsequence of man. They were tiny, even if most, including himself, had a hard time believing it.

Wylder Street in the early morning hours wasn't unlike any number of small towns he'd passed through on his way west. Most storefronts were shuttered, closed tight against any unsavory nighttime visitors. Few wagons rumbled along the rutted track, and there were hours before foot traffic brought color to the dusty landscape.

The ideal hour for a newcomer to get the lay of the land. Especially one who'd found a restful sleep impossible to obtain. He'd tossed all night, his mind filled with too much for him to comfortably ignore. Just before sunrise, he gave up the unsuccessful fight with the boardinghouse bedsheets and dressed for the day.

Time to get a feel for Wylder. He'd noted the jailhouse, mercantile, and a few offices on his initial swing through town, but he had been so tired and dirty he didn't spare the time to investigate any of them. Not that he wanted too close a look at that jail. No, he'd seen the wrong side of the bars once and it didn't bear repeating. Ever.

Up ahead, a man dashed out from between two buildings. His hat pulled low over his eyes, he kept his gaze on the ground and crossed the street so quickly Lane barely got a look at him. He didn't need to see the man's face to gauge his actions. The fellow had something to hide or else he wouldn't have run as if his feet were on fire.

He hurried to the spot where the man first appeared and turned into the alleyway. Gloom. He blinked to let his eyes adapt to the shadows. A movement a few yards in made his right hand move to the handle of the Colt holstered at his left hip.

"Who's there?" He heard shuffling on the dirt between the buildings. "Show yourself."

Two heartbeats' worth of silence. His eyes adjusted

to the dimness. Up ahead, a high wooden wall. Someone—or *someones*, perhaps—found themselves trapped.

One last chance for the person to show themselves before he drew his pistol and rooted them out. He didn't want to, but if his hand were forced, he'd have to go in with a mind that any man who wasn't willing to step forward had something to hide. And men with secrets could be dangerous. He concealed enough of his own to know.

"I'm gonna ask just one more time. Who's there?" The shuffle came again, so he tempered his tone a notch. "Are you hurt?"

The area between the two buildings offered several spots for cover. Odd lengths of wood leaned against the wall of one building, and piles of crates towered near the other side. In the middle of the tight space, cast-offs tossed haphazardly into the darkness. A no-man's land of refuse no one had a use for. It gave the person who emerged from behind a jumble of crates a hidey hole, a place to consider how it felt to be trapped like a rat on a sinking ship.

He expected a man to step out, but the form coming toward him had a sway to the hips and a waist that his hands could have ringed with an inch or two to spare. No man he'd ever met looked like that.

Dressed in baggy black trousers, dirty jacket, and scuffed boots, the figure pulled a dusty hat lower on its face. Head down, hands held up to show they carried no weapon. The person stopped with a little over an arm's length between them.

Barely five feet apart, almost close enough for Lane to reach out and grab the other's hat off. It crossed his mind to do so, but he had no right to uncover an identity that its owner clearly wanted concealed.

"Are you hurt?" The question bore repeating. A man had run from the alley. Who knew what he'd done before hightailing it?

A head shake. The jacket flapped and gave him a peek at the figure beneath it. Definitely a woman.

"Put your hands down." He took a step back. "If you don't need assistance, I'm gonna be on my way."

He backed out of the space, took one last look at the woman, and nodded. She'd raised her head a touch. Not enough that he could see her features but unless his eyes were playing tricks on him, a blonde curl had slipped from beneath her hat and dangled near her cheek.

****

Gertie couldn't help the tiny flutter that skittered in her belly every time she saw Thomas. He was the sort of man any woman would be happy to call her own. While Violet had worked her charms on him, he continued to work his on almost every female in Wylder, including her. That the man had no notion that the chiseled features, upstanding countenance, or financial security he possessed were the cause for many whispered conversations and appreciative, albeit covert, stares made him even more interesting. She knew, because she had whispered, and even stared, a time or two herself.

But now as she stood looking up at the man, her heart filled with thanks. That he shared his daughter with her and gave her the opportunity to feel, even in some small measure, a motherly camaraderie with the young woman brought joy that she'd never thought to experience. Gratitude warmed her insides and brought the edges of her lips high.

"Good morning, Gertie. Care to come inside?" He held the front door of his house open and took a step back. Beyond, a wide center hallway, staircase to the left leading upstairs, and a door on the right to a parlor. She had been inside enough times to know that the man and his daughter were more apt to gather in the kitchen, where a sitting area flanked a stone fireplace, than the parlor.

"No, thanks. I just dropped over on my way to town to leave this with you." She handed him a loaf of bread. Warmth seeped through the kitchen towel and a sugary aroma filled the air. "A small thank-you for Alexia's hard work on the buntings."

He leaned down and gave the bundle a sniff. A smile crossed his face. "She will appreciate this. And thank you for taking her under your wing with the sewing lessons, too." He shrugged, drawing the fabric of his gray jacket tight across his broad shoulders. "There are some things I'm not meant to teach my girl, and sewing is one of them."

"Well, it's my pleasure, so no thanks are needed. How did Alexia make out last night with the bundle of bunting triangles? Did she have any trouble with the stitching?" The girl had done so well in her dining room that she had no fear she'd done just fine on her own, too.

The tall man drew his eyebrows tight across his lined forehead. "She said they weren't anywhere to be found when she went for them."

"But I left a bundle on my front porch." She gestured toward her house. "When I got home from supper, the bunting pieces, along with the needle, pins, and thread, were gone. I assumed Alexia took them."

He shook his head. "Nope. I had a mighty disappointed girl when she couldn't find them. I told her maybe she misunderstood, and there weren't supposed to be sewing bits on the porch, but she insisted you said they would be there."

"She's right. I did say they'd be waiting for her." If the budding seamstress hadn't taken the bunting pieces, who had? Confusing to say the least, wondering who else would want triangle scraps. "Well, no matter. I'll pull together another packet for her and drop them off on your porch." She looked around, then pointed to a small table set beneath a window. It had an empty bottom shelf. "I'll leave them there, if that's okay."

"I'm sure she'll appreciate it." He smiled and held up the bundle of bread. "And thank you for this, too."

****

Gertie had more piled high on her plate than a starving miner with a tapeworm. Her chore list for the Founder's Day celebrations grew by the day, and no matter how much she did to gnaw at it, the darn thing refused to shrink. She sighed, thinking of how much she still had to accomplish—and how quickly the time between now and the celebrations dwindled.

As she hurried along the dusty street, she mentally calculated how much she would be able to accomplish today. If she went straight home after dropping off the second loaf of bread and conferring with Minnie, she might be able to cross one or two items off her list. Then again, maybe not. Now that the bunting pieces she'd left for Alexia were missing, she would have to cut some more. And that, like every other thing on her agenda, would take time.

But first, the Milligan home. Minnie and her husband had a half-dozen children. Brenda was the eldest, followed by two more sisters and then three brothers. Only the girls were school-age, which meant that the youngest trio were home all day. She couldn't begin to imagine how it might be, caring for a home and family with three little boys underfoot.

Despite her family obligations, Minnie found time to lend a hand whenever a need arose in Wylder. No one knew how she managed, although some suspected divine intervention.

The home had been built near the railroad tracks, in a less-desirable section of town. The exterior walls were unpainted wood, and the upper windows lacked curtains, but the porch looked freshly swept.

She rapped on the half-glass front door. The upper pane wiggled in the wood, so she took a step back. Footsteps sounded from inside and a moment later the door opened.

Her friend jiggled a baby on one hip while a toddler wrapped himself in her skirt. The baby's lower lip trembled, as if it were about to cry, and the one clutching his mama's skirts scowled in Gertie's direction.

"Why, Gertie, how nice to see you." The woman smiled as if she were wrapped in jewels instead of cranky young 'uns. She did a little foot-to-foot dance to keep the baby quiet. "Always such a pleasant surprise when a friendly face shows up at the door."

Manners went a long way toward softening frontier life. Acting as if they were somewhere less rugged lifted a woman's morale, and she returned the kindness with a smile as wide as one she'd offer to a visitor in their fancy Richmond drawing room.

"Well, that's kind of you to say. I see you've got your hands full—"

The baby took that exact moment as the perfect one to screw up its face and let out a wail. Minnie bounced a mite harder and patted the small back, but tears dripped down the little fella's red cheeks.

"I'm tendin' to Jacob for Kate Miller. She had to see Doc Sullivan, and I just thought it would make it easier on her if I kept her smallest one with me." She leaned closer and lowered her voice. "I'm pretty sure she's in the family way again. Pretty sick, too. So, it's the least I can do."

Typical, that one would offer to do for another this way. Women went the extra mile to help each other, even when it didn't prove convenient or the tiniest bit enjoyable. Life in the West didn't come easy, but if they pulled together, burdens seemed lighter. Gertie placed the bundle of bread on a table beside the door.

She held her arms out to the crying baby. "Here, why don't I hold him for a minute?"

The toddler tugged on his mother's skirt, his scowl turning stormy. He opened his mouth and hollered his displeasure at being kept waiting.

"Are you sure?" Minnie looked down at her son, giving his head a pat with her free hand. "I have an apple almost peeled for my boy. He's not usually this ornery, except he's hungry, and with the baby here, well, I'm running behind on feeding the others."

Gertie reached for the fussy babe and settled him against her shoulder. She began to sway, slow and steady, the way she'd like to be held and comforted if she felt distressed.

"I'm certain. Jacob and I are going to sit right over there." She nodded to a well-worn wooden rocker at the far end of the porch. "Take your time with your boys. I've got nowhere to go and nothing pressing to do." A tilt of her head to the bundled loaf on the table. "Maybe they'd like a taste of pumpkin bread with the apple."

The other woman flashed her a grateful smile, gathered up the bread in one hand, and scooped the howling child up onto her free hip. "Thank you."

The porch wasn't as wide as the one on the front of her own house but presented plenty of room for pacing with a fussy baby. She used every inch of it.

The small Miller child seemed intent on waking the entire town, he screamed so hard. She ran a hand over his clothing, checking that nothing poked him anywhere, but there wasn't anything wrong that she could fix. A slow, steady walk from one end of the porch to the other, and gentle pats on the baby's back as she wondered how on earth his mother would fare with another with an infant already at home.

Eventually, Jacob's cries lessened so she sat in the rocker. One press of a toe against the floorboards set it in motion. A few minutes worth of rocking and the little one snored gently against her neck. His cries were gone, his body at ease, and her own heartbeat finally began to slow.

Holding a baby, a blessing that had not come to her many times in her life, soothed her own nerves. Thoughts of the celebrations and to-do lists flew from her mind. All that mattered, everything that deserved attention at this moment in time, curled against her body with so much trust that all she could think of was how magnificent it would be to have had a child of her own to love.

Moisture pooled behind her eyelids, so she softened her gaze. When her throat tightened, she put her head back and closed her eyes. No time to cry about what might have been.

Grief claimed the baby she'd been carrying when she last saw her husband. Before she even had a chance to enjoy motherhood, the privilege had fled. Two losses in such a short period of time, double mourning...it had nearly done her in. But her spirit proved stronger than her sorrow. It amazed her that she survived those first devastating months.

A lullaby came to mind, more a melody than the actual words. Her own mother had sung her to sleep with the tune, and it brought back a wave of warm memories. They made her miss her mama, which closed her throat still more, so she swallowed hard and tried to chase sad images from her mind.

She held on to the lullaby's tune. Her voice creaked when she began, but as she hummed the sounds came without effort. The rumble in her chest against the small body, a reminder of how she'd pressed her face to her mother and listened to her sing. She'd asked if the words came from the heart, because they felt shaken from the center of her mother's chest. The reply, that yes, music and love both came from the heart had left its mark on her.

Now she put love into her humming and prayed the babe in her arms would recognize its touch and carry the feelings forward. If he did, she'd have left an imprint on one child, at least, and that was a blessing.

If only the child were her own...

But, as her mother had also taught her, not all dreams were meant to come true.

****

Lane leaned against the wide trunk of a cottonwood tree and watched the woman rock the baby in her arms as tenderly as if it were her own. When the breeze blew, he heard the sweetest whisper of a tune that turned his insides to jelly. His dear mother had sung that same lullaby to him when she rocked him in her sainted arms.

Gertrude had lost a child shortly after Will's death.

He only knew by way of her brother, Grant. The man could keep a sober secret, but give him a couple of whiskeys and he sang like a canary. One night at the Richmond gentleman's club over a few shots of fine whiskey, Lane had asked the other man whether he thought his sister might wed another someday, and Grant gave him the heartbreaking details of her short pregnancy. Grief for the father took the child, too. Her brother believed she wouldn't ever be comfortable sharing her heart again, which meant no more children for a woman who obviously was born to be a mother.

The last time Lane shed a tear he'd been wearing short pants. Nothing in life, not the death of his closest friend or the loss of the way of life he'd known, brought him this close to losing control.

But now his throat clenched as if the devil himself squeezed his skin, shaking him to his core and sending everything around him out of focus. The only thing that seemed clear, the woman on the porch. She stole his breath, and if he'd been able, he would have sold his soul to Old Scratch himself in exchange for a second chance for Gertrude.

Men made wars. Women suffered the dreadful consequences. All these years later, the woman paid for what he and her husband—damn, what the whole army had done—and there wasn't one thing about that that set well with him.

Not one single thing.

He pressed his palms to his eyes. Then, he stepped into the shadow of the tree and backed away. When he cleared the corner, he turned and headed toward Wylder Street.

If she were like most women, she would make a stop in at the mercantile. Maybe by the time they bumped into each other, his eyes wouldn't give his feelings away.

Chapter 6

Gertie steamed toward the mercantile. Rocking a baby put her behind schedule, but it had been well worth the delay. Nothing compared to holding a little one, and she never passed by that opportunity when it came.

But now she dodged riders on horseback and ducked behind wide, lumbering wagons in her hurry to make up precious time. The sun rose higher with every passing second, and it wouldn't be long before the whole town became as hot as the inside of a cast-iron skillet hanging over an open campfire.

Lord, she hoped it cooled down a touch before the festivities. It wouldn't do to have everyone melting as they danced or falling over in a heat-induced faint, instead of enjoying the games she'd planned. Excessive heat would put a damper on the decorations, too. Flags and buntings were meant to flutter and needed breezes to show to their best advantage.

She wished a breeze would touch Wylder Street and sweep away this hot, fetid air. Every breath she dragged in coated her tongue with a sour taste.

Her mind went to the reason for making her way through Satan's breath. She'd rather be home, sipping a nice glass of lemonade, but her responsibilities didn't allow that luxury. They would have, had there not been a thief in town.

Where in tarnation had that stack of triangles gone to? Who would want them? Useless for much save bunting making, it defied logic that anyone would take such an ordinary bundle.

The front door of the mercantile stood propped open, so she swept inside and raked her gaze across the large space. She had to hand it to Finn Wylder. The man ran a tidy business. Almost anything a soul could want, he stocked, and if he didn't have it, he placed a special order—with a smile, no less. He never acted as if any request were too large or small. The man's kindness and fine business sense benefitted Wylder, and she wasn't the only one who thought so. She'd never heard one harsh world said against the man.

The Wylder family made this town. And years later, they hadn't deserted it. They had stuck around. A commendable accomplishment and one of the many reasons she worked so hard to make their annual celebration a success.

A handful of shoppers walked between the well-stocked aisles. Finn must have gotten a fresh shipment of produce, because several local women stood near the bins of fruits and vegetables. She heard one woman declare an orange "too firm" and another say it felt "just right when I squeeze." Funny how no two people had the same standard of acceptance, and that went for everything, not only food.

She resisted taking a peek at the offerings. With her luck, she'd get sucked into a discussion on the differences between ripe and overripe. She didn't have time for dallying with anyone or listening to opinions on how firm one's fruit should be.

A flush crept up her neck. Her mind had wandered

into territory she generally kept off-limits, and now she heated at the memories that rose without warning. Recollections of how a man's body responded under a woman's touch... She shook her head, chasing the images away. It wouldn't do to bring all that up, not with Will dead and buried. It almost shocked her that carnal thoughts invaded her mind now, after they'd been absent for so long.

Lane Hutchins. Lord, but his appearance had stirred emotions inside her that she'd forgotten about. The blame for her wandering thoughts landed squarely on his shoulders. His big, broad shoulders...

Her cheeks heated so much that she put a palm against her skin. Damn, but she had to leave off thinking about men and their parts unless she wanted her cheeks to burst into flames.

With a final look toward the produce where the women had moved on to discuss the merits of tomatoes, she turned and headed toward the yard goods. There hadn't been much of the bunting fabric left on the bolt when she'd purchased the initial yardage. She went to the wooden shelf where Finn kept the cottons and scanned the stacks. No sign of it. On the adjacent shelf, muslins. Maybe it had been improperly stored so she looked at each bolt, to no avail. A quick check of the rest of the yard goods didn't turn up what she needed, so she headed for the counter. A silent prayer that somewhere in this building hid the exact fabric she came in for.

"Miss Gertie, it's good to see you today."

Finn Wylder's eyes were kind, and despite being a tall man, he had an air of friendliness about him that pulled her in and made her feel comfortable. He smiled and that pushed her sense of security up a notch. Surely, he had more fabric somewhere.

"Why it's good to be seen." She smiled, despite feeling a line of sweat making its way down the center of her back. Best to get what she needed and go home before she ended up in an unsightly puddle on the man's floor. "I came in for more of that bunting fabric I bought the other day." She shot a finger toward the bolts on the shelves. "I checked, but it's not over there, so I'm guessing you maybe have it here, near the counter. Someone bought a length, and you haven't had a chance to return it to its usual spot, perhaps?"

"You're talking about the blue-and-white-striped fabric? I remember you bought quite a good bit of that the other day."

A nod quick enough it tilted her sunbonnet, so she reached up and pushed it back in place. "Yes, that's the one. It's what we are using to replace the Founder's Day buntings that the mice ate over the winter. This year, I'll have to be more careful about storing it."

The man's gaze gave his reply before he opened his mouth. "I hate to tell you this, but I don't have any more of that yard goods." A sad shake of his head. "I sure wish I could help you, but I sold it. Yesterday, in fact. Right before closing."

Her heart fell, and she wished she had bought the entire bolt when she had the chance. But there might be a chance that whoever bought the fabric hadn't cut into it yet. Yesterday and today were almost the same, weren't they?

"Do you remember who bought the fabric?" She gave him a friendly smile, hoping it might entice him to talk. "And if you do, would you share the information with me?" When he hesitated, she added, "After all, the buntings are going to be used for the Founder's Day festivities. And since your family is the founding family of our great town..."

The mercantile owner sighed. "How can I refuse you when you put it that way? Besides, I don't think Missus Harvey will mind if I tell you she's the one who took the last of it. Said something about it making a nice pair of lightweight overalls for her boy."

Her boy. So, Lily had bought the fabric. She and Theo had a toddler.

A last smile before she turned for the door. "Thank you for your help. I'm going to see if Lily won't mind using something different for her boy's britches so I can get that school bunting finished."

****

Lane couldn't have timed it better if he'd coordinated every pocket watch in the Wyoming Territory to coincide with the exact moment that Gertrude Jackson pushed through the front door of Wylder's mercantile. He stood just beyond, so close that it proved impossible for her to avoid running right into him.

"Oof!" The sound came as a high squeak.

He put his hands out and steadied the woman as she bounced back from the wall he presented. When she looked up at him, her eyes were so round they looked like two of those extra-large marbles young children used as prizes in competitions.

"Whoa, there. I didn't mean to startle you." She had found her footing, but he kept his hands on her shoulders. A gentle squeeze and a grin to soften his words. "It wasn't my intention to put up a wall for you to run into. I guess my timing's to blame. I'm sorry."

She gave a small nod. When she raised her shoulders, then pulled them back, he took his cue to remove his hands.

Gertie took a step back and shook her head. "No need to apologize." She looked around and lowered her voice. "Actually, I'm glad it's you. Not every man in Wylder smells good enough to bounce off of, if you catch my meaning."

Well, now if that didn't catch his attention.

"Good to hear that I'm, ah, not quite as unsavory smelling as some folks." He chuckled. Lord, but she did have a way of putting things. "I'd say it's nice to run into you this way, but you're the one who's doing the running. Where are you off to with such a head of steam?"

A blush stole across her cheeks. The woman might be on the other side of her maidenhood, but she still had enough charm and beauty that his heart warmed at the sight of her.

It shouldn't, but it did. He'd left off fighting his attraction. He wouldn't be in Wylder long enough to do any damage to her reputation, but he could show her some fun, if she'd let him. Before he delivered her brother's package, of course. After she received it, she might not want to see him again so he wouldn't rush to give it to her. Grant hadn't told him when to put it in her hands, only to please do so. Which he would. Eventually.

"It's the craziest thing, really. The garlands for the Founder's Day celebration were eaten by mice, so I'm trying to replace them in time to hang them at the schoolhouse, only the pieces I cut and set on my porch for someone to pick up and work on disappeared."

He narrowed his gaze. "Disappeared? Do things like that happen in town a lot?"

"You mean folks walking off with what's not theirs? No, hardly ever, actually." She pulled in a breath so deeply that her shoulders rose high enough to brush the bottoms of her ears. "But it did, and now I don't have enough fabric left to cut more triangles. But Finn, the owner of the mercantile, remembers who bought the last off the bolt, so I'm headed out to see if I can prevail upon Lily to give me the yardage for the buntings."

She let out a long breath. The recitation had brought high color to her cheeks and reminded him of how she'd looked years ago, in the full bloom of young womanhood on her wedding day.

"Sounds like you've got it all figured out. Maybe you won't mind if I walk with you to this Lily's house. I could use a stroll."

A quick shake of her head. He thought she would refuse his request.

"You don't want to 'stroll' all the way out to Lily and Theo's homestead. Why, it's clear out of town and a couple of miles toward the frontier." She sighed. "I'm on my way to rent a wagon to ride on out there."

Ah, an even more enjoyable way to spend time with her. The day got better by the minute.

"How about if I run on over to the livery, get us a nice little buggy, and then ride out with you? If you don't mind my company, that is." He gave her a wide smile, but not too wide. She'd shown herself to be somewhat skittish around men—or maybe just around him, he couldn't be sure—and scaring her off wouldn't do. He tipped his head back and closed his eyes for a few seconds, letting the sun's warmth wash over his skin. When he dropped his chin and met her gaze, it warmed his heart to see she had been watching him with a tiny smile on her face. He decided to press on. "It sure is a nice day for a ride."

"It is. But are you sure you don't have something to do? I mean, I can't let you squander your morning away running errands with me. The Founder's Day decorations aren't your problem."

He leaned a few inches closer and lowered his voice. "It would be my pleasure to accompany you." As he hoped, her upper body tilted closer to his. Now he smelled the sweet scent of apples and lavender. Coming from her hair, maybe, or perhaps her dress. He didn't know and didn't care where it originated when he took a deep breath. A quick internal head shake to gather his wits, then he stood tall and gave her a nod. "I'll go fetch a wagon. Be back for you in less time than it takes to shoe a mare."

A tap to the brim of his hat before he turned and walked away. Give a female time to consider and she might find a reason to keep him from the plan. While he respected the fortitude and strength of a woman like Gertie, he believed in providing assistance when possible. He knew that if she thought on it too long, she'd decide to take the drive on her own.

And that would put him in a precarious position. Grant wouldn't appreciate him letting his sister ride off into the wilderness on her own. And he hated the idea, too. So he'd have to follow her covertly and run the risk of being found out. He'd known some Native trackers who could tail an animal or human without ever being detected, but his skills weren't nearly that good.

No, better to take her to this homestead. Sitting beside her would make every mile fly by, no matter how far into the frontier it sat.

****

Gertie had no idea how the morning had gotten so spun around. All she wanted, blue-and-white fabric and the time to cut new bunting pieces.

Instead, she directed Lane out of town and rode along a narrow trail toward the Harvey property. He'd rented a nice little buggy, complete with black leather canopy, so she sat in comfort. And, in very close proximity to the man himself.

Every time the buggy hit a rut in the lane, or they rounded a curve, their shoulders brushed. Not a distasteful situation, but it sent shivers up her spine. Good tingles. Ones that oughtn't be there.

Sensations like no man since her beloved Will had brought to her body. It had been a long time since she'd been touched by another, even in this harmless sort of way.

Her tongue felt glued to the roof of her mouth, and she searched for something to break the silence.

She swallowed hard. Wracked her brain for a topic of discussion. Wondered what interested him. It had been so long since they'd sat across a table from each other back home in Richmond. It seemed like another lifetime when they laughed and chatted with ease. Conversation used to come easily, but now she sat mute, scrambling for a bit of harmless nonsense to fill the silence. She'd used her best conversational topics over dinner at the Wylder Hotel. Now her mind sat empty.

The black gelding clip-clopped along at a steady

pace, seemingly unaffected by those in his care. Lane had an eye for beautiful horseflesh. She never would have engaged such a big animal, and she certainly wouldn't have splurged on the fancy little buggy. A reliable work horse and a wagon with serviceable wheels were all she required.

It crossed her mind that men liked compliments, so she said the first thing that came into her head. "That is one large animal, isn't it?" She instantly regretted that she hadn't given more consideration to the words before they shot from her mouth.

Beside her, his shoulder shook when it brushed hers. She felt his struggle to keep from laughing, even without his saying a word. A glance at his profile to confirm her suspicions.

Talking with men was much more difficult than she remembered it being.

He cleared his throat. His tone held a hint of mirth, but he did not outwardly laugh. "I suppose he is, at that." Another short throat clearing. "I wanted the ride to be as smooth as possible for you, so I chose the horse that looked the sturdiest."

"Well, that wasn't necessary. I don't need anything fancy." She couldn't remember when anyone had given her comfort a thought. "But that was very kind of you, Lane."

He turned his head and dipped his chin. "I'm glad you noticed. It was the handsomest horse in the livery, and I thought you might like him. And the buggy? Are you comfortable?"

Considering the conveyance had cushioned seats, instead of a hard wood bench, and a crisp leather canopy above their heads, they rode in luxury.

"Very. But you didn't have to get so extravagant on my account." She ran a hand over the brass fittings beside her head that held the top in place. "I'm used to making do with much less, you know."

The smile vanished from the handsome man's face. Instantly she wished she hadn't spoken so much. She had not meant to insult him.

"Just because you can do with less doesn't mean you need to, at least not when I'm around. Tru-ah, Gertie, you are a woman who deserves the world. And this—" He gave the reins an extra hard jiggle. "—isn't excessive by any stretch of the imagination."

"Well, that's kind of you to say but as I've tried to tell you, I'm not the same woman you knew. I've changed since coming out west. A lot. And this woman, the one sitting beside you, isn't in the habit of being pampered. Not one bit, really."

Lane shook his head, a slow, thoughtful motion that reminded her of old times. He and Will shared discussions that brought that measured movement so often just seeing it again tugged at her heartstrings.

He didn't respond to her proclamation. Instead, he pushed the conversation in a new direction.

"I remember one evening an apple pie hit the dining room floor."

Good Lord, but that had been years ago. The memory brought a smile. She slapped a hand onto her cheek. "How on earth do you recall things like that?"

He smirked. "Oh, I recall a lot more than that."

Thankfully, the only witnesses to her pie disaster were Will and Lane. She'd waxed the dining room floor earlier in the day, and when she walked over to place the pie on the dinner table, her heel slipped. Her feet flew out from beneath her, the pie dish went flying, and in the few moments when no part of her touched the floor, she felt sure she was about to break her neck.

But her husband leapt up and caught her in his arms. Their dessert, however, hadn't been as lucky.

"What a mess that pie made on my clean floor. And unless I've forgotten, I served cookies I'd baked for the Reverend Whipple. Poor man, he missed out on a treat that week."

His smile grew. "The reverend had enough sweets brought to him by the church ladies. Rounder than a watermelon, the man could barely fit into his Sunday coat." His voice turned serious. "But what I remember most about that day is how Will acted."

She took a deep breath and let her mind wander back to those precious moments. Her husband hadn't cared one lick about the pie. His only concern had been for her safety. He'd even helped her clean the mess, right in front of his friend. Come to think of it, Lane had done a share of mopping up, too.

"He always was a good man." She sighed. "The greatest blessing in my life."

"He loved you, and if he were here, he wouldn't think it wise for you to choose to deprive yourself. We both know his passing left you well-tended, money-wise. Will would want you to splurge a bit here and there, Gertie." He stopped, then gave a slow shrug. "I'm sorry, but it's a big stretch to not call you Trudy."

"More than my name has changed." She looked down at her hands where they lay in her lap. Her white gloves were growing thin in the fingertips but would last a while longer. She had the means to replace them, but it didn't seem important. Keeping up appearances here in the territory didn't top the must-do list the way it had back east. "I'm really not the same woman you knew."

"You keep saying that, and I get it. What happened to you had to have an effect, a profound one, but inside, deep in the center of you, I truly believe the woman I knew from our time in Richmond exists. She can't be gone forever. I won't consider it." He paused and ran his free hand across his brow. Even with the canopy, the warmth affected them. "I told Grant you might not want to see me, but the fact that you did and are still spending time with me tells me that you're not so awfully changed. You only think you are, dear Trudy."

She let his words settle over her. Some truth in what he said, but he didn't have any idea how hard she struggled to present this semblance of normalcy to the world. Inside where it mattered most, some days she wanted to scream at the injustice that brought her life to this point.

"You have no idea who I really am."

He slowed the horse and turned to face her. "Then give me a chance to get to know who you are now. Please, all I ask is a chance."

Before she could speak, she heard a click.

****

If he'd been able to do it, Lane would've kicked himself for being so damn stupid. In a preventable situation, one that no self-respecting war veteran should encounter, he hated that his careless inattention had brought them to this point.

He'd let romantic feelings for the woman beside him distract him.

A potentially deadly mistake, dropping his guard. It

wasn't called the Wild West for nothing, and here he'd gone and sashayed over the plains as if it were a Richmond dance hall. Bile rose in his throat from the acid churning a hole in his gut. His eyes narrowed, and he swallowed down more anger than he'd felt in years. The worst part? Most of it he directed toward himself.

If they died here on this dusty stretch, it would be his fault.

Chapter 7

"Keep them hands where I kin see 'em." The man rode up beside the buggy near Lane's elbow, his Winchester rifle pointed their way, on a horse whose head dipped low. The hand that held the firearm wobbled a bit, and the business end of the barrel shook. But shaky or not, it stopped them in their tracks. "I mean what I say, y'hear? I'll shoot ya both deader than a cow patty if'n ya give me reason."

Gertie didn't doubt he meant what he said. Desperation drove men to do what they wouldn't ordinarily consider, and the robber looked desperate. Had they been on a street in Wylder or passing in the mercantile, she might have had some pity for him, he and his horse being so downtrodden and all. But they were alone on a stretch of prairie, with no one in sight who could help them, facing a man whose motives were clearly unsavory. Her heart hardened against him, but not as completely as it should have. Despite the situation, compassion for the unfortunate soul seeped in.

Even astride a horse, the man looked ready to fall through his pants. Nearly as slender as the rifle barrel, his shoulders jutted out against a raggedy gray jacket, and the legs of his blue jean trousers fluttered in the warm breeze, slapping the horse's lean flanks. She could make out the outline of the animal's ribcage beneath its dull brown coat, and she wondered how long it had been since either had a decent meal.

Hard to tell the man's age with his cheeks and jaw covered with a tangle of whiskers while the rest of his face showed a layer of grime so thick she doubted lye soap would cut through it. Dynamite, maybe, but the filth would make any soap bar cry. She'd always believed herself a compassionate woman, but she couldn't stop a shiver of disgust from running up her spine when her mind wandered to the rest of the man. With such a dirty face, the other bits of him must be grimy, too.

No human should exist in such dirt.

Still, that didn't give him the right to accost them on the road.

Lane's tone did not challenge, but he also didn't show fear. She imagined he didn't have any, knowing him the way she did. Neither he nor Will were ever frightened, not that she recalled, although there were times when she was sure they should have been. One of the reasons they were so close, that they had the same kind of dispositions and that included their courage.

"No one's gonna shoot anyone here." Lane held the reins in one hand, but the other rested on his thigh. Close enough to his hip, but far enough from his revolver that it would be hard to get to it before the rider got a shot off. She glanced down at his fingertips, dancing on the fabric covering his leg. "We know you don't want to do us harm, so why don't you turn your horse around and ride off? We'll continue our way, you'll go yours, and no one will be hurt by this little, ah, meeting."

"You think I'm stupid?" A bump of the rifle butt

against the saddle made Gertie flinch. Suppose the man's finger slipped and the damn thing went off? Aimed toward the man beside her more than at her, it would surely hurt him. "Turn around and ride away?" A snort, followed by a barking cough. "Lookee here, I mightn't be the brightest star in the sky but I'm no eejit. I turn around, and you pull that shiny piece at your hip out 'n nail me one right in the middle of my back. Nossir, I ain't doin' that."

Indignation pulled her forward. She leaned past Lane's body, which he'd angled away from her the minute they were waylaid. She supposed he did it to protect her, but the rider's words were enough to push her past concerns about her safety. "Watch what you're saying! Lane has never shot a man in the back in his life. Only cowards would do that, or even consider saying something so weak-minded."

A shoulder nudged her back, and she didn't fight him.

"You'd best check ya woman." The rider leaned sideways and spat. "She's a mite too big fer her britches, looks like. Hell, mebbe she's the one wearin' the britches in your fam'ly. Mebbe she's the one who'd shoot me in the back."

The man beside her sat up straighter, and she felt anger coming from him. The air in the buggy grew charged, and it had nothing to do with the midday heat.

"Now you're on shaky ground. Don't malign the lady's character. Leave her out of this. Whatever you're thinking of doing, it's between us." He paused and calmed his tone a hair. "Why don't you tell me what exactly you want? Then we can all be on our way."

The cackle that came from the other man surprised

her. Almost a howl, the sound put the ears of both horses up. Their livery horse took a step back, so Lane gentled it with a tug on the reins and a low murmur.

"Whaddaya think I want? Hell, man, my pockets're so empty the only thing in 'em is air. My belly, the same, and Chester here, well he ain't ate nothin' in longer'n I can say." His howl had left a tear trailing from his left eye. He wiped at it with the heel of his hand. "What do I want? I want what ever'body else has, that's what. A place to lay my head, a woman to keep these bones warm at night. Food…what I wouldn't give for some good grub…"

The man's demeanor rapidly descended from stiff-lipped, gun-toting robber to a rambling, almost incoherent figure. If he kept losing control, no way to tell what he'd do.

Violet Bloom taught the children of Wylder their arithmetic and writing, but she had also schooled the local women on a few things. While the six-shooter Will had given her when they were married lay in her delicates drawer along with her embroidered nighties in the bedroom of her house, the Remington over-under derringer she'd gotten on the teacher's advice nestled in her skirt pocket. She inched her hand toward the break in the cotton seam, hoping the man didn't come to his senses before she could grab it.

He didn't. When her fingers closed around the small firearm, she reminded herself that it did not have a safety catch and one wrong move would fire the thing. Violet warned that its size made its power misleading and that if she aimed it well, it had the ability to kill its target.

She remembered that now as she slipped it from

her pocket and into the folds of her skirt.

"Look, we've all fallen on hard times now and then." Leave it to Lane to try to find a bond with the man. The tactic reminded her so much of her departed husband. "You're not the only man down on his luck these days."

That brought a second howl from the man. "Down on my luck? Hell, man, I ain't got no luck! Never had, not even as a baby. Papa said I nursed my mama to death, that's what did 'er in. Me, with my damn luck so bad it'd kill my own mother." Tears leaked from the man's eyes in a sad stream. He didn't bother to wipe them, and she wondered if he even knew they were there.

"You've had it hard, then. I'm sorry for that but 'bout the only thing I can do is try to help you now." Lane transferred the reins to his other hand and went to reach for the inner chest pocket of his jacket.

The man waved the rifle in the air between them. "What're ya doin'? Stop it right now! Don't force me to blow yer head off!"

There's only so much a woman can take before she pulls things into her own hands, and she'd reached that breaking point. The robber came unwrapped right before their eyes, and who could tell how much more his tired, hungry mind could take?

She raised her hand and closed one eye the way Violet told her to do. With so little distance between them, her extended arm came close enough to the arm waving the Winchester that she had a good shot. So, she took it—and the man howled louder than before as he lost his grip, the rifle hit the dirt, and his horse skittered sideways.

Lane pulled his Colt from its holster, but he needn't have. The man wasn't a threat to anyone with his hand clutched to his chest.

"You shot me! You went and shot my damn hand, woman!"

The wounded man hollered as if she'd taken the whole hand instead of one small finger. Pretty sure she'd hit the pinky, if her aim had been true. And really, how much did that little end finger do, anyhow?

When the man beside her turned to face her, she gave a smile. His brows shot up, so she shrugged. "We can't dillydally here all day. I need to get that bunting fabric from Lily, remember?"

****

Even though he'd seen it with his own eyes, Lane could hardly believe that Gertie shot the man the way she had. No warning. No indication that she had a firearm in her possession, let alone her hand.

The woman baffled him. Yes, she surely did. But he had to admit, the bafflement tasted sweet.

They had relieved the wounded man of his firearm, something that didn't sit easy with Lane, but the fellow had already shown he couldn't be trusted to use it lawfully. And now that he'd been shot, he might take it into his head to come after them in a vengeful manner. No, they couldn't chance that. So the other's rifle lay beneath the seat where it wouldn't do any harm.

They'd watched the man bandage his hand with the dirty scrap of fabric he wore around his neck. Gertie offered him a clean length, but a scowl refused her kindness. He'd been directed to stop in to see Doc Sullivan and tell the doctor that they'd be in later to explain. Lane told him he'd cover the medical bill and added that the injured man should stop in at the café for a meal, and to tell the owner of the establishment to put the charges on his account.

Some might think it strange that he would foot the bill for a man who attempted to rob him, but he saw the other's reduced circumstances. He felt it essential to have compassion for humanity, despite the finer details of their meeting.

It had been nearly a half hour since they'd watched the rider disappear down the dusty trail. He had to be sure the man headed away, and then waited to see if he doubled back. He hadn't, so they'd continued toward the Harvey place.

They had been on the homestead for a few minutes, but neither spoke. Companionable silence, and the view from the carriage supported it. A mountain range in the distance, endless plains sweeping away toward the craggy brown boulders. Beside the lane, a bubbling creek. Prime land, with its own water source and all. He guessed the Harveys pulled a good living out of their claim.

The home came into view when they rounded a slight curve. Two stories, painted white, with a wide front porch and shutters beside the windows. Yes, the man did well for himself, to own a place this nice.

Gertie shot him a smile. "Pretty, isn't it?"

He nodded. "A fine day for a ride, and the homestead is something to be proud of. How long have Theo and Lily, did you say her name is, lived here?"

There were too many folks in Wylder to keep track of all their names. He'd never been good at that, anyway, but once he met someone, he'd remember the face. No guarantee on the name, though.

"Yes, Lily and Theo Harvey. They haven't been married too awful long, about a year or so. They've got a little boy named Cade. Cute as a button, that one is."

A chance to step into uncharted waters. Bold of him, but their years of friendship gave him courage. He took a deep breath.

He gentled his tone and hoped his question didn't wound her. "You've got a soft spot for children, haven't you?"

Beside him, her shoulders lifted, then dropped. The movement brushed her sleeve against his with a feathery rustling sound that reminded him of butterfly wings.

"Doesn't every woman?"

The words were low, so he leaned toward her. They were nearing the house. A couple stood beside the porch, watching their progress. He slowed the horse.

He shook his head. "I've met some who went to great lengths to avoid having a child. So no, not every woman takes to little ones the way you do."

Another shrug. Her sadness filled the buggy, and he wished he'd kept his mouth shut. What sort of man asks a woman these kinds of questions? A stupid one, that's who.

Whatever had he been thinking, opening this conversation? Well, they were in too deep now for him to change the subject. Besides, he knew better than most that painful thoughts never healed on their own. They needed to see the light, and he owed it to his best friend's widow to offer that to her.

"Look, Gertie, I know about the child you lost after Will died."

Her head whipped around, so he turned and met

her gaze. The beautiful eyes he knew so well flashed, and for a moment, he thought he'd made her angry.

"How do you know?"

He couldn't lie. "Grant."

A long, shuddering sigh that made him want to place an arm around her shoulders. He resisted, but just.

"That makes sense. He never could keep his nose out of my business." She ran a hand over the fabric covering her knees. Despite the heat, her skirt fell in crisp waves. "I had to move across the frontier to escape his interference."

She had turned the conversation from one matter to another with ease.

"You seem happy here, so does it matter how you ended up in Wylder?"

"I am happy." They drew near enough to the house that she gave the couple who waited for them a small wave. "And you're right about children, too. I do love them."

There had to have been men who would consider themselves lucky to have such a fine woman, who would love to have a family with her, but she remained single. It astounded him that no one had swept her off her feet yet.

He pressed his luck as he brought the horse to a stop in the area near a small barn. A hitching post near the open door stood in a puddle of shade and would serve to keep their horse in comfort. "But you don't have any of your own, do you?"

The couple drew near. A fast shake of her head, then she met his gaze. Her words were quiet but weighty. "No, I don't."

The door stood open. He had to walk through. A

quick look at the folks making their way to them, then he asked the question that dogged him every mile between Virginia and the Wyoming Territory. "Why not? Surely you've had opportunities…men who would be honored to take you as their bride. You love home and family so much, why haven't you begun anew?"

Gertie glanced at the homesteaders. They were a few feet shy of hearing the conversation in the buggy. For a moment, he thought she might refuse to answer him.

She lowered her voice and met his gaze. "If I could have children without a man, I would. But we know that isn't possible, now don't we?"

****

The ride to the Harvey homestead proved fruitful.

Lily gladly handed over the fabric which she, fortunately, hadn't touched with a scissor yet. And bless her heart, she accepted the length of midnight-blue cotton offered in its place. The fabric came from Gertie's stash of prized material, yardage that she hoped to use on special projects. She'd held on to the blue waiting for something important to come along, but so far nothing had. Time to let it go, she figured.

The littlest Harvey would look good in the deep color. He'd flashed her a shy smile and she'd seen his cornflower-blue eyes. Any outfit Lily made with the dark-blue yardage would bring out the stunning feature. The boy had baby charm now but with those eyes, he'd grow into a real handsome young man. Take after his daddy, for sure.

Lane didn't ask any more personal questions on the ride back to town, and she was grateful. In fact, he hardly spoke, and it didn't bother her one bit that they rode in peace. After a short visit with the Harveys, she realized the wind had gone from her sails. Tired, hot, and done in by thinking about all that she didn't get done in the day, she preferred the quiet.

It seemed the man beside her did, too. She caught him looking at her a few times, but he didn't offer to share whatever he had on his mind. And she didn't ask. Better to leave things uncomplicated between them. Lane would move on sooner than later, she suspected. When he did, there should be no unfinished business holding him back.

But she did have to admit that she liked having the man around. His presence comforted her, a reminder of the life she once led without bringing any of the sadness of what she'd lost. Strange, really, that he affected her this way. No other man ever had found a sweet spot to offer her, a place where she could relax and not worry about whether she might be inviting unwanted interest by being herself and speaking her mind. He let her drop her guard, and it came as a relief after having been so conscious of her standing as a single woman for so long.

And Lane was easy on the eyes, besides. She wouldn't admit to anyone else that she had thoughts like that, but then, who would ask? She was a widow, yes. Dead? Far from it. As such, she noticed the way he walked. How he held his head at an angle when he listened to her reply to one of his questions. The deep timbre of his laughter, which came without reservation. His hands, lined from years of hard work, yet looking as if they could touch as gently as a feather.

She wondered how it would feel to be stroked by one of those hands. Held by the strong arms that tested the seams on his shirts. Cradled in the warmth of his embrace. Those thoughts, more so than the others, were for her alone. She'd sooner go to her grave than admit she entertained any of them. Her allegiance still belonged to her dead husband. It always would, as long as she had a breath left in her body. But still…she wondered. For the first time in all the years since her Will had been killed, she speculated over how it might feel to lie with another man.

Probably a good thing that Lane would be leaving Wylder soon. What swam in her mind could only get her into trouble, and Lord knows she'd already had her share of that. More than enough to last a lifetime, certainly.

When they reached town, he directed the buggy to her house. The horse stopped at the end of her front walk, beside the hitching post at the painted white fence.

For a long moment, neither she nor the man beside her moved. Then, he turned to her and met her gaze. She couldn't read the look in his eyes, only saw that it had changed during their outing.

"Trudy, ah, Gertie, thank you for allowing me to accompany you to the Harvey homestead. They're nice folks, and I'm glad I got to meet them." He scrubbed a hand across his chin and looked up at her house before he trained his eyes back on her. "You've made a fine life out here for yourself. A good home, decent friends, a place in the community." He sighed. "Yeah, you've done real well for yourself. Will would be pleased if he could see this."

She swallowed around the lump that rose in her throat at the mention of her husband. Funny how that happened. She could be perfectly okay one minute and near tears the next, all at the sound of the man's name.

"Thank you for saying that. I always hope he'd be proud, but how can I ever really know?" She held the bunting fabric tight against her bosom. "I can never really tell, but I do pray he somehow sees me."

"I think he sees. And he'd be proud, I'm sure." He paused, then added, "Grant would be happy to see how well you're doing, too."

Grant again. Would she ever be free of her brother's shadow? Was she destined to have the man and his opinions about how she lived her life hang over her forever?

She pulled her eyebrows together. It probably didn't do a lot for her appearance, but she didn't care. They'd been having a sweet conversation until he'd brought her brother into it. Now he could suffer the consequences of her sour expression.

"I don't care what that man thinks. Not one bit!" She turned on the cushioned seat and reached for one of the metal struts that held the canopy in place. A tug, and she moved enough to dangle her shoes over the step. "My brother has no bearing on my life. None, do you understand? When I needed his support, he denied me. Now, I don't need anything from him, and I'll thank you to remember it. I don't want to hear his name again!"

She heard him move behind her, but before the man could come around the buggy, her feet were on the ground. She made it to the front porch without looking back, and when she heard him call her name, she stuck the key in the lock and turned it.

In a heartbeat, she stood in her home with her back

pressed against the front door. The cool wood touched the back of her neck, sending a shiver down her spine. She'd run like a scared schoolgirl, but he'd turned the day from fine to annoying in one word. Why had he mentioned her horrid brother?

Her pulse raced, and the thoughts inside her head whirled.

She wished she didn't wonder when she'd see Lane again. But, as with so many other bits of her life, that fell far from her control because if she had any question she'd like answered, the timing of the man's next appearance fell at number one on her list.

It felt like an eternity before she heard the horse's hooves carry the buggy down the street. In those long, quiet minutes, she fought to not open the door and invite the man inside. She'd only left him behind, and yet she wanted to see him again.

I'm losing my mind—addlepated by the heat.

What else could it be?

Chapter 8

The baby nestled against her bosom, a warm bundle whose heart beat in time with her own. Her gaze pinned to the wee one's face, savoring the sweetness of him as he slept. So innocent, so pure...that he'd been entrusted to her came as a miracle. The answer to one of her greatest wishes, to have a baby of her own to love.

He stretched one small arm out of the blanket that swaddled him, a fragile limb that would grow strong. Her vow to him, to love and protect him, watch him flourish, and see him take his place in the world. And always, she would walk beside him. Provide a safe home for him to feel the love that bound them together.

His mouth opened, the rose-colored lips separating as he stretched. A murmur of contentment, so soft and pure, came as he settled against her. Her heart sang, as if he held the notes to a symphony that only the two of them shared.

A sigh. This time, her own. It sounded loud by comparison to the inhales and exhales her little one produced. She counted his breaths, falling more deeply under the spell of his existence.

One. Then two. Another, slow and steady.
Four breaths, the exhalation long and peaceful.
Five—but no!
A hand reached out to grab the baby, catching the

tiny, exposed arm first, then scooping the rest of his body from her arms. She reached, but the thief was quicker and snatched the boy child away before she could tighten her hold.

"No!" Her voice tore from her throat as she struggled to stand. Her legs were cemented in place. Her arms, heavy on her lap. Empty now, no babe in her embrace. "No—he's mine—no, you can't have him!"

The babe was torn from her sight. Gone, whisked away on that sweet breath. Lost in one moment, leaving a gaping hole in her chest where her heart had been. She struggled to breathe, to make sense of the loss.

"No!" Another scream, this time so raw and agonized she barely recognized it as her own.

Tears streamed down her cheeks. Her vision blurred, but in the distance she saw him, and her heart stuttered.

Will. Her Will.

In his arms, their son.

She tried to lean forward, struggled to reach for them but could not. Immobile, stolen of everything save sight and the ability to plead.

"Please, don't take him. Please, I beg you—"

Without a word, her husband turned and walked into a white haze. It surrounded him and the child. In half a heartbeat, they were gone.

"No..."

Gertie woke with the scream on her lips. Her nightgown clung to her sweaty body. Tears turned the hair at her temples wet. She struggled to breathe through the congestion in her nose and swallowed hard against the heat left in her throat. Raw, from the surface of her being right down to her center.

A hand over her chest, between her breasts to be sure her heart still beat. It did, but not the nice, easy rhythm that usually carried her through her days. No, this thrumming came hard and fast, as if she'd been running.

Chased by invisible demons.

There would be no rest for her tonight, so she rose and draped her wrapper around her shoulders. Turned to pull the rumpled bedcovers into place. Tucked her feet into her slippers and padded toward the doorway.

Sometimes her life wore her out. She sighed, grateful that her breath came without a hitch now, as she wiped a hand over her cheeks. No reprieve for a broken heart, shattered dreams, and remnants of a previous life haunting a tortured mind. The struggle to go day after day feeling broken, and the weight of hiding that brokenness from others, exhausted her.

Sleep. Wonderful, dreamless rest, the kind she used to find wrapped in Will's arms, that's what she needed now. The truth of it slapped her again, that she would never find solace and ease in a man's arms. Hardly seemed worth living the remainder of her life without those comforts.

She chided herself for entertaining such thoughts. Surely, a reason for going on could always be found, if only one were to look hard enough. For now, she had the Founder's Day preparations to finish. No time for feeling sorry about what couldn't be changed.

****

By the time the street outside her house buzzed with morning activity, Gertie had all the triangles for the remainder of the bunting cut from the fabric Lily had surrendered. The tidy pile sent a wave of satisfaction coursing through her. The morning may not have gotten off to an auspicious start, but she had salvaged it.

She believed in keeping busy, and with the festivities bearing down on her, she had plenty to do. The afternoon would be a perfect time for sewing the banner pieces together. She would sit out on the front porch. If fortune were on her side, Alexia and Brenda might spot her after their school day ended and offer to help. She could use all the extra hands she could find.

Remnants of her nightmare hung like a nasty-smelling cloud over her head. No matter how she tried to shake it, it clung. Disappointing to be so afflicted by one's sleep terrors but there was no help for it. Maybe tonight she'd find peace, but until then, she took shallow breaths and concentrated on getting through the day.

She turned her attention on the tasks still on her mental list. With any luck, she could tackle a few before school let out and, hopefully, her sewing girls were available.

A glance through the dining room window at the sky. The day's warmth tempered by some clouds. Not the fat, fluffy kind so often evidenced back home in the south, but the grayish, almost ominous, low and flat type that sometimes hung over the plains. Well, she didn't have far to go, so even if those clouds let loose a sprinkle, she would wait it out in a doorway.

Her reticule sat on the table beside the front door, so she grabbed it and went out onto the porch. Another peek at the sky. Not promising but not so horrible it chased her back inside.

No, she would not be chased. Not in the light—or

cloudy gloom—of day, anyhow. Nighttime had its own set of rules, but during the waking hours she determined her destiny. And now, that meant calling on the food committee members.

****

Lane turned to the woman beside him in the bed. She lay face down, her hair spread across the pillow. He didn't remember her name. Hell, he wasn't sure she'd even told it to him last night before she invited him into this room.

He looked around. Most likely, she rented the room above the saloon or gave someone part of her earnings for the right to use it. It didn't have a lived-in look. More a flopped-in atmosphere, without any real sense of its occupant's character. No trinkets or geegaws. No evidence that the woman snoring lightly on the flat pillow resided in its four walls. She probably didn't, seeing as the only dress hung over the back of a wooden chair beside the door.

She'd been wearing a scarlet dress last night, and he'd been attracted to it like a bull in heat. The interest grew with each shot of whiskey he consumed. He'd joined a poker game and had a good run of luck. Every winning hand brought a fresh round of drinks. The more he won, the more whiskey he poured down his throat. And the greater his interest in the friendly woman wearing the low-cut red dress.

He'd been too intoxicated to get back to the boardinghouse, so when she offered to take him upstairs he didn't decline. The woman—damn, but he wished he knew her name—had been laughing. Joyful. If she had a sad past, she kept it a secret. No heartstrings pulled, none of the responsibility he felt yesterday with Gertie.

Gertie. A different woman from the Trudy of years gone by, but similar enough that the familiar tug to get close to her had not disappeared. With her, there were layers of feelings. Some tender, others melancholy. Still more that sparked happiness and hope, emotions he hadn't known for far too many years.

He reached for his pants and stepped into them. With as much stealth as his aching head allowed, he took his shirt off the bedpost and slid his arms into it, then tucked it into his waistband and did up his fly. Movement brought a brass band alive in the region above his eyes, but he leaned forward and grabbed his vest.

"Well, good mornin'."

Damn it all. He'd hoped to escape without having to make small talk.

The woman turned onto her back and rubbed her eyes. When she raised her arms, the sheet slipped low enough to reveal one rosy nipple. She smiled and waved him closer when she saw his gaze drop.

"Like what you see, honey? I tried to share it all with you last night, but you wasn't havin' any of it." She pulled the sheet down and ran a hand over her left breast. Her fingertip circled that deep areola, bringing it to attention beneath her touch. She grinned. "That's all right, though. Don't mean we can't have ourselves a little mornin' fun. I promise you'll start the day with a bang you won't forget any time soon…c'mon back to bed, and let's get these springs singin'."

She threw the sheet down toward her feet, exposing her body to the waist.

His gaze drifted over the woman. Firm, with high

breasts and a flat belly. Tiny waist, the kind he liked most. A man should be able to put his hands around a woman's midsection when he held her close. Leastways, he enjoyed the feel of gripping a woman when they came together, a tender connection to enhance the other, more primal, joining.

He hadn't joined with this woman last night, and despite her enticing invitation, he wouldn't do so now. No, he'd merely needed a spot to sleep, and this bed had given that.

He reached for his hat and set it on his head. His feet slid into his boots as his hand dipped into a front pocket.

"That's a mighty fine offer, ma'am, but I'm afraid I have places to go this morning."

She scowled. "We could be real quick about it, if you want."

Lane pulled some of his poker winnings out and tore a couple of bills from the wad. A shake of his head as he dropped the money on the bedside table. At the sight of the cash, her expression softened. "I appreciate that, but I need to leave." He touched the brim of his hat and headed for the door. "Thank you for your hospitality, ma'am. Have a nice day now."

When he closed the door behind him, he breathed a long sigh.

The woman had been pretty. Pleasant. Charming, even.

But she wasn't Gertie. And for now, the only woman he wanted to share a bed with, his best friend's widow, wasn't on speaking terms with him.

Just as well, maybe. Once she found out the whole truth about why Grant sent him to Wylder, she'd hate him for sure.

****

Gertie hurried along the boardwalk.

In front of Thomas Harvey's office, she glanced in the wide window and saw him hunched over some paperwork at his desk.

Then, Addison Merriweather's law office. Closed up and dark, the man was not in evidence. She imagined he might be spending time with his wife, Daisy. The pair was often spotted together during the day when most men were busy working. That's what wealth brought, she supposed. Hours to do what one enjoyed, rather than what must be done for survival.

Rumor about town, that Merriweather's fortune filled the vault at the bank, didn't intrigue her. Money couldn't fix a broken heart or fill empty arms. Some needs went beyond the capacities of silver and gold.

A lot of families in the territory scrabbled to eke sustenance out of the harsh landscape and challenging circumstances of frontier living. That they surmised about the man's wealth she understood. To them, any hint of excess gave cause for speculation. But it also gave rise to considering grabbing some of that so-called extra wealth, what they perceived could be snatched and never missed, and that gave her cause for concern. No, better to avoid giving the impression of enhanced circumstances. Staying far from thinking about others' bank accounts would serve her best, as well.

Still, it brought a smile to think the strong attorney might be passing a peaceful morning with his curly-haired bride. She hoped they were having fun. This close to winter, taking time to enjoy the year's last weeks of sunshine seemed vital.

A few minutes of brisk walking brought her to the Milligan home where she felt certain there were joyful moments nestled in among the lean ones. This modest abode housed six children, as well as the two adults. It hardly seemed possible that so many could fit in a space so small, but they did.

Despite its position near the railroad tracks, the place looked far from neglected. As she'd noted when she'd comforted a crying baby, the porch boasted an old rocking chair, its unvarnished wooden seat worn into the shape of a posterior from hours of use. The porch had been swept clean, and a lone flowerpot held a tuft of sage. She ran a finger across the tips of the silver-green foliage and inhaled the comforting scent.

Minnie answered the door on the first knock. Today she held a sleeping baby in her arms, her red, chapped hands curled protectively around the little one. When she spoke in hushed tones, she offered a smile.

"Gertie, so good to see you. Care to come inside?" She took a step back. Beyond, a hallway that sat as bare as a turkey's carcass after a feast. Clean, but empty. And dark, without the light from windows to brighten it up.

She shook her head. "No, thanks. I can't linger." A nod toward the little one. "And you've got your hands full, besides. I just wanted to check on the food tables. Have we got everything covered? Enough for all?"

Minnie took charge of the food tables at both the Christmas party at the school and the Founder's Day celebration. Her planning skills were unrivaled, and she somehow managed to conjure mouth-watering displays out of seemingly thin air. Every family who could contribute did, and she had a donation fund to make up for those who were unable to provide a dish for the tables. More importantly, almost, that she sent the neediest families home with food after every event, and acted as if they were doing the town a favor by accepting the leftovers so they didn't go to waste.

One of Gertie's favorite people, this mother of a half-dozen and caregiver to countless others, had the soul of an angel.

Now, she tucked a tendril of hair behind one ear and nodded. "Yes, we'll have plenty."

"I'm thinking we may have more mouths to feed than we usually do. Out at the Cruesdale ranch, there are extra hands. I hear they're putting up a couple of last-minute barns on the far edges of the spread to provide shelter in case their people get caught out in bad weather and can't make it back to the bunkhouses."

Since the cholera outbreak in July 1879, which started at the ranch and killed the elder Cruesdale and several who worked for him, the handling of the place had gone to the eldest son. Windham had a gentler touch than his father and compassion for his workers. The transition had made for better relations between the townspeople and the family. With the nasty old rancher dead and buried and his son running things, all who worked the large holding were welcome in town. All the unprovoked brawls the dead man brought to Wylder were gone, much to everyone's relief.

Branch Wylder, the sheriff, had said more than once that he hated that the yellow fever came to his town but that it did leave him with less trouble. He made no secret about his meaning, either.

"I heard that, too." Minnie swayed gently from side to side, holding the baby close. "But I accounted for a stampede of hungry ranch hands. And I've got a good amount in the donation fund. That Mister Harvey can be generous. And Doc, now he's always ready to open his wallet when we have an event." She smiled. "I never need to ask. Somehow, the funds just show up, like magic."

Gertie glanced from the woman's pleasant face to the dim interior behind her. In that instant, she wished she could find some magic to help the Milligan family. Not that they'd ever take charity, they were too proud. But pride didn't put food on the table or windows in the walls.

Time to turn her attention back to the subject at hand. She hadn't forgotten about the dark gray clouds scudding overhead.

"Well, that's good to hear. But you just let me know if you need anything at all." She hitched her reticule higher on her forearm and spun on one heel. "Violet has her eldest students ready to help you set up the tables and lay out the food, so you should have plenty of hands to make the work light. Still, if you need anything…"

"I won't." When the baby stretched, Minnie danced from side to side, shifting her feet without making a sound. "Why, you shouldn't worry so. I'm sure this celebration will be wonderful, the way all the others you've overseen have been. Wylder knows the woman for this job is you, Gertie. You give us the best time, every time."

Heat flooded her heart, and a lump filled her throat. It meant so much to hear the words, although if no one ever thanked her for her work she would still take on the organizational tasks. Wylder had given her a home when she was lost, and she'd be forever in its debt.

"Aww, you're making me tear up." She dashed a fingertip beneath one eye, then the other. "Thank you for all you do to make these events a success. Without you, we'd all be hurrying home to find dinner."

The baby shifted in its sleep again, waving a tiny, fisted hand in the air beside its cheek as if in agreement. "Well, I guess that's what we all do in a small town—we help each other. And I'm always glad to help." She shot a look at the sky. "I hope you're goin' straight home from here. It looks like it's gettin' set to storm."

She glanced up. It did, indeed.

"You're right." She offered a fast wave and stepped off the porch. "Thanks again. Remember, let me know if you need anything before the celebration."

As she hurried down the street, away from the railroad tracks and toward the center of Wylder, she wished she'd been wise enough to grab an umbrella before she left home. But, as was her way, she acted first and thought second. A bad habit, she knew. It would likely get her drenched before she hit her own front porch again, but there was no help for it.

She turned and headed for the boardinghouse, moving as quickly as her long skirts allowed. At times like these, she wished she could pull on a pair of trouser pants and move the way men did, instead of stumbling over yards of fabric.

Life just wasn't fair sometimes. She reached a hand to raise the front of her skirt enough that she didn't trip and quickened her steps.

Chapter 9

Lane ran the hunk of bread in his hand over the last dribble of his soft-boiled egg, then popped it into his mouth and chewed. He'd practically licked the cracked white ceramic clean.

Damn, but the little diner on Wylder Street knew how to feed a man. If he had to guess, the cook in the kitchen might either be a woman with a houseful of children or a retired wagon cook. Meals came out of the kitchen faster than greased lightning. He looked at the nearest tables. Plates were as empty as his, barely needing a dip in a dishpan before being filled again.

He'd anticipated frontier food to be terrible, a steady stream of hard tack and wormy, stale biscuits. That the menu exceeded his expectations filled him with gratitude. Some men could live on fried dirt and creek water, but he wasn't one of them. He appreciated a good meal.

He grabbed his hat with one hand and dropped silver on the table with the other. He could've eaten more, but too much food weighed him down. He couldn't afford the luxury of feeling as full and lazy as a spoiled cat. Not today, when he had to find Gertie and have a serious discussion with her.

He hated to do it, but every day that passed without his opening up about Grant and the reason behind his sudden appearance in Wylder ate at him. The woman he came to see treated him with respect. She deserved the same and hiding his full reason for the trip did her a disservice. Today he aimed to come clean. Sure, she'd be angry, but he hoped she'd see past that.

On the walkway in front of the diner, he craned his neck back and looked at the sky. Clouds this ominous in Virginia typically meant a gully washer. Clearly, Mother Nature had stormy intentions, but he had no idea how bad they'd be. He'd heard stories of harsh frontier weather but that came mostly with snow. Still, this dark gray cloud cover did not sit well with him.

Best get a move on.

He planted his hat firmly on his head and took off toward the mercantile. He'd noticed most women stopped in the place at least once a day, and Gertie was no exception. If he got lucky, she'd be there, giving him an opportunity to walk her home and get to explaining the circumstances of his visit.

A visit. Because that's all it could be, right?

He'd meant to deliver the news and take off for the coast, but now that he'd seen Wylder—and more importantly, Gertie—he wasn't sure about leaving. Nothing waited for him in California, and he didn't know a soul there. But here, he knew someone…a pretty woman with a heart of pure gold. Maybe he'd plant some roots in town, see what grew.

There weren't many riders on the street. A few wagons, but a lot fewer than he usually saw.

Usually. He'd been in town only a few days, and already he had a feel for how things worked.

He'd misjudged the number of women shopping at the mercantile. The place stood nearly deserted. Finn Wylder wasn't even behind the counter in his customary position. He found the man restocking goods in a center aisle.

The shop owner looked up when Lane's bootheels broke the silence.

"Well, nice to see you again, Lane."

The man must see countless folks in a day, yet he recalled names and faces without difficulty. A sign of an expert businessman.

He pulled his lips into a smile and gave the merchant a nod. "Finn." He waved a hand to the space around them. "A slow business day?"

"It always is when there's a storm brewing. Folks know to hunker down, leastways most do." He straightened the packets of Arbuckle's coffee on the shelf. The man kept a neat business. Every shelf tidy, and things where people could see and help themselves, mostly. "No one wants to be caught out in the bad weather. Sometimes it can't be helped, but most try to avoid it if possible."

"Seems wise." He glanced around the store again, but the only other person present, an elderly man with a hat tipped over his eyes, napped in one of the rocking chairs near the belly stove. No wood burned, and there wasn't a need for heat, but it still looked like a cozy spot to rest. To his eye, the stove looked like it might even be one of those expensive coal-burning models. But that wasn't the important part of the area, the chairs were. That the owner of the establishment didn't chase older folks from their rest brought Lane's estimation of the fellow up a notch. It took a good man to recognize a person's need for a safe, peaceful spot to relax. "Well, I guess I'll be on my way."

The other man stood and wiped his hands across

the apron he wore over his clothes. They were both nearly the same height, so their gazes locked. "Looking for anything special? I'm here to help you out, you know."

He shook his head. "Nope. Thanks, but I didn't come in for anything."

An eyebrow went up on the other's forehead. "Looking for anyone special, then?"

Either the man was exceptionally observant, or he'd been too transparent. He'd thought his feelings hidden, but as he felt heat rising from his collar to his jawline, Lane realized he'd been wrong.

"Ah, no, not exactly." He shook his head and turned on his heel. One step toward the front of the building before he glanced back and met the other man's gaze again. "But I appreciate the help."

"Any time. Now, take care out there." Finn nodded toward the wide front glass window and the view of the street beyond. "I've got a feeling we're going to get a hit before the day ends."

He nodded, then went for the front door. Outside, the air had grown warmer. And still, as if Mother Nature held her breath. That couldn't be a good sign, so he turned and began walking. The debate in his head, whether to go to the livery and get his horse or continue on foot, raged. He'd waste time if he went for the mount, and chances were good that the object of his search had tucked herself in at her home.

No time to waste on the horse. A fast walk and he'd be on Gertie's porch. Surely she'd let him in on such a God-awful weather day. And when she did, he'd let the truth fly. Hopefully, she'd understand his side of the situation…and not toss him out into the weather that the blackening sky seemed intent on dumping on them.

****

Gertie scowled at the sky. The clouds felt lower, and the air had turned so still that walking gave her an idea of how it felt to be a knife slogging through an overdone loaf of bread. Tough to move and harder still to breathe.

She should have gotten out sooner. Or, maybe not at all. But the Founder's Day celebration drew closer with each passing day, and she wasn't ready to have the entire town see anything less than another spectacular event. She had to put on something to give everyone good recollections to remember until next year, at least.

Food under Minnie Milligan's care would be plentiful. Tasty, too. The woman brought out the best in folks.

Decorations were stored in the small building behind the schoolhouse, ready to be strewn about the schoolyard the morning of the event. Violet Bloom promised her pupils would help with setup, decorating, and clean up afterward.

Buntings were a sticking point, but she would put in extra long hours working on them, if need be. Anything to get the new ones sewn.

One of the big draws to the celebrations, the apple pie contest, still demanded her attention. Women waited all year to try their newest recipes on the judges in the hopes of taking home a blue ribbon to hang on their kitchen wall. The apple pie contest was one of the most highly anticipated events and as such needed her consideration.

Wylder's Mercantile always arranged to get in bushels of apples in as many varieties as Finn could find for the competition. She hadn't checked with him yet, but the man ran his store so efficiently she felt certain he'd taken care of the ordering. Why, the apples were probably waiting in his mercantile already.

Still, she couldn't leave anything to chance, so she scurried along Buckboard Alley. Made it past the boardinghouse without being spotted by its owner, thank goodness. The woman's tongue was sharp enough to peel every apple in town, and Gertie had no patience for that kind of interaction today.

The stale air affected her, and she wanted to get this last item ticked off her list, then head home. Another look at the darkening sky. Home, where she'd be safe.

There was hardly anyone on Wylder Street when she turned right and headed toward the mercantile. No foot traffic in front of the hotel. The actors who usually milled about near the open-air theatre were nowhere in sight. Hitching posts empty and not even one wagon drove along the rutted road.

I'm the only one in Wylder foolish enough to be out on such an ominous day.

Well, no help for it. Founder's Day meant enough that she would take her chances.

She wondered who would win the competition this year. For the past few, the coveted ribbon had been awarded to Sarah Adams. She and her husband Harry had gold rushed in California and hit a vein before moving to a place about a mile outside of Wylder. They relocated to a nice homestead before the town's founding, and their apple orchard and few plum trees were a hobby, as well as a source of fruit for Sarah to use to perfect her pie-baking skills. Their Chinese cook,

Wei, spoke broken English but was a crack shot. Scuttlebutt around town, that he'd killed a man over a recipe, circulated, but neither the man himself nor his employers ever addressed the subject. Mostly, the Adamses kept to themselves—that is, until Founder's Day when Sarah garnered so much attention for her perfect pie.

Sarah had once confided to Gertie that she and Harry wanted a quiet life. They were well set for funds but had no desire for expensive clothing or finer home furnishings. A comfortable, calm living situation, with their good cook to cater to their needs, kept the pair content.

She understood the other woman's feelings. Hers had been the same at one time, to live her life in peace with Will. Maybe a grandchild or two to bounce on her knee, but nothing fancy and certainly no wealth to flaunt. No, a simple life seemed a blessing.

The wind picked up, chasing away musings about the celebration. She fought to keep to her feet, grabbing a nearby hitching post for support. It wouldn't do to go hurtling down the street like a tumbleweed, skirts flapping and underdrawers on display!

She clenched her eyes shut against the sudden swirl of dust that pelted her. A hand to her head, to keep her hat in place, and the other fingers digging into the wooden post. No need to glance at the sky to know the storm would be upon the town in no time—if it wasn't already here.

A voice startled her.

"May I help you?" The accent gave the man's identity away. Gus Wright, the kind undertaker. A quiet, humble man who was widely respected for his attention to both the living and dead. A good man, one she'd liked from their first meeting.

She turned toward the sound of his voice, dipping her chin into her chest and opening one eye. The man held onto his own hat but held out a hand between them.

"Yes, please." She released her hold on the hitching post when his free hand went to her upper arm. "This wind, it came up so fast. It took me by surprise."

They leaned into the tempest and made their way over the uneven wooden walkway. She tried to keep her footing but stumbled once. The man's hand tightened on her and kept her upright. After what seemed like an age but had been only a few minutes, they reached the mercantile. Gus pulled the door open, and she ducked inside ahead of him.

It took a full moment before she felt safe enough to open both eyes. When she did, she met Gus' gaze. His kind face looked at her with concern etched so deeply on it that he had two vertical lines between his eyes.

She managed a small smile. "Thank you. I'm sure you saved me from tumbling down Wylder Street, and I'm grateful. Lucky for me that you came along when you did."

A nod. He removed his hat and ran a hand through his hair.

She noticed he had long fingers and work-worn hands. It crossed her mind that his hands were used to handle the dead. It seemed a fine profession, caring for those whose mortal lives had come to an end. A pang of remorse shot through her as she remembered her poor Will hadn't had the kind of care this good man gave to others.

Gertie chased the sad thought from her mind. No going back, she reminded herself. What's over is over, and no amount of sorrow could change the facts.

"I am glad that I was able to help. Pardon my boldness, but the weather doesn't seem fit for a fine lady to be out in it. Surely, you're headed home from here?" His tone held so much concern, she struggled not to cry. It had been so long since anyone cared this much for her, she hardly knew what to do.

She cleared her throat and pulled some starch back into her spine. Sure, it had been scary outside, but she'd been brought to safety. No time for wobbly knees now.

"I appreciate your concern, really, I do. And I am grateful for your help." She adjusted her hat, remembering it must be hanging at an odd angle after its windy beating. "I only have a small matter to discuss with Mister Wylder, about the Founder's Day celebration, you know. Then I'll be off home."

He smiled, turning his plain features handsome. "Ah, yes, the festivities. I know it will be wonderful again this year." He paused, as if choosing his words carefully. "Will there be, um, dancing?"

So, the quiet undertaker must have his sights set on a woman, then. Otherwise, why would he inquire about something that seemed far from his nature? Or at any event, the character he presented to others, herself included.

"Why certainly, there will be dancing." She had a piano player, as well as a string quartet, lined up to provide music at the event. "And I trust you'll be a fine figure on the dance floor, if the surefootedness you just displayed is any sign of your talent."

The man blushed, and she almost wished she

hadn't teased him. But he had saved her and that should give them some degree of familiarity, after all.

But to make him squirm further wouldn't do, so she waved a hand toward the counter along the far wall. "Please forgive me, but I must consult with Finn about apples."

An eyebrow rose and dipped behind the lock of hair that hung across his forehead. "Apples?"

He didn't need to ask with such a surprised look. It wasn't as if she mentioned anything exotic, like mangoes or pineapples.

"Yes, apples. For the apple pie competition?"

Understanding showed in his eyes. "Ah, yes. The apple pie contest is one of my favorite parts of the festivities. Excuse me, my mind was otherwise occupied…"

Gertie smiled as she turned toward the counter. "On dancing?"

The man gave her a sweet smile in return. "Perhaps." A shrug that brought the shoulders of his jacket high. "After all, doesn't everyone dream of dancing?"

Chapter 10

Lane pounded on the door so hard his hand stung. He'd knocked several times, but Gertie had not responded, and it worried him.

He'd dashed into the mercantile, hoping to find her there. Finn Wylder said she'd been in, looking to check his apple supply. The merchant said he thought she'd been headed home when she left his store.

Home. Where she'd run to from her former life, the place that nourished her so well no one would ever guess what she'd endured. Now it stood empty, and his nerves were stretched taut. No amount of pounding would bring her to the door, but frustration won out and he banged once more anyway.

Hell's bells! Where could she be?

A few steps took him to the edge of the porch, where he tipped his head back. That sky, so menacing that it turned his blood cold. He'd faced a lot of adversaries in his short time as a gunslinger. Trepidation came as part of the job. But this? No way to beat this kind of foe. Impossible to stare it down or make it doubt itself the way he could with a man.

"Hello?" The word carried on the wind, from the porch on the house beside Gertie's. A young voice he recognized as Thomas Harvey's daughter.

Her name danced beyond the edges of his memory. He searched for it as he turned to face the other house.

She stood on the porch, the front door wide open behind her. Arms wrapped around her midsection as tendrils near her temple flew around her head.

"Mister Hutchins, isn't it? You're Miss Gertie's friend, aren't you?"

So his appearance in town hadn't gone unnoticed.

The girl's name appeared on the tip of his tongue, as if by magic. "Alexia, right? You're helping Ger—ah, Miss Gertie with some sewing for the celebrations, aren't you?"

Her hands went down to her hips as a gust swept up the porch steps and made her skirt flap. Her lips sealed against the wind, she nodded. When the breeze died down, she said, "That's right. I heard someone at Miss Gertie's door, so I came out to see who it was."

Nice of her to not mention he'd practically pounded the door down.

"I don't think she's home." He shot a look up, then down, the street. Deserted.

"She's not. I saw her leave a little bit ago."

Damn it all! Exactly what he didn't want to hear.

A struggle to keep his voice even when he would have liked to scream. The idea of her being out beneath this hellacious-looking sky just about drove him mad. Anything could happen. He had to find her, and quickly.

"You saw her leave?" He thought fast. "On foot? Or did she take a wagon or buggy?"

The girl shook her head. "No wagon. She walked down the street toward the railroad tracks." Still clutching her skirts with one hand, she brushed hair off her face with the other. "Looked like she was in a hurry to see Missus Adams, too. Maybe there's trouble out there at their place."

Adams. He'd never heard the name before.

"Where is their place? In town? Near the Social Club, maybe?" Trouble on the wrong side of the tracks? He could see that happening. And he could picture dear Gertie rushing to help someone out. "Is that where she went?"

Alexia shook her head. "No, the Adamses live 'bout a mile out of town. Past the, ah, the…"

Color rose on her cheeks. When she couldn't bring herself to name the establishment, Lane realized she may have been taught not to refer to places like the Five Star and Social Club. Hell, but bringing up female children must be hard. Lord knew he didn't even have sense enough not to mention the town whorehouse in front of a young girl.

"Past the telegraph office, right? They live beyond that, um, part of town?"

A smile crossed her face and she answered in a rush. "Yes, that's it! Out past there, that's where they live."

He took the steps at a run. With no idea where to look for the Adams' homestead, he'd be best served to stop at the livery and saddle his horse. He hated to waste precious time, but he'd get farther on horseback than on foot.

"Thank you, Alexia." He touched the brim of his hat. "You've been a great help."

"I hope you find her. I don't think she should be out in this kind of weather. It's getting ready to get ugly, I think."

Ugly. Now, that was one way to put it.

He hightailed it for the livery. No time to waste.

No telling why Gertie had headed out of town on an afternoon like this.

****

Loose rocks dug into her palm as she hit the ground hard. Tears bit the backsides of her eyes. She sat back on her heels and wiped her hand across her skirt. This certainly wasn't going well.

No need to look at the sky. The wind told its tale and left no room for misinterpretation. The air that had been so oppressive and still earlier had transformed into a whirling dervish. Red dust flew past her face. Tumbleweeds, usually so delicate and graceful, jettisoned across the plains like shots fired from a cannon. They lifted off the ground, projectiles destined to damage whatever unfortunate obstacle stood in their paths.

She'd never seen the wind kick up this way. Living in the territory, she'd dealt with her share of snowstorms, blizzards, gully washers, and, of course, searing summer heat. But this? Never in all her time in the West had she seen the likes of this.

Gertie pushed to her feet, spreading them wide to help keep her balance. The wind came from behind and pressed against her back, but she stood firm. The heel of her hand dripped blood, so she wiped it across her skirt again and took a few tentative steps.

Each came at a cost. Her muscles strained, fighting the brutal gusts.

The Adams' homestead lay a mile or so outside town. She and Sarah weren't good friends, but she'd had cause to make the trip a few times. There had never been any need to use a wagon. Once clear of the railroad tracks and the businesses beyond, she merely had to walk toward Medicine Bow Creek to find their place.

Never any trouble—before now.

She wished she didn't have to make the trip.

If wishes were diamonds, we'd all have rings on our fingers.

There were enough wishes dashing through her mind to embellish the fingers of every woman in Wylder, including the youngest ones. The ladies at the Social Club, too, now that she thought about it. The never-ending series of wishes for her safety that ran through her head would cover everyone's fingers. Maybe their toes, too.

The stupidity of this trip couldn't be denied. She never should have set out, but going back wasn't an option. The wind blew from behind, so if she turned, it would blast her full in the face. So fierce, it would probably rub her bones clear of skin, muscle, and fat.

No, she had to press on. Her eyes squeezed tight against the gritty onslaught, she concentrated on putting one foot before the other. And again. And, yet again. Every inch of progress took all her strength. Most were lost to the backward push of the wind, the steps when she stumbled behind, into the footprints she'd just left in the rocky soil.

Still, she kept going. Temptation to leave the trail and look for shelter beckoned, but she stayed the course. Many had been lost to the unforgiving frontier, souls who might have been rescued had they kept to the well-worn trails.

Gertie wouldn't allow that to happen to her. Too much had happened, too many trials to overcome and grief to bear. She'd come west with a plan to find her way and she wouldn't give up that dream now.

She hadn't come this far to only get this far.

****

Lane and Belle had ridden into many messes in their years together. The strong, reddish-brown animal had never shown fear before, not even when gunshots whizzed past or outlaws threatened to run them down. She'd even kept her head the time they were caught in a cattle stampede just west of the Mississippi. Had held her ground, still as a statue, while the herd thundered past them.

Apparently, she'd saved an entire lifetime's skittishness for now. She tossed her head and whinnied her discontent. When a tangled cluster of tumbleweed came at them, she stepped sideways and nearly dumped them into a gully. The wind blew fierce, so Lane leaned down close to one of the ears she had pinned against her head.

"Easy, Belle! I won't let anything happen to you." He pulled the reins to the left, hoping to calm her by setting them back on level ground. Her hooves slipped on loose gravel, but she dug in and stepped back onto the trail. He breathed a sigh of relief. While the gully would protect them from the wind, it wouldn't help him locate Gertie. And that's all he needed to do, find the woman.

The woman who'd stolen his heart all those long years ago. The object of his dreams. The one person he thought he could spend forever with…if only he had the guts to tell her how he felt. Since he'd been in Wylder, he'd been tempted, but so far the opportunity for baring his heart hadn't presented itself.

But he knew the truth. He'd known forever, it felt

like. Oh, yes, his heart and soul understood there would never be another woman to claim his love.

So, he had to find her. And even if he didn't ever tell her the truth, he'd see her safely home to that snug house in town. The least he could do after disrupting her life. And he had no doubt he'd done just that. He knew his appearance would affect her before he left Richmond, but he'd come anyway.

He'd turned her life on edge and made no apologies for it. Probably for the best if he didn't tell her that he loved her. Why would she believe him?

But that could all wait. No need to decide now what he'd do when he found her. The real objective— the only one that counted—was to track her down.

His knees tightened on Belle's flanks as he urged her forward into the swirling dust storm. The horse went, but the rigid body beneath him and the tentative steps gave away her apprehension.

Lane ducked his chin toward his chest and squinted. The storm had kicked up in a heartbeat, leaving no time for preparation and lots of opportunity to think fast. He searched the area beyond the trail for shelter. Gertie had a good head on her. If she could find a spot to hunker down, she'd take it. Now, if only he could find her hidey hole, they could both wait out this mess together…

****

The breath rushed from Gertie's lungs in a loud whoosh. Her knees burned, despite their covering of cotton, as if the scrub and rocks beneath them scratched at the tender skin. Her hands went out in front of her and kept her face from hitting the ground, but she'd fallen so many times she wasn't sure any flesh remained on her palms.

It felt like the hundredth time she'd gone down.

She realized she wouldn't make it to Sarah Adams' house while the storm raged. She wanted to, enough to pick herself up and contemplate continuing on the trail, but foolhardiness had never been one of her character flaws. She had others, everyone did, but no one ever accused her of not being levelheaded.

But in this moment, she didn't feel all that smart. What had possessed her, to think she could outrun such nasty weather? Wind whipped her hair loose and sent it flying about her head. A hand to hold it from her eyes while the other shoved against the hard ground. A stifled cry of pain as rocks found delicate flesh already scraped raw. Still, she pushed until her throbbing knees supported her and she stood almost upright. A lean into the wind to keep from being thrown onto her backside as she contemplated her options.

A mile hadn't seemed a long distance when she started out. How deceiving miles could be when grit blasted the traveler!

Sarah Adams probably wouldn't answer her door on an afternoon like this, even if she did somehow miraculously make it to the homestead. And who could blame her, if she looked out her front window and saw a wild woman? Surely, she looked a fright by now, and it could only get worse the longer she stayed in the weather. Gertie sighed. No chance of talking the woman into doing the town a favor while she likely looked insane.

The wind came at her fast, from behind so she adjusted her stance. Walking back to Wylder seemed the best decision on the surface, but with the howling gales coming from that direction, it might prove impossible.

Her best bet, to find a spot to hunker down and ride out the storm. But where?

She scanned the sides of the trail, looking for any kind of shelter. Nothing save some cottonwood trees and the brambly brush that grew from the berry seeds birds dropped. None of that would protect her from any of this.

Her legs felt like jelly, but she forced them to move. One step. Then another. And a third.

As she lifted her toes from the ground, she paused.

Was she losing her mind? Or had she heard her name? Slight, and more a sigh on the wind than an actual word, but it sounded as if—

There! Again, louder this time.

She turned to face the onslaught. One closed eye, the other's lid dipping as low as possible without shutting all the way. Her eye strained to see into the reddish-brown haze, to look past the foliage flying by and the dust pelting her body.

Rushing wind, cracking branches, and the thud of stones being lifted then dropped. They were the sounds that reached her ears, but she leaned forward and forced herself to search for something—anything—more than the storm's rage.

"Ger…" There, again! Her name—and it wasn't her imagination playing tricks on her. A man's voice—

Oh dear Lord, could it be Will calling to her from the hereafter? Was her time in this lifetime up? Had he come for her?

A spark of joy burst from her heart at the thought of seeing her beloved again. An instant flash of relief that this life without him ended. She'd endured enough and waited for their reunion...

Then, her heart fell into her feet. She had endured. Lived life as well as she could. Worked hard to find her way, to lose the mantle of grief, and appreciate the happy moments afforded her. Even after she lost the baby, their dear child, she pressed on.

Had it not counted for anything? Why had she struggled to remain alive if she were going to be swallowed by a horrible storm? It hardly seemed fair.

Her mind swirled as rapidly as the world around her. She shut her eyes tight and prayed for deliverance. She didn't want to die, not yet. Not even if it meant she could see Will again.

"Gert...ie..." The voice came louder now, pulled out by the wind. She cocked her head to the side, hoping to hear it one more time so she'd know which direction it came from.

She opened her eyes as wide as she could and saw the outline of a horse in the distance. Big and as reddish brown as the sand, it blended with the storm.

She raised one arm and hollered. "Over here! Help me, please!"

The horse drew near enough for her to see a man on its back. When he called her name, she recognized him.

Not Will, after all, but Lane.

In that moment, when she realized she wasn't about to die but be rescued by the strong man and his faithful horse, her knees went weak. She folded to the ground, placed a hand over her heart, and looked toward the sky. Gratitude filled her soul.

Her throat hurt, but she whispered, "I'm sorry,

Will. I'll see you someday…just not today, my love."

****

Lane jumped from Belle's back to run for Gertie. A gust came up and pushed him against the horse's flank as his boots hit the dirt. One step back, the stirrup bumping against his thigh, before he tilted his torso into the wind and hurried to the figure lying in the center of the trail.

A crumpled form, a heap of dust-covered fabric, tendrils of chocolate brown hair streaming from her head. It could be anyone, but he knew better. That still form belonged to the woman he searched for. The distance between them, only a few paces, felt like miles.

"Gertie! Good God, Gertie!" Her body felt weightless in his arms when he turned her over and pulled her onto his knee. A hand over her face, to clean some of the dirt away, before he grabbed her shoulders and gave her a shake. "Can you hear me?" The roar of the wind stole the words from his mouth as soon as they left his lips. He bent close and placed his face near hers. "Gertie—damn it all, do you hear me?"

She inhaled and nodded, her cheek brushing his in a gritty stroke. "I thought I'd die out here." A cough, then another big inhale.

Her lungs. Hell, but with every breath she sucked grit into them. He'd tied a bandana around his face to cover his nose and mouth. Now he reached into his back pocket and pulled out another. It might not be clean but would filter some of the sand from finding its way inside her. Without asking permission, he tied it around her face.

Her gaze met his, and he saw fear. The woman had

always been so brave, without wavering regardless of what life threw her way, but this storm had her spooked. He couldn't blame her, although it occurred to him that had she been at home, safe and snug, she'd have no reason to be frightened.

"Can you walk?" He shouted to be heard.

A nod, so he stood and pulled her to her feet. He guided them both to the waiting horse by looping an arm around her and tucking his head down. A few near-blind steps brought them close. Belle hadn't moved, and when he lifted Gertie onto her back before climbing into the saddle, she stood as serene as if they were getting set to go on a summer's afternoon jaunt. Only her ears and flared nostrils gave her mood away.

When he reached for the reins, the woman snugged up against him fell into the circle of his arms. He'd wanted to hold her close so many times, yet when it finally happened, all he could think about was finding a way to get them out of their current situation.

"Where were you going?" A whiff of something sweet came from her hair when he dipped close to speak beside her ear. "Is it far from here?"

Her hair whipped around her head and across his temple. His fingers itched to run through the strands, to hold them in a loose bundle, maybe even drop the bandanna and inhale the scent of her.

"The Adams' homestead." She shook her head. Shouting against the wind, she added, "I only know it's out this way. About a mile."

Not much help there. A scan of their surroundings offered little in the way of refuge. He turned the horse in a full circle, searching for someplace to shelter. Lining the trail, cottonwoods and scrub. A few boulders, but none large enough to get them out of the weather.

In the distance, trees gave way to an outcropping. Large boulders, a stand of trees, and perhaps a spot to weather the storm. He turned Belle toward the horizon, gave her some slack as they descended into a culvert beside the trail, then coaxed her up the other side. When she made flat ground again, he urged her forward.

The less time they spent being buffeted by the frontier storm, the better. He put pressure on the horse's flanks and hoped the animal wouldn't die trying to save them.

Chapter 11

Fear did not come often to Gertie—at least, not under the light of day. Night, with its darkness and terrors, told a different story, but in her waking hours, she rarely saw any reason to be scared.

Losing a husband, finalizing her affairs in Richmond, traipsing clear across the wilderness, and settling in a town that, when she arrived, could barely be termed "civilized" had given her enough life experience to laugh in the face of danger.

She'd turned her six-shooter on men when they'd made it necessary, never wavering in her determination to survive any nefarious intention they might entertain. When liquored-up ranch hands raised hell in the dead of night just beyond her front window, she steadied herself to confront any marauder who dared enter her home. A cholera outbreak in Wylder claimed lives and kept townsfolk home, but she refused to be intimidated by a disease and delivered soup and other necessary items to afflicted families.

She did not scream over mice or start at the sight of bats or snakes.

But this tempest from the sky? It sent her heart hammering in her chest. Not at first, but when it flung her face down in the red dirt she thought for sure her time had come to an end. A horrible, dirty, disastrous finish to the life she'd tried so hard to lead with courage and integrity.

Now her unease dropped as she nestled against the strong man who held her. Astride the horse, it proved impossible to keep distance between their bodies, so she settled into his embrace, her backside snugged up intimately against the front of him. Whether gratitude or excitement, or some other emotion she'd yet to identify, shot through her, a tingling sent shivers up her spine. She'd thought herself dead, imagined taking Will's ethereal hand and flying up to Heaven with him, leaving her body behind for vultures to feast on. But by the grace of God or maybe the tenacity of the man behind her, all that changed. They still were surrounded by howling that sounded drawn straight from the bowels of purgatory, but companionship put her fears to rest.

Gertie wiped a hand over her eyes. Tears, also uncharacteristic without the cover of darkness, threatened to fall, but she swallowed twice and steadied her resolve. She didn't like tears. They were a sign of weakness she refused to indulge. Fine for others, especially small children and elderly women, but she was neither of those and would not succumb to the maudlin activity.

Besides, her eyes puffed up like cotton bolls ready for harvest when she wept. Not a look she wished to share with anyone, least of all Lane Hutchins. He'd never seen her lose her composure, and she intended to keep it that way.

So she sniffed and scrubbed a palm across her face. If he asked, she'd say grit got in her eyes. But he and the horse were intent on reaching the outcropping in the distance. He didn't question her. A good thing, most likely. She didn't have any answers to give him, had he inquired about anything at all. Right now, she knew nothing, and that sat well with her. Too tired to think, she let herself lean into his strength.

The horse beneath them moved steadily onward, negotiating around downed tree limbs and rolling tumbleweeds as if she did so every day. Gertie thought for sure the animal a mare. The glimpse she'd gotten when she'd been thrust onto its back included a momentary gaze into its deep brown eyes. Wisdom and bravery, and a willingness to put other lives above her own, showed from the depths. All characteristics she associated with women.

Lane tugged his bandana down, then leaned close and spoke near her ear. His hot breath caressed her cheek, a welcome change from the harsh biting wind.

"There's an outcropping not too far from here. I see it through the haze." He came so close his lips brushed her temple. "We'll take refuge in the shelter and wait for the storm to pass."

The only logical solution to their situation, the one way they might survive nature's assault. No reply needed, so she pressed her body closer to his and put her chin down toward her chest. Even with the bandana, breathing took effort, so she saved her strength and put herself in the strong man's capable hands.

What other choice did she have?

****

There were moments he wondered whether Belle's strength and stamina were enough to get them safely to their destination. After all, the animal had already walked many miles in her lifetime, and one could only expect so much from any living being. He would have hated to lose her, especially in such a brutal manner, but he would have understood.

But the horse's determination matched his own, and she kept putting one hoof before the other. The distance between them and the cluster of rocks and trees closed. Not fast, but steadily.

He held Gertie as tightly against his body as he dared. He wanted to shelter her so completely, keep her from harm that if it were possible he'd envelop her with his body and clothes. Give her the shirt off his back and wrap her in an embrace so secure that nothing could penetrate.

He'd gladly allow his flesh to be scoured by the biting wind-blown grit if it would spare her.

But he couldn't do that, so he held her close and urged his mount forward.

And he did something he hadn't done in many years, not since the war. Then, he realized that the faith he placed in an almighty, loving being had been misguided. No matter how much he or the men standing shoulder to shoulder with him begged for mercy or fell to their knees in the soil and asked that the fighting stop, the war continued. Bloody, horrific, deadly. Men died calling to Heaven, to the divine spirit who they'd asked to protect them.

Lane saw with his own eyes that religion and a supreme deity weren't enough to change the course of events. If God was real, as he'd been raised to believe, the omniscient one had His own plan. He didn't consider the pleading of mortal men. Whatever fate befell humanity, it had nothing to do with their supplication, despite their believing it had an effect.

No, he knew better.

But in times like this, when the life of one he loved hung in the balance, his willingness to try even those practices he'd scoffed at for so long increased. He'd do anything to save her, including talking to a being he didn't believe existed.

He tightened his arms around the woman and closed his eyes. For a long moment, the only sound in his head came from the wind buzzing past his ears. No words came to mind, nothing that would help him get the attention of an almighty god or influence Him to help them.

Screwing his eyes closed even more forcefully, he searched his brain for the proper words. Back in Richmond in the big brick church he'd attended until the war took him away, praying had been simple. And, when he came to a point where words failed him, the prayer book tucked into the back of the pew ahead of him saved him.

Now there was no one to rescue him.

Gertie shifted in his arms, burrowing even closer. Her unwavering trust hit him like a hammer to his heart. Her life literally rested in his hands. Damn it, but for that he should be able to pull a prayer out of the part of himself he'd locked away after the war.

Lord, you know I'm not a praying man.

He bit the inside of his cheek. How stupid could he be? If a god existed and deigned to listen to him in this moment of need, he already knew their communication had been non-existent. The last time he prayed had been on a battlefield all those years ago.

He began again.

Lord, I need your help.

Well, that fell short, too. His teeth worried his

lower lip. Didn't everyone who prayed ask for help? He couldn't be that stupid, to fall in with what everyone else did. No, if he were to get noticed, he'd have to stand out.

From the heart, that was it. If there was a deity who could see into a man's soul, he'd best begin by speaking from the heart.

I need you now. Not just for me, but for this beautiful woman in my arms. She's lived some difficult days and doesn't deserve to die out here. If you could just help us make it to shelter, I'll do the rest.

The words echoed in his head against the background sound of grit slapping his legs, body, and the horse beneath them. Wind keened now, louder than ever.

Repetition. That had to be helpful. Nothing more to do, their fate depended on reaching safety.

I need you now. Not just for m—

Belle stumbled. The terrified cry that escaped her made the wind seem like nothing.

He held on to Gertie as the horse pitched forward and tossed them over her head. When they hit the unforgiving ground, he circled the woman's body and rolled away from the animal. They cleared the fall by inches.

"Lane!"

He gazed down at the woman beneath him. He'd protected her from being crushed by the horse with his own body. She looked up at him with terror in her eyes.

"Are you okay?" He would have run a hand over her, but he needed his limbs to press up from the ground. "Are you hurt?"

A quick nod. The bandana moved when she spoke.

"I'm fine. Are you?"

He nodded as he looked over at Belle. The horse lay panting in the dirt near them. She didn't struggle, and her legs were tucked beneath her. Grateful to not see her thrashing about, he hoped she wasn't hurt.

Gertie reached behind her and shoved herself to a seated position. Her eyes were wide but to her credit, they were not filled with fear. She pointed and shouted over the wind. "Your horse?"

Lane looked over his shoulder. They were near the cluster of stones and trees. He grabbed her hand and got to his feet. She rose with him and when she did, he bent low, beside her ear. "I'm going to carry you."

She shook her head. "I can walk."

The wind came from the direction they were headed. It would be slower if he carried her, so he agreed. "Wrap your arms around me and tuck your head against my back. Close your eyes and follow me."

When he turned, she grabbed his arm. "What about your horse?"

Choices weren't always easy. He'd learned that years ago. He wouldn't lose Gertie trying to save Belle. "I'll come back for her. She'll be fine."

Please, let that be true.

The prayer came without thought as he took the woman's hands and snugged her up against his back. When her fingers locked in his, he began to walk.

****

The wind could not easily penetrate the natural circle of trees and boulders. Within its shelter, a warm breeze without any of the ferocity offered on the open plain. Tumbleweeds stuck at the bases of the outermost pines, a barrier for blown grit or any of the other debris sent airborne by the storm.

Gertie pulled the bandana low, so her nose and mouth were exposed. She sucked in a deep breath, then coughed. Sand in her mouth and some from her throat came up, so she walked toward a boulder and spat into the scrub at its base. Another big inhale produced a second round of coughing, and more of the prairie came up, so she spat again. Finally, she drew a long breath and exhaled without issue. The constriction in her lungs eased.

She leaned against the boulder and welcomed the warm stone on her shoulders. Her legs wobbled, so she slid down to a seated position and dropped her head back. Closed her eyes, this time in relief rather than for survival.

A moment to rest, a gift after the terror of being caught in the storm.

A look at the sky. Still dark, with gray clouds hanging low. But here, in the circle, a reprieve.

Lane had gone for his horse. She wished he hadn't but knew he must.

Without his strong presence to steady her nerves, vulnerability created fear that swept over her again. Like a tiny whisper of wind, it found its way past her barriers and under her skin. She found strength for facing most matters, but this cacophony created by the earth itself brought so much unease she fought the urge to go after the man. Standing with him against the storm had not been as difficult as sitting alone in this refuge.

How had she allowed herself to become such a shrinking violet? She barely recognized the shivering female pressed against the unforgiving surface behind her, the one who waited for a man to return and chase away her fear.

All these years, she'd taken pride in her fearlessness. It had been the steel in her spine that kept her moving forward, defying those who said she would not survive on her own, and what kept her from faltering when others would have surrendered. Pride in her strength, the asset that turned the liabilities in her life to her favor, gave her the gumption to hold her head high, regardless of what happened.

But gumption had been swallowed by the howling wind and spat out with the biting sand.

Tears slid from the corners of her eyes. A struggle to breathe around the thickness in her throat made her gasp for air. Small, quiet swallows at first, but as the tears flowed more quickly, the tiny gulps grew.

A wail escaped her lips, a sound that pulled her knees to her chest with its intensity. She wrapped her arms around her legs and dropped her head down. Anger that she gave in and sobbed this way mixed with hopelessness. She'd lost her way in the storm, not only physically but spiritually, as well. How to reclaim a part of herself that had been carried off by the wind?

****

Belle gave a whinny of recognition when he reached her side. The familiar sound went straight to his heart. Leaving her behind had torn him in two, but seeing her again relieved some tension.

She hadn't moved, which both comforted and alarmed Lane. For a second, he wondered if she'd taken her last steps trying to carry them to safety, but when he ran his hands over her, there were no signs she'd been hurt. A big steadying breath to calm himself, then he smoothed his palms over her a second time to be sure he hadn't missed anything.

A pat to her neck to soothe them both.

"All right, old girl, we're going to get you up." The reins dangled so he took them in his left hand and kept his right on the horse's neck. A careful touch, meant to encourage her to give up her seat. Down low where she'd settled, less brutality from the wind, but he couldn't leave her here. A tug on the reins brought no response, so he leaned his head against hers. "Come on, Belle. You know I won't leave you, but if I stay here, Gertie's all alone. And that woman's been alone for far too long. Please, let's get to her so we can all rest."

He stood. The horse met his gaze, as if an understanding passed between them. When he tugged the reins a second time, she came to her feet. Dirt and grit fell from the saddle.

"You'll get an extra long rubdown when we're back in town, I promise." He swung himself into the saddle, turned them around, and touched his bootheels to her flanks. "Now, let's get to Gertie before she has a chance to become frightened."

The horse put her head down and began walking. To his relief, her stride didn't seem affected by the fall. Surefooted and stable, she headed in the direction of the outcropping. No need to direct her, she moved as if she knew the precise location of the trees and boulders that would shelter them.

He kept his chin down and gave the animal her head. Time to trust her instincts. They'd saved the pair in the past and looked like they'd do well by them again.

Such a relief that she hadn't been hurt. The whole

way back to her he'd wondered if he'd be able to pull the trigger if something had broken when she fell. The thought of unholstering a pistol and aiming it at the one who'd travelled so far with him…even now, astride and with the knowledge they wouldn't have to cross that horrible bridge, his heart hurt.

He'd killed men when pushed into a position of having no other alternative. The world could be harsh and kill-or-be-killed situations arose. He'd never backed down and didn't plan to ever do so.

But ending an animal's life came with a heartbreaking cost. She trusted him and had never done him or anyone else harm. He had never been in a position to kill an animal and hoped to never stand in that spot. This brush with the fragility of Belle's existence would not be forgotten. From now on, the mare would get extra special treatment. That is, if they managed to get out of this storm alive.

When she breeched the pine trees and stepped into their sanctuary, he leaned forward and placed his arms around her neck. Silky fur caressed his cheek.

He glanced up and saw the dark sky through the tree branches. No telling how long it would be before they could get back to town, but for now, all three were as safe as he could keep them and that was enough.

****

Gertie had reclaimed some composure by the time Lane appeared in the circle of trees and boulders. Her eyes felt swollen, either from crying or the storm or a combination of both, maybe. She must look a sight, but she didn't care.

Before she could get to her feet, he was on his knees beside her.

"Are you okay?" His gaze swept over her and probed without words. She felt seen in a way that she hadn't in so long, as if layers were peeled back to expose the hidden nature of her true self. "I got back as soon as we could."

"Your horse?"

"She's fine. Tied to one of the low branches, out of the storm." He held up a gray woolen blanket. "I always carry this in my saddlebags. C'mon, let's get comfortable."

"We'll be here a while, won't we?" The trees formed a canopy, but when their uppermost branches swayed, patches of dark sky showed. And the wail from the wind diminished within the circle, but nothing could make it disappear. "The storm's still raging."

He stood and flapped the blanket open. He placed it on the ground and sat before motioning for her to sit beside him. "I'm afraid so. If anything, the wind's picked up. We won't be outta here for a while."

She scooted over and settled next to him. When she did, he wrapped the blanket around them. His arm circled her, so she leaned against his body. Warm, smelling of man and horse, and strong enough that she didn't feel as exposed as she had when he'd gone for the animal.

"That's okay." She tucked an edge of the blanket over their knees. A comfort to see the man's blue jean trousers snugged up against her skirt. "We can wait it out."

Tension seeped from her body, bringing her shoulders down and settling her nerves.

She looked up at Lane. The frown lines between his eyes were gone, and a smile tugged the corners of his mouth upward. He'd lowered his bandana, so she got a view of his whole face. A stubble of whiskers covered his cheeks, chin, and upper lip, and she wondered how they would feel against her skin.

"We'll have to wait it out." He spoke softly so she leaned closer. "Pretty sure Belle would refuse to take another step in that swirling mess. Can't say I blame her, either."

His eyes were dark and focused on hers. They drew her to him as forcefully as if she were an ordinary tack and he a magnet. The attraction took her breath away.

I should look away.

Should and can were two different things, though.

Impossible to break a connection so strong.

"Me, either." Her voice came as a whisper. She cleared her throat, searching for some of the sense she'd seemingly lost to the man's good looks and tender character. He'd saved her, after all. No surprise she felt indebted, was it? "Maybe we should, ah…"

"Rest?" He smiled as the suggestion slipped from his lips.

A small word that offered a chance to slow her heartbeat, so she nodded. "Yes, I think that would be a good idea."

****

Wind shook the treetops, and the sound of grit washing up against the far sides of the boulders made it impossible to forget, even for an instant, that they were trapped in a storm. One glance at the gunmetal sky brought the reality of the situation home.

But storm be damned. His heartbeat quickened, not because of the threat from the clouds. The woman beside him caused a shift in his being that left nature in the dust.

Lane had never felt closer to Heaven than he did when he pulled the edges of the old blanket around them, and Gertie snuggled in beside him. Room inside the woolen cocoon was limited. Their bodies could not lie together without touching, not that he'd want them to. Sure, if he were a better man, he might cover her and lie on the dirt beside her, but she didn't seem to mind his presence. Besides, the storm might rage for hours, and he'd already been sandblasted by its fury.

When she rested her head on his shoulder, he closed the circle of his arm about her form. Her womanly curves pressed up against him, and the sweet scent of her hair swept up his nose. A deep inhale, to pull her closer as he shut his eyes. With each breath, he felt her breasts against his side above his ribs, a welcome pressure that calmed his galloping heart.

They were safe.

She shifted against him, so he opened his eyes and met her gaze. "You okay? I'm not squeezing you too hard, am I?"

Her smile turned her pink lips into a tempting bow. "Nope, you're not."

"Good to know." He held her gaze with his for a long moment. "Wouldn't want to do anything to make you uncomfortable, Gertie."

The name came easily now. Back in Richmond, she'd been Trudy, the woman who married his best friend. But out here in Wylder, Gertie fit her. A new woman, different from the one he'd known but similar enough to be familiar. A strange feeling, that he'd known her in two incarnations.

"You're not." She placed a hand on his chest above

his heart. "I'm not uncomfortable, Lane."

She caught her lower lip between her teeth and looked at him, long and hard. The kind of stare that shows a woman's got something on her mind but doesn't know how to give a voice to it. He'd seen the expression enough to recognize it, so he waited. Gave her time to order her thoughts, then set them free.

It didn't take but a few minutes.

"I haven't been this close to a man since the war." Her fingertips danced in small circles over his shirtfront. "I never thought I'd feel, ah, safe in someone else's arms the way I did with…"

Her husband. His best friend. Here on the solid ground of the unforgiving plains, the man's presence insinuated itself between them. It should have felt intrusive, but it didn't. Lane spoke the name they both hand on their minds.

"Will."

Something passed over her eyes, a fleeting emotion that disappeared almost the instant it arrived. She nodded, her hair whispering against his shoulder as she moved. "Yes, Will." A pause to swallow, then she nodded again. "I never thought I'd feel this comfortable with another man. I know it must sound silly to you, but I thought myself incapable of letting down my guard or…"

When she hesitated, he waited. This unburdening should come on her terms, not his. It was, after all, her grief that she laid bare.

"Trusting." She pressed her hand on his chest, an emphasis on the word that came with so much effort. "That's it, you know. The faith in someone, well… I didn't think I'd trust another man again."

He should pull away. She spoke of trust and comfort, but she had no idea why he'd journeyed to Wylder. He wasn't a man deserving of her confidence, something she would realize when he came completely clean about the reason for his visit.

But he was only a man, after all. Not a god, but an ordinary human who had loved one woman almost all his life.

A tendril of hair sat on her cheek, so he reached out a hand and brushed it back with a fingertip. Sleek and smooth, skin exactly as he'd imagined. Words failed him so he wrapped his hand around the back of her head and tangled his fingers in the locks at the base of her neck. A fingertip found a hair pin, so he slid it out. Most of her hairdo had come undone in the wind. These last pins barely held anything in place, so he sought out another and removed it, too.

Her gaze softened as her hair came fully undone. He threaded his fingers in the silken waves to loosen and spread them across her shoulder. The sight of her natural beauty, without restraint, took his breath away.

A crackle between them, a sensation that they'd been waiting for his instant forever, charged the air. The storm fell away. Noise, chaos, wind…none of it existed. All that was important to him, everything that made sense or mattered, he held in his arms.

Gertie's hand rose on his chest. It glided slowly along the front of his shirt until it brushed his collar. A pause, then she ventured a fingertip inside the fabric and slid it across his neck. His skin tingled at the feel of her touch.

She lifted her face to his, so close he felt her breath against his lips. His gaze dropped. Those lips, so full and pink, open and inviting.

"Lane…" A whisper. "I…" Her tongue swept out over her lower lip.

Good Lord, but how much could a man take? The feel, scent, and sound of her all played with his senses, enhancing his desire to know her. Touch her. To show the effect she had on him.

He wanted to pull her closer but resisted. No, this had to be her choice. He wouldn't put her in a position where she felt she had no option but surrender. Her life had given her far too many situations that were out of her control, and he respected her too much to do that.

Still, it was getting mighty hard to breathe with her so near.

The air between their faces dwindled when she moved toward him. He watched, first her lips, then her eyes, as she cut the distance. With an inch separating her nose from his, she paused. Her gaze searched his, so he didn't try to shield his feelings from her.

When her eyes closed and her lashes fluttered against her cheeks, he leaned in and claimed her lips with his. His whole body came alive at the connection. Every nerve ending tingled. Heat spread from his center outward, sending blood to his groin and stealing it from his head. Thoughts fled as he lost himself to the experience of kissing her. After so many years, he had her mouth on his, and all he could think was that the wait had been worth it.

Their lips were never hesitant. They joined as if they had always known each other, as if there had never been any wall between them. As if they were made to come together, their mouths rejoicing at having found each other, finally.

Her tongue slipped between his lips to explore the recesses of his mouth. It surprised him, but in a good way. He liked a woman who knew what she wanted and wasn't afraid to go after it. He rose to the challenge and reciprocated and found the taste of her mouth as sweet as he'd dreamed.

A shift onto his side brought them closer, so her feminine curves met the solid lines of his body. If she objected to the feel of his desire pressed against her hip, she didn't show it.

Instead, her hand moved across the front of his shirt to undo its buttons. A moan, so delicate and low it came as a sigh. Her hand slipped beneath the fabric and skimmed his chest. She paused above his heart, holding her hand in place as if she held the beating organ in her palm.

Lane floated his hand down her side, touching her tiny waist before resting on her back. He took care to move slowly, in case she had second thoughts. If she did, he would be disappointed but would respect her feelings.

Tiny bits of sand stuck to the back of her skirt, but he palmed the fabric and pressed. There, the curve of her buttocks, in his hand.

Enough to drive a man wild. Still, he kept from moving too quickly. He'd never forgive himself if he scared her. So, a smooth, gentle sweep of his hand to bring her hips closer to his, to tuck her against him and eliminate all space between them. That is, all except for what their clothes took up.

"Oh, yes." A murmur, as delicate as the sigh, against his lips. "Yes…"

Time lost its meaning when he kissed her. Minutes

melted into each other, and with each sweep of her tongue over his, his desire heated.

She unbuttoned his shirt and tugged the ends out of his pants. Her fingers found his chest and combed through the light cover of hair.

Lane dragged his hand from her buttocks and inched it toward her bosom. The moment when he'd either drop her to her senses or inflame her passion, he hesitated long enough to give her a chance to push him away. When she didn't, he placed a hand over her breast and held it there for a heartbeat, savoring the way she filled his hand so nicely.

Oh, my dear Gertie, a perfect fit.

Her nipple pressed the cotton fabric over it. He ran a thumb across the peak, excited when she groaned her approval. Emboldened by the response, he tugged her blouse from the waistband of her skirt. Pushed aside the thin chemise and swept his hand along her bare flesh.

He wished she were naked beneath him, without their blanket for cover, so he could take joy in the sight of her. For now, a touch would suffice. It had to.

Encouraged by her moans, his palm covered her breast, the feel of her skin fueling his desire. He brought his mouth to her neck. He wanted to taste her, all of her, from lips to all that lay lower. His tongue trailed a line down the side of her neck toward her collarbone. She squirmed against him, urging him forward, so he undid the buttons at the top of her blouse and exposed her breasts.

The sight of her rose-colored nipples stopped him. Exquisitely beautiful. So much so that he could hardly think, but when she met his gaze, he saw they were both beyond thinking. This lovemaking swept thoughts aside, driven by emotions and sensations that defied words.

Her lips were swollen, and her eyes glazed and dreamy. Lane thought she'd never been more beautiful than she was in this moment.

He kissed one breast, pulling the nipple between his lips. The taste of her made him want more…so much more.

Gertie's hand had fallen from his chest. It went lower, over his abdomen and down to the bulge in his pants. She cupped him, then her fingers went for the buttons.

No time to waste. He needed to feel her against him.

His fingers joined hers, and the second he undid the last button, he reached for the hem of her skirt and pushed it high. Underthings, lacy and ruffled, against his fingertips. He found the waist string and untied it, then pushed the bloomers down over her hips.

Her legs opened, and he traced a line up the inside of one. A chuckle when she shivered against him before he placed his hand higher and cupped the apex of her thighs. Her desire was evident, the warm welcome as she opened herself to him. A fingertip found the jewel of her at the same instant she wrapped a hand around him.

She squeezed, and he groaned his delight. Good Lord, but the woman knew her way around a man. Her fingers teased his hard length, stroking and fondling until he nearly lost his mind.

When her hand moved faster, he matched the tempo and slid against her slick folds with the same intensity. Her breaths came in jagged pulls as he sent her closer to the edge. Bearing witness to her pleasure kept him from losing control, but just barely.

"Oh…oh…oh…" Her lips formed a perfect circle as she moaned her delight.

He had to feel her. Had to know how it felt to gather her close and sink into her warmth. A shift brought him onto his elbows as he positioned himself between her legs. She put her hands on his shoulders and pulled him close. He rocked against her, pressing his swollen length to her.

Gertie opened her eyes. For an instant, he thought she would push him away, but then he saw his need mirrored in her gaze. She wanted him as much as he did her.

"Please…" She pulled back a bit, her body angling to take him inside.

She didn't have to ask twice.

The first thing he thought when he slid into the warm, wet center of her came as a shock. He'd never bedded a woman and thought *I've come home*.

But that's how it felt, as if he'd been waiting his whole life to be in this spot with Gertie.

No time for thinking, though.

Their hips moved in unison, the timeless rocking that brought them nearer their release. Each breath, he came closer, yet he held back. Her climax, just as important as his own, neared. The look in her eyes and the way her hips bucked against him told the tale, so he thrust harder and faster, excited to see her breathing quicken.

Then, he felt it, the first ripples of her orgasm that made her quiver beneath him. Her muscles gripped him so tightly that he gave himself up to the sensation. As they neared completion, he had only one thought in his head.

Home. I've come home.

Chapter 12

Warmth kissed Gertie's cheek, so she opened one eye. Day claimed night and all seemed quiet. She had the blanket to herself, so she pulled it tight and closed her eye. Squeezing both against the memories that flooded her mind, she held her breath and swallowed a groan.

A lifetime of behaving as an upstanding woman thrown into the fire in one frenzied blur of poor judgement. What must Lane think of her?

She wouldn't be surprised if he'd ridden off and left her. He probably considered her a cheap, barroom wench, someone who opened her legs for any man.

No, he knew her better than that. Embarrassment over her behavior pushed her to entertain thoughts that had no basis. She may have behaved out of character, but she certainly wasn't any soiled dove. And he wouldn't believe she casually invited men to take her the way she'd done with him.

Lane.

Her eyes shot open. Who knew when he'd return? When he did, she wanted to look as respectable as possible, given the circumstances. It wouldn't do to have him find her with her blouse gaping and her hair billowing down around her shoulders. She pulled the blanket snug about her, reached for the hair pains that lay scattered nearby, and pushed to her feet.

A dash behind a large boulder to set herself to rights. There wasn't much she could do, given that she didn't have fresh clothes or a hairbrush, but she did her best. At least her clothes were buttoned, and her hair somewhat done up. A last swipe of her hand down the front of her skirt, then she grabbed the blanket and walked around the boulder and back into the clearing.

Lane leaned against a rock wall. His hat brim dipped low over his forehead which suited her just fine. She didn't have any desire to look into those eyes. They knew each other too well for him to hide his feelings from her. He must think even a little less of her, surely, now. Why see it written in his gaze?

He cleared his throat, but she ignored the sound. Even if she could take seeing his diminished appraisal, her cheeks felt hot. It wouldn't do to let him see her shame. Better to get home and put this out of her mind.

The blanket hung from her arm, so she let it claim her attention. She folded it until it flattened into a neat package, then hugged it against her bosom.

Oh, her breasts. They tingled still, hours after the man had kissed and fondled them. The recollection sent a sharp thrill through her. He had enjoyed them, that had been obvious.

She gave herself a shake. Of course he did! That's how men acted, they went wild for bosoms—everyone knew that. If they didn't, the Social Club would be out of business. She couldn't for one minute think his response to her naked body special. He'd reacted as any man would, and that was the truth of it.

But good Lord, he sure knew how to make love to a woman. Beneath her skirt, the evidence of his attention, a sweetly sore reminder that she'd been satisfied. Heat bloomed right from her core at the memory of their passion.

A second throat clearing. She could hardly ignore him again, especially seeing as he'd be the one to take her back to town. Oh, dear heavens, she'd be forced to look at him when they were riding. Then again, maybe not. If she kept her gaze lowered and didn't hold on too tight…

"The storm broke in the night." He paused, as if he expected her to reply but she kept her gaze on the sky beyond the boulders. "Probably a good time to get to town, if you're ready to go."

She nodded. "Yes, I think it's time to head to Wylder."

****

Lane wondered if he'd confessed the particulars of his visit during his sleep because by the way Gertie acted toward him, he must've done something wrong. He'd had morning-after talks with women that covered all kinds of behavior, but nothing prepared him for this.

She acted mortified by what they'd done. It made no sense, not really. Of course, Will hung like a shadow over them, but they hadn't disrespected his memory by their actions. And he hadn't done anything, well, out of line to her. He knew some men preferred roughness and others had peculiar leanings, but their lovemaking had been consensual and considerate. He'd been gentle with her, before, during, and after the act.

Whatever she had on her mind kept her as stiff as a length of fresh-cut oak. Not a comfortable curve to her spine or an inclination to share a laugh. And by the time they'd reached the cemetery at the edge of town, it showed as clearly as if he'd gazed into a bucket of fresh water that she had no intention of letting him kiss her goodbye.

She'd insisted he leave her at the cemetery. Said she'd had Founder's Day items to attend to, which made absolutely no sense seeing that none of the folks in the cemetery could lend a hand with the festivities. Still, he did as she asked.

Belle held back a bit as Gertie slid off her back and walked into the cemetery. No small nicker of farewell or friendly nudge with her head.

Why, even the horse had sense enough to know something wasn't right between them.

****

Gertie sat at the base of the cemetery plot. After the long hot summer, brown grass clung to the red dirt. Flowers had been planted up at the head near the wooden cross, but they were wilted, turned to sticks that sprawled beneath the modest marker.

Naomi K Wylder Died 1870

Whenever she saw the chiseled inscription, she pondered what the middle initial stood for. Today it crossed her mind, again. Not that it mattered, but curiosity brought the question to her thoughts.

At the base of the cross, a fist-sized square of granite to further mark the woman's existence.

Beloved Wife and Mother

Once more, the mystery middle initial claimed her thoughts, but only for a second. No way of knowing the truth at this point. Most likely no one remembered the woman's middle name. Her husband, Ralph, had entered the declining years, and his mental faculties were severely compromised. Lucky if the man knew his own name. Forget anyone else's.

She didn't imagine she would ever find out the truth of it. Maybe some things were meant to remain a mystery.

She turned to survey the surrounding gravesites.

The Wylder Cemetery lay just south of town, a short walk to the railroad tracks and all that stood beyond. Quiet, with the distant mountain range and acres stretching toward the horizon. Not big or fussy, it served the town well. Wylder had been incorporated in 1869, and Gertie guessed that most of the town's dead found this their final resting place.

Many homesteads had private family cemeteries. Thomas Harvey's wife and baby were interred in a plot out at the homestead where Theo and Lily lived. She'd seen it the other day when she and Lane went to confer with Lily about the fabric. Many families, like the Harveys, placed their plots close to the main house, so those left behind could visit without difficulty.

She wondered how that might be, to have the departed near at hand. It still grieved her that she hadn't gotten Will's body back after he'd been killed. She would've liked to have him in the family plot in Richmond. But if she'd had him buried, would she have been able to leave him behind? Probably not. So, as awful as it had been to not have him returned, maybe it had been for the best.

A shadow fell over the ground, so she looked up and flattened a hand above her brows. Violet Bloom stood at the bottom of the grave, a smile on her face and her bonnet dangling from one finger by its ribbons.

"Well, I'm not surprised to find you here." The schoolteacher motioned to the ground. "Mind if I join you? I could use a little rest after the walk over."

"I'd love it if you sit with me for a bit." She patted the ground and watched as the other woman folded her legs and sat. "A cemetery always seems lonely to me. Too quiet. I welcome the company."

Violet placed her hat on the ground beside her, then smoothed a hand over her cheeks. They were flushed, as if she'd hurried. She patted her hair, but every strand remained secure despite the heat.

She became conscious of her own disheveled appearance. Her skirt bore wrinkles and traces of yesterday's grit, and her blouse could not be sparkling white any longer. And her hair—well, she had lost more hair pins than were currently holding the tendrils in place.

No help for it.

If her friend noticed, she didn't let on. She swept a slow gaze over the nearby plots as she gave a satisfied nod. "I'd hoped there wouldn't be too much cleanup to do out here." She turned to look behind them, then nodded again. "I like when it's tidy. It shows respect for the dead, and since that's part of our Founder's Day celebrations, I wanted to be sure everything is as it should be."

Tradition dictated that the schoolchildren, the next generation of Wylder citizens, place flowers in the cemetery. Gertie left the organizing of that part of the festivities up to the schoolteacher, but she always made sure the cemetery looked presentable before everyone showed up to witness the flower ceremony.

"I'm here for the same reason, but we're in luck this year. Not too many graves need tending, and there aren't any whose monuments are leaning." She crossed having grave markers straightened off her mental to-do list. One less thing to worry about. "It makes me feel good to see everyone is taking care of their dead—and those who don't have anyone to tend to them, too."

The schoolteacher had arrived in town to find her intended dead—or so he would have her believe. But when Jasper Abraham appeared on her doorstep to confess and show himself as a married man, she—and the rest of Wylder—wondered who they'd buried. The man in Abraham's grave wouldn't be missed by anyone. That's how he had managed to trade places with him. Even though the man resting beneath the stone that read Jasper Abraham wasn't Violet's intended, he didn't have any kin, so she continued to tend the grave as if he were hers, and no one in town questioned it. Gertie admired her for doing the duty to a dead man she'd never met. Many others did, too.

Now Violet pointed toward the Abraham gravesite. "I sit there a lot and think." The admission, so soft it blended with the birdsong coming from a nearby cottonwood tree. "It might be strange, I suppose, to sit in a graveyard with people you mostly never met, but it makes me feel connected to Wylder in a deep way. Some of these folks were the first to settle here, and because of them, I'm able to call this place home."

Gertie remembered when the other woman had first come to town. She'd been an odd duck, determined to fit in but struggling to figure out how best to do that. Her association with Thomas helped townspeople accept her. Also, she took her situation seriously. The children in her care not only learned their reading, writing, and math, but they were taught how to be mindful of others and how to be good citizens of their town. The woman drew admiration from all, herself included.

"I don't think it's strange, Violet." She ran her fingers through the sparse grass beside her. "I'm so glad you feel connected to the place. Believe me, when you first arrived, a few of us wondered if you'd stay. We hoped you would but wouldn't have blamed you if you didn't."

"I wasn't sure I'd make it here, especially before I met Thomas." She smiled, a twinkle in her eyes. "And that's when I met you, too. My life changed for the better after I fell into that snowbank."

When Thomas rescued the woman from a fall in the snow one early morning, he'd brought her home to his house. Doc Sullivan checked on her and advised they let her recover in place, so she'd stepped up to help the widower tend to his houseguest. She'd cared for Violet through the worst of her recovery.

"The whole town benefitted from having you arrive in Wylder. We could've done without that episode in the snowbank, though. Nearly lost you that week."

A head shake didn't loosen Violet's hair, and not for the first time, Gertie wondered how on earth the woman managed to get those pins in so tightly. She never looked disheveled, not even on the hottest afternoon in the schoolyard.

"You, Thomas, and the good doctor saved me. I'm so grateful, because I love living here." She pulled in a deep breath, then sighed it out. "To be honest, life isn't easy for a woman on her own. No one knows that better than you. But in a place like this, with so many fine people, it's worth living." She held her hand out, palm toward the sky, and waved it to the graves beyond where they sat. "And it's because of people like Naomi

Wylder that we get to be here."

"You're right, as usual. It's tough making it without a man." She shrugged. "At least you've got Thomas, and we can all see how much happier he is now that you're here. Alexia, too."

"Thank you for saying that. I think I'm the one who's better off now that I've got Thomas and sweet Alexia in my life. They bless me beyond measure."

"Blessings go both ways."

Her cheeks colored. "That's kind of you to say." Violet raised one eyebrow. "What about you, my friend? Any thoughts about men in Wylder? Or more to the point, do any draw your attention?"

The other woman's powers of observation were well-known around town. Gertie had no doubts that she'd seen Lane, and that this line of questioning targeted him.

She chose her words carefully, not sure she should say too much. Still, it would be good to confide in someone…

"I haven't thought about, well, about getting involved with a man in years." She swallowed. The truth came without trouble, but the reason for that required some strength. "I lost my husband in the war and thought I'd never find a man to hold a candle to him. All these years I've been happy to have my memories. They've sustained me but now, I'm not so sure about my choices."

A short silence let her gather her thoughts, and she appreciated that the other didn't press.

When Violet spoke, she did so without a trace of judgment in her voice. "I am sorry for your loss, Gertie. I can't imagine how hard that must have been for you.

Why, when Thomas came down with yellow fever and I nearly lost him…well, I came close to losing my mind, too. Love runs so deep, it's impossible to forget how much of your heart you've given to another." She paused, then cleared her throat. "But I'd think a heart as big as yours might have room in it for another without doing any disrespect to your first husband."

First husband.

A chill swept up her spine, as if someone walked over her very own grave.

She'd never considered having a second husband, but hearing the words come from the other woman's mouth planted the idea in the fertile soil of her mind. Could she cling to another the way she'd given herself to Will?

Why, she'd done more than that just a few hours ago.

She felt herself turn hot at the memory of how shamelessly she'd clung to Lane. How on earth could she think for one minute that man might see her for anything more than a loose woman?

She shook her head and forced herself to speak. "I don't think so. One man is my limit, and I'll keep my life this way until I join him in the hereafter." Before the other woman could take the conversation further, she pushed to her feet. "If you'll excuse me, I've got many errands to run."

****

Lane rubbed a hand over his chest, hoping to chase the ache away. A futile effort, but worth the try. If a horse had kicked him squarely and sent him flying, he felt sure it wouldn't hurt nearly as much as this did. Hour after hour, and the pain did not subside.

Damn, but the woman had punched him straight to the heart, and now he could barely breathe.

He sank lower in the tin bathtub. Its water had been heated to almost scalding, which he imagined was what happened when the woman who did the heating had her amorous advances turned aside for the second time. She'd offered to help him undress when he'd come for the bath, but he assured her he'd manage on his own. A huffy exit before a return with steaming kettles.

Well, he'd rather steam a bit than have sex with the woman. If she shaved him without cutting his throat, he'd tip her well. Maybe next week's bath wouldn't be so hot. Better yet, perhaps she'd just do what he paid her to do and stop grabbing at his pants.

And that train of thought brought him back to the ache in his chest. More precisely, the woman who gave it to him. As it turned out, she was the only female he wanted unbuttoning his blue jean trousers.

Heat that did not come from the water swirling around his body rose in him at the memory of their lovemaking. His cock came to attention beneath the suds. He kept his hands on the edge of the tub and left it alone. That part of his anatomy had been well loved and deserved a bit of rest.

But his mind…now that came at him differently. He closed his eyes and there, right against the backs of his eyelids, he saw her. Lying on the blanket with her hair spread around her shoulders. And lower, her legs open and inviting.

Despite their being stranded in the middle of that God-awful storm, lying on the hard ground without any comfort at all, last night had been the best sex he'd had. Ever. Hands down, the absolute most earth-shattering, heart-clutching experience of his life.

So how could it have taken a bad turn so quickly? He understood a woman being a little bit embarrassed over behaving without inhibition. Not that he minded her losing her calm, cool demeanor in favor of becoming a vixen.

He'd been with women who blushed come sunup. Most men had, he figured. But it went way past that with Gertie. Not only did she refuse to look at him, but the loving softness she'd shared so freely became encased in steel at daybreak. If he didn't know better, he'd think he'd done something inappropriate.

Another fast look back at their relations solidified his feelings that he hadn't done anything out of line. He'd been gentle and caring, moving with tenderness and not rushing her. And he'd been sure she found her release before he took his pleasure.

He'd heard stories from men who got their kicks from slapping women or forcing them to do, in his eyes, depraved acts, but he did not abide that kind of behavior. He'd done nothing along those lines, and still Gertie acted as if she'd been offended.

The door pushed open, and the bathing attendant entered. She didn't exude friendliness the way she had earlier, but he watched as she dropped her gaze to the bathwater. A slow grin spread over her face.

Unfortunate, the way she earned her living. He didn't imagine that she'd grown up hoping to someday bathe strange men and try to fondle them for tips. A sad state of affairs, the world they lived in, but he couldn't change the way of things and he knew it.

"Seems like you could use a hand there." She pushed the door closed behind her and came closer.

Interesting how a stiff penis made the woman smile. From surly to friendly again, all in a heartbeat.

She'd nearly boiled him alive like one of those fancy lobsters he'd had at a restaurant in Richmond one time. He'd heard they were thrown in the pot while they still lived and served on a plate after they stopped thrashing about. Well, he wasn't a lobster and hadn't forgotten she'd tried to cook him.

"I'm hoping your hands are steady, ah..." Damn, but did she ever give him her name?

"Lara."

"Right, Lara." He shot her a smile and wished there were bubbles in the tub. "I need a shave, and I'm thinking you've got nice, steady hands."

She raised an eyebrow toward the water. Or, what lay beneath it.

"Nope, I'm fine, thanks. Just need a shave, nothing more." He linked his fingers over the water, his elbows on the tub's rim. They hung just about over the middle of the bathwater, in a spot that he hoped concealed at least some of his anatomy. "And if you don't nick me, there'll be an extra bit of silver in it for you."

A shrug sent her lightweight cotton blouse high. It exposed an expanse of smooth skin at her waist before it dropped into place.

"If you're sure that's all I can do for you..."

He scooped a handful of water up and washed it over his cheeks. "I am. And it is."

****

Gertie didn't take the time to bathe when she got home. Instead, she changed her clothes, combed the snarls from her hair and twisted it into a tidy bun, and washed her face. She wasn't her Sunday best by any means, but it would do for the call she had to make.

And this time she wasn't going to walk to the Adams homestead. Nossir, she'd been silly once. She stopped at the livery for a horse and buggy before setting off.

She hoped the drive would clear her head but as the horse clip-clopped along she didn't find any clarity. Not one teeny, tiny bit.

Embarrassment, lots of that filled her. Lane must think so little of her now that she doubted she'd see him again. Why, she'd acted as if she were employed by Miss Addie over at the Social Club. Not that she really knew what those ladies did to get their transactions going, but she had an idea. A good idea. She probably rivaled their skill at unbuttoning a man's fly.

The thought of how she'd behaved was mortifying at the same time it sent a bolt of sexual lightning right to the very part of her that had been so well-loved. Good Lord, but her mind had become tangled, and she knew no way out of the mess.

Concentrate on Founder's Day, she reminded herself. The only thing that should occupy her mind, the celebrations and all she had to do to be ready for the town's biggest day.

The horse slowed when she tugged on the reins. The Adams' home was not pretentious, but it couldn't hide the fact that its owners were well off. No unpainted wood or bare porch. The place could have been at home in Richmond, it sat so beautifully on its manicured garden lawn.

Late-blooming roses perfumed the air surrounding the front porch. They grew in a dazzling pink-and-red row, each plant pruned into an appealing round shrub.

What she wouldn't give to have roses like that in her own yard. Missus Adams must've brought clippings from somewhere else, because plants like these sure didn't grow naturally on the frontier.

She and Sarah weren't overly friendly, but she wondered if the woman might be persuaded to part with a cutting or two. She could probably get them to root if given the chance.

Well, first things first.

Apples. Then, roses.

She climbed the front steps and knocked on the door. Footsteps echoed inside the house, coming close as if their owner had little more to do than sit about and wait for visitors.

Sarah pulled the door open. A fashionable pink-and-cream-striped dress that most would consider too elegant for an ordinary afternoon in the West made her appear younger than her years. Gertie knew the woman to be older than she, but being financially set had its benefits. She supposed expensive creams kept the other's face unlined, and of course, her dress must have cost more than most Wylder women ever spent on themselves. Still, she had the good grace to not look put out that someone stood on her porch, so Gertie didn't hold the woman's show of wealth against her.

"Why, what a surprise to see you." Sarah put a hand to her hair to pat the immaculate updo. "Would you like to come inside?"

The offer came with a tight smile that made it clear the woman only asked out of common courtesy. For an instant, she considered saying that yes, she'd love to go in and visit, but the truth, that this visit had many more to follow, stopped her.

"No, thank you. Maybe another time." She looked back at the horse and buggy, as if they pressured her to hurry. "I have several other errands to run so I'm afraid I can't linger."

Sarah didn't hide her relief. A smile that came more easily now. "I understand. Well, then, how can I help you, Gertie?"

Time for luck to shine down on her. With the mercantile fresh out of apples, the fate of the Founder's Day apple pie baking contest rested on this woman's shoulders. Hopefully, she felt generous enough to share her bounty.

A deep breath, then she plunged in. "Well, it's like this, Sarah. You know the apple pie baking contest is one of the big draws of the Founder's Day celebrations."

Pride shone from the other woman's eyes. "Well, of course it is. We all enjoy putting our pies on display for judging. A little bit of friendly competition never hurt anyone, did it?"

"No, it certainly did not. And we all respect the way you've taken the top prize in the contest in years past."

"Several years, to be exact." Sarah crossed her arms over her bosom and smiled. She looked as if she'd just feasted on the bones of past pie contestant losers. "Not to be shouting my own praises, I certainly would never do that, but I have been taking home top spot for as long as most of us can remember."

So much thinly disguised arrogance in the words...

Gertie didn't have time to bolster the other woman's opinion of herself—not that she needed any bolstering. The glow on her cheeks could have lit the night sky.

She didn't much take with overinflated self-opinions but couldn't run the risk of deflating this one and jeopardizing her chances of getting what she'd come for, so she smiled and spread her hands wide. "Why, you're right, of course! Everyone knows you bake an apple pie to perfection. I've always thought the angels in Heaven must look down at our pie table and wish they could snatch a bite of yours."

"Oh, that's kind of you to say." A shimmer in her eyes made her look even younger than she had just a few moments ago. "I don't know about angels, but as long as the judges agree I bake the best apple pie in Wylder, I'm happy."

Time to press in. "Well, since we all know how you have the judges' favor, I wonder if you wouldn't mind sharing the good fortune with the other women in town?"

A furrow appeared above Sarah's brows. "Whatever do you mean?"

"We need plenty of apples for the pies for the contest. I went to see Finn Wylder over at the mercantile yesterday, and there's bad news, apple-wise. Seems this year's growing conditions were off, not enough rain, he said. So the shipments he gets from back east didn't arrive. Not enough apples, they said." She paused and took a deep breath. Asking for a favor didn't set well with her, but there was no other choice. Besides, she asked for the town, not herself. "But you have an orchard here, so I wonder if you wouldn't mind supplying the other ladies with apples you've grown?"

One eyebrow lifted so high on Sarah's face that Gertie wondered how on earth it was possible to even make a face do that. She didn't have time to linger over the absurdity, though.

"Why, that's impossible." The other woman crossed her arms over her chest and drew her lips into a thin, straight line. "Simply impossible!"

"But, Sarah, you don't want the other women to be unable to bake their apple pies, do you? I'm sure you have enough fruit to help the other ladies."

"I'm sure I don't." A haughty sniff. "We had an exceptionally dry summer. Don't you remember how the dust blew off the plains and creeks ran dry?"

As much as she hated to admit it, the other woman spoke the truth. The previous months had been insufferably hot.

Sarah didn't wait for a reply. She shook her head, as if there were no changing her mind on the subject. "We only have three trees that produced fruit, and I'm certainly not going to give any of it away."

Chapter 13

Gertie crossed the final "t" on the sheet of paper and added it to the others in the pile on the table beside her. She looked over at the porch railing. Her empty glass sat there, its lemonade long gone. Funny how a throat could parch when the mind was busy.

She considered going indoors for another glass but decided against it. Too much trouble. Instead, she closed her eyes and let her head fall back against the wooden rocker. A warm breeze touched her cheek as her mind wandered.

Like a bird returning to its nest, her thoughts went straight back to the man who had so recently made passionate love to her. Her heart gained a beat thinking of what had transpired between them. The feel of his body against hers, the way he moaned when she took him inside her…the energy of their encounter lingered and sent tingles dancing along her skin.

So many emotions swirled through her, she could hardly breathe. Was Violet right? Did she have the capacity to hold two men in her one heart?

The sound of footsteps on the path leading to the porch grabbed her attention, so she opened her eyes and sat up. Goodness, but she'd lost track of the time. School must be out, because Alexia and Brenda both had big smiles on their faces and looked as if they hadn't a worry in the world.

Gertie remembered how it felt to be so carefree. It had been so many years since she had known such lightheartedness, but one didn't forget the way walking on air touched a heart.

"School's out?"

Both girls nodded, their grins growing wider.

"We couldn't wait to get here." Alexia held a slender book in her arms. She tapped her fingertips on its cover as she nodded to the side table. "Are you busy? Did we come at a bad time?"

Gertie stood. She placed a hand on her back and gave it a little twist. Sleeping on the ground hadn't done much for her minor aches and pains, although they really hadn't slept much. Heat touched her cheeks, so she shook her head and focused on the task at hand. There would be moments to look back on all that, but now wasn't the time.

She handed a stack of papers to Alexia and another to Brenda. The girls had arrived after school, hoping to assemble the new bunting, but she had this more pressing issue for them to work on. The bunting could wait.

"You've arrived at the perfect time. I need these put up all over Wylder. Everywhere."

She watched them read the notice. Saw their eyes widen.

Brenda looked up at her with a hint of panic in her gaze. "No apples? But Mama will be so disappointed."

"We have lots of other options to choose from. And, really, it can't be helped." She tapped the paper in her hand. "Remember, girls, put the announcements in as many places as you possibly can. Anywhere a lady might look needs to have one of these in plain sight."

It had taken precious time to write all the notices by herself, and her fingers were sore. Overseeing the celebration came with obligations including this completely unexpected one. She'd been to the mercantile and spoken with Finn. They'd assessed all the available fruit and compiled a list, which she'd added to the bottom of each notice. Hopefully the women of Wylder would not be put out at her changing their apple pie baking contest to a general pie baking event.

And if they were upset, they'd have to get over it. Without a good supply of apples, she couldn't hold an apple pie contest. And with this surprising twist to the usual event, who knew what interesting pies might show up on the judges' table?

Maybe Sarah Adams would lose her title this year. After the way she'd behaved, Gertie wouldn't feel sorry for her if she did.

"Don't worry. We'll get them tacked up all over town." Alexia held the bundle against her chest and nodded toward her companion. "Won't we?"

"Sure will, ma'am. Then we'll be back to help sew the bunting."

"Oh, you girls won't have time for that today. You'll need to get home for dinner."

The two young ladies exchanged a long look. Their excitement over completing the project couldn't be hidden. Gertie remembered how it felt to be so all-fired up over something that little else compared. She smiled at their enthusiastic faces and relented. "Well, if you get done before dinnertime, come on back, and we can at least begin sewing the bunting together. How does that sound?"

"Perfect!"

"We'll be back, you can count on it!"

They took the front steps at a run and dashed down the street. She watched until they turned the corner headed toward Wylder Street before she sat in one of the rockers and breathed a sigh of relief. One less thing on her must-do list. She hardly dared consider how she would manage to get everything done. She only knew that she would.

****

Lane knew better than to try to push a woman into doing something against her wishes. He'd seen the consequences of that type of action by observing friends and it never ended well for the man. Nossir, a fella might better try to prod a constipated bull than a woman who had a belief not to do a thing.

And Gertrude Jackson had her mind made up to not speak with him. Poke her now and she might dig her heels in and never even look his way again. He wouldn't put it past her, not that he had a clue about what bee had flown into her bonnet and hatched its own hive of angry baby bees—or more importantly, why she suddenly had a hatful of hateful bees.

After a night of lovemaking, she should have been pleased. Instead, she treated him as if he were a pus-filled blister on the end of her toe. He couldn't fathom why she did, but he knew better than to make her madder.

The Five Star Saloon caught his attention. After the other night and his morning-after killer of a headache, he had no intention of getting drunk again anytime soon. That didn't mean a man couldn't quench his thirst, though.

Besides, a saloon offered a spot to think for a while. And maybe that's what he needed to do, sit and ponder what had gotten into Gertie. A few shots of whiskey might give him some insight.

He turned and strode up the wooden steps. Before he pushed the batwings wide, he leaned over and peered inside.

Not too crowded. A few poker games going at corner tables. Couple of fellas at the bar. No sign of the woman he'd woken up beside after his last dance with the drink.

Good. As much as Gertie didn't want to see him, he didn't need to run into the woman he'd shared a bed with. Thankfully, that's all they did last time. He wouldn't take a chance like that again.

No, if he were going to bed any woman, it would be Gertie. After being with her, he couldn't imagine sharing passion with anyone else.

A push sent the doors swinging open. He stepped inside.

Time to stop thinking. He'd done enough that his brain hurt and all of it had gotten him no closer to uncovering the mystery surrounding the woman's behavior.

Maybe the time for thinking had passed.

A game of poker, now that would take his mind off things nicely…

****

Minnie Milligan gave her permission for Brenda to spend the night at Alexia's house, so once they had hung all the fruit flyers, the girls returned to Gertie's dining room to sew the bunting.

They hadn't stopped for dinner, so she insisted they

eat some of her potato soup and cornbread before they started working. Both girls ate well. As they were clearing the table, Alexia paused after she placed her bowl in the kitchen wash basin.

She knew the girl well enough to recognize she had something on her mind. Hopefully it wouldn't be another anatomy question, like her last one. "What's got you looking so thoughtful? Anything you'd like to talk about?"

Brenda stepped up to wash the few dishes they'd used. The other girl grabbed a dish towel and dried, before passing the items over. Gertie placed them in the cupboard.

"Well, it's just that for a long time I thought I wouldn't ever know how to do certain tasks. Like sew or cook, the kind of things that get a girl a husband." She colored slightly but continued. "I thought that, without a mother, I'd never be able to learn all there is to know." She handed over the last bowl. "There's a lot a woman needs to understand before she can get married and care for a house and a…well, a husband."

Brenda turned and held out a hand for the dishtowel. She used it to wipe her hands, then hung it over the side of the empty dishpan. "There's so much. I've been watching Mama, and I don't know how she manages. So much work." She shook her head. "And that's why I want to be a schoolteacher like Miss Bloom. No husband, just a lot of children in a classroom. When I leave at night, I won't have to look after anyone but myself."

Given that the girl had been helping her mother with her younger siblings and the house since she was old enough to sweep, it came as no surprise she would feel that way. She knew from experience how laborious caring for a big family could be.

"I think you'll be a wonderful teacher, Brenda, if that's how you decide your future." She paused and looked from one girl to the other. She met the aspiring teacher's gaze again. "But it's okay if you change your mind and decide you want a family. You've got plenty of time to give it more thought."

A nod, but the girl didn't look like she would have a change of heart. The firm set of her lips and look in her eyes showed determination.

Well, time would tell.

Alexia sighed. "I don't want to be a spinster. I want a man of my own, and a house and children. Lots of children, not just one. One is lonely, and I don't want a lonely house." She met Gertie's gaze.

A question hung between them. She felt the young woman's hesitation, so she urged her to speak her mind.

"What is it, Alexia? It's clear as day that there's a matter you want to ask about. Go on, honey. Ask away."

Time marched on, and they had buntings to sew. She didn't want to rush the girl, but they didn't have hours to spare.

"Do you mind being a spinster?"

Well, good heavens, but she hadn't expected that!

She had never made a big deal about her past when she arrived in Wylder. There had been a few questions from some of the nosier residents, but she gave short answers about her history and turned the topic around. Eventually, no one bothered interrogating her, because they realized she wasn't going to offer a lot of information. And then, new folks moved to town, and she became an "older" Wylder resident, someone whose background hardly rated as pressing news.

But this young woman wrangled with finding her way in the world. And for her, a motherless world. She could use all the insight everyone who cared about her would provide.

Gertie pulled the edges of her lips upward as she reached into the neckline of her dress and pulled out a gold chain. Two gold bands dangled from the chain. She held it up for the girls to see, then tucked it back inside where it belonged.

"I don't think I would mind being a spinster, not if I were happy and productive. Many women decide not to marry, and there is certainly something to be said for that." She sighed. "But I'm a widow, honey. My husband died before I moved to town. Those are our wedding rings."

Brenda and Alexia shared a fast glance.

Alexia smiled. "We thought you had to be married, but we figured you might've run away from a man." She lowered her voice. "And, you know, been in hiding. But we knew you must've done some housekeeping, because you know everything." A pause, then the girl put a hand on Gertie's arm. "And you're teaching what you know to us. You're helping me get a husband, training me on how to do wifely things. Thank you. I am grateful."

A lump formed in her throat for the sweet, motherless child. She pulled the girl in for a hug, then reached a hand out to Brenda. When she had both in her arms, she kissed first one brow, then the other. "I am the one who's grateful. You two are like my own daughters, and it fills my heart with joy to teach you simple skills."

Alexia giggled, a reminder of how young they really were. "I need all the help I can get with sewing. My fingers should be made of stone, so they don't bleed the way they do." She cast a rueful eye at her fingertips.

"Well, if you'd stop pricking them with the needle, they wouldn't bleed so." Brenda slung an arm around her friend and led the way back to the dining room. "And the more you practice, the better you'll get."

Gertie followed, wiping a tear from her eye. They blessed her, and gratitude filled her heart. Too bad she'd not been meant to have her own child to love and care for. She would've treasured that opportunity.

****

It hardly seemed real that they'd managed to sew the whole bunting for the front side of the schoolhouse, but they had. The girls had been so excited they wanted to hang it immediately, and Gertie, despite being bone weary, didn't have the heart to turn them down.

She held the lamp before them as they walked to the schoolhouse. It wasn't her habit to walk the streets of Wylder after dark. But seeing as they weren't going near the saloon or Miss Addie's place—not that Miss Addie's business ever spilled out onto the street, but still, the girls were young and impressionable—she thought it would be okay. They'd hang the garland, then she'd have them home with no one the wiser.

The girls wanted the decoration to be a surprise for everyone to see in the morning. Tomorrow the other buntings and a banner across Wylder Street would be hung, but they were determined that this new one be the first to go up.

"Won't everyone be shocked to see our pretty garland hanging when they wake up tomorrow?" Brenda held the project clutched to her bosom, as if she carried a baby.

She had sewed the bulk of the part the girls worked on. Alexia had been diligent, but the other's fingers flew over the fabric, her experience making the task come to life with ease. Her stitches were fine and straight, and if she wasn't so intent on becoming a teacher Gertie thought she'd make a naturally talented seamstress.

"Everyone is going to be even more excited for the festivities now that the decorations are going up." Alexia dropped her voice to just above a whisper and leaned close. "No one knows we're planning a surprise for them. It's like we're Santa Claus, swooping in to deliver a gift and leaving before anyone sees us."

Gertie's heart warmed, listening to the two chatter about the festivities. It had been a wise move to involve them in the preparations. Someday she'd be too old to head up the committee and keeping the Founder's Day traditions would pass to others. Either young woman would do a fine job of honoring their founders and the beginning days of their frontier town.

But she wasn't ready to step aside yet, so she hurried them along, mindful that the longer three females were out past dark, the higher their risk of stumbling into an unfavorable situation. Lord knew she'd already done enough of that stumbling in her life. No need to involve the girls in any sort of mess.

The schoolhouse stood quiet in the darkness. Hard to believe that come morning the place would be loud and lively, filled with children of assorted ages whose educational needs were being met by their young but capable schoolteacher. They'd been blessed with Violet Bloom's arrival and the following appearances of her other sisters. The women were assets to the town, and it brought a smile to Gertie's face now when she imagined the happy surprise the teacher would get tomorrow.

"Okay, girls, let's sort the bunting out here, and then we'll walk it over to the front of the building." A stone wishing well stood near the street, so she stopped and waited for the others to join her.

To her mind, a wishing well near a schoolyard made little sense. What purpose did it serve? She wouldn't be surprised if the bottom sat filled with torn school papers and the tiniest pencil nubs. What other use would schoolchildren have for a wishing well?

Well, now the thing served a purpose. A nail stuck out the side near its top, so she looped one end of the string holding the bunting together around it and handed the other end to Alexia.

"Here, you go walk it out. Brenda and I will make sure there aren't any tangled triangles. When we've got it straight, we'll hang it above the double doors."

It took only a few minutes to straighten the fabric streamer. She grabbed the middle section while Brenda took the end off the wishing well, and they walked toward the front of the building. Hooks from previous years were embedded in the wooden siding, so they reached up and looped the ends of the bunting in place, then adjusted the way it hung.

When they stood back to survey their handiwork, a collective sigh escaped into the night air. Even with only a small lamp to cut the darkness, the bunting stood out against the building.

"It looks as if the schoolhouse is a package that we've decorated." Alexia placed a hand around her friend's shoulders and leaned against her. "We really sewed it, didn't we? Like a bow on the building so others will know we're celebrating."

She placed her arm around the girls and pulled them close. Pride swept through her in such a wave she could hardly control the wobble in her voice. "I am very proud of you two. So much hard work and dedication, and all for the joy it will bring others."

Brenda tilted her head to the side, as if giving the decoration a critical appraisal. "We didn't do badly at all, did we? My mother says this celebration is as much for the original Wylder family who stopped here to build the mercantile and begin the town as it is for the rest of us. She says we need to remember where we've come from if we're ever going to have an idea of where we're going." She paused, then turned and met Gertie's gaze. "What do you think of all that? About the first Wylders and all?"

"I think your mother is a very wise woman." She turned them toward the street. "Now, we'd best get home. We want to be well rested for tomorrow. That's when our preparations really begin."

Her list of things to do before the festivities dwindled. Tomorrow the bulk of it would be done, and then she, along with the rest of the town, could sit back and wait for the big day.

But the next twenty-four hours would be challenging, and that's if everything went exactly as planned. And that, she knew from years past, never happened.

****

Lane hadn't counted on staying at the Five Star for so long, but luck favored him, and the hands dealt his way were winners. He won so many times that he practically cleaned the table. But as a gesture of good faith, he'd bought the last round of whiskey for his fellow players.

When you're walking out with a pocketful of money, it's better to leave the men who you've taken it from smiling than looking for revenge. He'd learned that lesson a long time ago, and in a hard way. He still wore the scar from a knife belonging to a man who had nothing left in his pockets but the blade after he had lost everything else.

So now he always ended a night of poker by buying the final round before he stood up.

The last whiskey had put him a tiny bit over the line between just happy and slightly intoxicated. The soft glow that warmed his insides turned his judgment hazy, but he didn't stop to consider his actions when his feet moved toward Gertie's place instead of the boardinghouse.

Maybe by now she'd chased the bees from her bonnet. He sure hoped so, because one day of not being in her good graces had taken its toll. Tough to admit, even to himself, but he missed the woman.

Her pleasant ways, wise talk, and lovely smile felt miles away now that she withheld them from him.

Well, it wouldn't do. How could a man atone for a sin he didn't know he committed? He couldn't, so she left him no choice but to press her for the truth. Then, he'd do whatever it took to get back on her good side.

A thought, that she would be angry when he

divulged his full reason for being in town, nagged near the back of his mind, but he shoved it away. If he played his cards right, the way he'd done in the Five Star, he still had time with Gertie before she sent him packing.

A knock on her door brought no response. He tipped his head toward the thick slab of wood, hoping to hear footsteps coming from inside, but there were none. A step back, to see if she walked past a window, but the place showed no sign of activity.

He removed his hat with one hand and ran the other through his hair. Now, where could she be at this time? Decent women weren't out and about after dark. It wasn't safe, and besides, he knew she'd been up with the sun. Didn't the woman ever get tired?

He stepped over to the far end of the porch and leaned against the railing. His lips twitched at the memory of what tired her out. Just last night, she'd lain in his arms, her breath feathery upon his cheeks while she slumbered. Their lovemaking left her sated and ready to rest, and he'd been happy to hold her close.

They should be twined together now, making love and murmuring tender words in each other's ears. Neither should be alone on such a night, when stars shone brightly and romance danced in the air. He sighed and turned his gaze upward.

Then, he shook himself.

What in tarnation had happened to him? He'd gone from soldier to gunslinger to law-abiding citizen to soppy mess, all in one lifetime. It wouldn't do, being intoxicated by love, as if he'd been impaled by Cupid's arrow. He wasn't a schoolboy, after all.

Get yourself together, man.

Resolve straightened his spine. He'd come here to talk with Gertie, to get to the bottom of her current prickliness, and that's exactly what he'd do.

He leaned back against the porch pillar and folded his hands in his lap. Sooner or later, she'd come home, and when she did, he'd be waiting.

****

Gertie hugged each girl before they went into the house. Alexia's father had been waiting on a porch rocker when they arrived.

She and Thomas looked at each other for a moment, listening to the excited conversation as it became swallowed by the house's thick walls. The sound of footsteps on the stairs. A giggle. Then a closing door.

"I'm sorry to keep them out so late." She raised an apologetic eyebrow and held her lantern high. He didn't look angry, just concerned. "They were so caught up in surprising everyone tomorrow morning with their new bunting hanging on the schoolhouse that I just didn't have the heart to deny them. I should've known, though, that you'd worry."

The man shook his head, a compassionate smile coming to his lips. "Nothing to apologize for. Why, we're good friends and neighbors, and I know you'll care for Alexia as if she's your own. Don't get the notion I worried. It's a nice night to watch the stars, is all." He nodded toward her house. "Would you like me to walk you home?"

"I appreciate the offer, but my house is only a stone's throw from yours." She tipped her head back and looked toward the sky. "And you're right about the stars. I think I might sit on my porch a spell and watch them myself."

"Enjoy the quiet, Gertie. It is soothing." He put a hand on his front door. "But don't linger too long. It's getting later, remember."

"Good night, Thomas."

She held the lantern up and took the steps with care. No need to rush, the stars weren't going anywhere.

"Good night, Gertie. And thank you for spending so much time with my darling girl. She needs a woman's influence."

"My pleasure."

The walk between his yard and her own took less than a minute. She climbed her porch steps, set the lantern on a table beside the front door, then settled into one of the chairs that faced the street.

One of her favorite times of day, these quiet moments before she turned in for the night. They felt sacred, as if the veil between worlds thinned. A big star caught her attention, and she focused on it, wondering if Will could see it, too, from wherever he had gone.

The view from Heaven. Could it be the same as the one every mortal had?

"Beautiful night, isn't it?"

Lane's voice, as smooth as the Kentucky bourbon she kept in the cupboard for her special holiday cake, came from the darkness. Maybe she'd grown too weary to jump at sounds this late at night, or perhaps her body had already grown accustomed to the sound of him, but she didn't move when he spoke.

Silence stretched between them while she considered her options.

Finally, she turned and saw him. Seated on the top

railing, leaning against a pillar, he looked like something pulled right out of her imagination. Strong, able to protect a woman from harm. Stable, unflinching in his steadfastness. And here, which counted more than the others, even. A good man who hadn't gone off to leave her, who lived and breathed…and who made her feel more alive than she had felt in years.

"What are you doing here?"

He chuckled. "Well, seeing as you're not rushing to spend time with me, I figured I'd come to you."

Had she not been busy reminding herself why she avoided him all day, she would have been swept away by his reply. Imagine, a man coming after her. Why, in her younger days, she would have believed it possible, but at this point in her life? Shocking, almost. And on the same night when she'd been regarded as a spinster, too.

The man touched her in places she'd considered long dead, but that didn't change anything. The reality of her life, and the way she'd behaved when they were stranded in the storm, could not be denied.

"I thought I made myself clear." She swallowed and willed herself to go on. "I don't want to see you again, not after last night."

He rose from his perch and walked across the porch, his bootheels tapping against the wooden floorboards. When he reached her, he removed his hat and placed it on the table beside the lamp. Then, he knelt in front of her and met her gaze.

Stubble covered his cheeks, upper lip, and chin. The fresh coat of whiskers made her want to run her hand over his face, so she fisted her fingers and shoved them down onto her lap.

He reached for her hands as he met her gaze. He unfurled her fingers and held her hand in his.

"I got that much out of you." He ran a slow thumb across her palm. "But I don't understand why. Did I do something to offend you?"

Good heavens, the man had saved her life! How could he think anything so far-fetched?

"No, of course not. You were…" What could she say? All the words that came to mind would only show her to be as loose as she'd acted last night. She couldn't very well tell him what she really thought of him, but she couldn't let him believe he'd wronged her. "You were a hero, Lane. You saved my life, and I am grateful."

His brow furrowed. "I'm hardly a hero, honey, but I sure do like hearing you say so. But tell me, if I saved you why are you acting as if I'd just about murdered your cat?" He gave her a mischievous grin. "I promise, I didn't touch Boots."

Back in Richmond, she and Will had a big old cat named Boots. She loved the animal, although both Will and Lane, and Grant, too, teased her about how bad it smelled and how they'd be happy to take it down to the stream and give the old man a "bath"—before assuring her they would do the cat no harm and were only teasing.

She hadn't thought about Boots in a while. Nice to have someone who shared her history and remembered the small things that made a life interesting.

"You're not the one who did anything wrong." She hesitated. "It's me. I'm the one who acted badly."

The lines in his forehead deepened. She focused on them, not trusting herself to meet his gaze. "What are you talking about? You didn't do one thing last night that I don't consider incredible. Beautiful. Fascinating."

Lane tucked a fingertip beneath her chin and gave a gentle nudge. She met his gaze and saw the world in his eyes, and for a moment, she believed him. Then, she remembered.

Heat rose in her cheeks.

Goodness, but she was tired. The day had been a long one, and tomorrow promised more of the same. They couldn't stay out here going back and forth forever. Time to stop hiding behind her own embarrassment.

"I threw myself at you like a common, well, like a woman who should be working at the Social Club." She gave a small sniff and hoped he knew what exactly went on behind the closed doors at Miss Addie's place. "I didn't act the way a southern-born widow should have acted, and I'm sorry."

"Whoa, hold on a minute. Are you saying you regret what happened between us last night? Because I've got to tell you, last night was the best night of my life." He stared into her eyes as if he wanted to bore into her soul. "The best ever."

Her own eyes filled with tears. She hated it, but they came without warning. And since he held her hands in his, she couldn't wipe the tears that fell and trailed down her cheeks.

"But I didn't act like a lady…and you were Will's best friend. I must have shocked you…I don't know what came over me, I've never done that before." She sniffed. "I swear, Lane, I have never lain with a man except for my husband. And now, you."

He held her gaze for a long moment before he

reached out and ran a tender hand over her face. First one cheek, then the other, wiping her tears away.

"What happened last night was beautiful, like nothing I've ever known before." He paused, looking off to the darkness for a moment before he met her gaze again. "It was what I've always hoped love would be. I've just never experienced it—love, I mean. And honey, it blew me completely off my feet. I've walked around all day wondering if I dreamed it and feeling so full and alive that it's almost as if I never lived before now."

"Me, too." She had to admit the truth. All day she had felt in a daze, as if what she shared with him had been a fantasy, something she conjured in her mind to help escape the loneliness of her existence.

He cleared his throat. "Except I couldn't figure out what I did to make you turn from me. It's been dogging me all day, eating away at my gut." He shook his head as if to clear it. "It pains me to know that you've spent the time thinking I took you for common. That's the furthest thing from my mind, honey. That you gave yourself to me, a man who will never come close to deserving a woman like you, well, it's the best gift I've ever gotten."

Her breath caught. Had she heard him right? "A woman like me?"

He nodded. "I don't think you're aware of how incredible you are, Gertie. You're strong and unafraid. Moving out to the territory on your own, well, that took a whole lot more spine than most people—man or woman—ever have. You pack a six-shooter as if it were a rolling pin and are as capable of using one as the other." He grinned. "When you walk through Wylder, you have a kind word for everyone, and everybody in town knows who you are. And you're humble, which is a fine quality in a person."

She tugged a hand from his grasp and put it to her cheek when he spoke. Her face felt hot to the touch, and her mouth had gone dry. She never expected such high praise from anyone, let alone a man who lived such an upstanding life. Why, he had fought in the war. He'd come home a hero, had shown his courage in defending the south. Even though the north had won, they still recognized their southern men as fearless and brave.

"Why…I'm speechless."

When he smiled, the night stars looked dim by comparison. "Are we better? That's all I need to know, that we're okay."

She nodded, still at a loss for words.

"Good." He placed a hand over hers on her cheek and rubbed his fingertips across her skin. "Because I intend to court you, Gertie. Proper calling and walking about, if that's what you want. Or we can go directly to the preacher, if you'll have me."

She gasped. The preacher?

Lane chuckled, but he didn't back down. "Oh, yes, you heard me right. I love you, Gertrude Jackson. Always have, and always will. And if you'll let me, I aim to show you just how much you mean to me."

The world tilted as she looked into his eyes. Had he really said all those things?

And what would Will say if he could hear them now? Good God, could Will hear them?

As if he read her mind, he rubbed a lazy thumb over her cheek. "And I know that right about now you're wondering what your special man would say to all of this." He swallowed hard and blinked twice. His eyes looked glazed, but he went on. "I admit, I've had the same thoughts, but I believe, deep in my heart, that Will would be happy for us. He loved you with his whole heart and soul, and when you love someone like that, you want the best for them, always. Now, I'm not saying I'm the best, but I am saying that I love you. I think that would make him pleased, and if you think about it, you'll see the truth in it."

She didn't need to think. He was right, Will would want her to go on.

When Lane leaned in, she closed her eyes and melted into his kiss.

Chapter 14

Soft blue light held her in a warm embrace. There was no fear, trepidation, or loneliness. Peace surrounded her.

From the swirling pool of light, a figure appeared. She didn't need to see his face to know him.

"Will."

He stopped before her and held out his arms. She wanted to go to him, but something held her back. The holding wasn't painful, and she didn't struggle, but she couldn't move forward.

"It's okay, Trudy. It's good that this finally happened. You've found a reason to stay where you are." He smiled and the familiar expression cut across the distance and held her heart. "You deserve this second chance at love."

The blue darkened as Will faded. She reached for him, but he moved farther from her with each heartbeat.

She dropped her hands and watched as he dissolved into the light.

When he was gone from her sight, she placed her hands over her own chest. Beneath her palms, a strong, steady beat.

She woke in the darkness and scrubbed at her cheeks. They were dry. No tears, but the vivid memories of the man who she held in her heart lingered. A good trade. Better to take the remembrances of their love than suffer the ache of their loss.

A snore beside her ear reminded her she shared the bed. A strong arm lay over her side, and Lane's hand cupped her breast. They'd fallen asleep that way, and neither moved throughout the night.

Well, his nearness prompted her to move now. She covered his hand with her own and swished her hips. The masculine feel of him, all muscles and warmth, sent a shiver of delight running up her spine. She moved again…and he responded.

His hips pressed against her as he came awake.

A kiss on the back of her neck, then a trail leading toward her shoulder.

"'Morning." His deep voice held the rasp of sleep. "My, but you sure know how to wake a man up, don't you?"

"Hmm…I like the way you, ah, rise in the morning."

A chuckle sent tremors from his skin to hers.

She rolled onto her back, and he shifted so his body covered hers. She felt the hardness of him where it lay against her hip. It had been far too long since she'd been touched by a man's morning arousal. Until this moment, she hadn't remembered how special it felt, this intimacy at the break of dawn.

Night surrendered to day…and she surrendered, too. She placed her arms around his neck and gave herself to him. A lift of her hips, one smooth slide, and they came together as naturally as if they'd been making love with each other for years. No need for words, their bodies knew the way.

Just hours before they had made love so

passionately that Gertie imagined she'd be sated for a good, long time. How could she have been so wrong? Had she forgotten the craving of one for another? She had to admit, the hunger for the man who even now brought her body to new heights would not be satisfied with only one night. She wondered if a lifetime of nights and sultry mornings would be enough, then tossed the musing from her mind.

Better things claimed her attention.

Lane's tempo increased so she wrapped her legs around his waist and pulled him closer. He rose onto his knees and lifted her into his arms, never taking his lips from hers. Every thrust brought ripples of pleasure, sending her nearer the pinnacle.

A struggle to control her breathing. Her heart beat so fast that her words came in ragged gasps. "I—oh, I—Lane—"

He chuckled, then thrust harder. Faster. She could tell he danced on the edge, the same way she did, so she squeezed her thighs against his sides and met him stroke for stroke.

When he moaned, she closed her eyes and dropped her head back. Unrestrained, she gave herself over to the sensations that exploded like a bright burst of fire within her.

Lord, it had been too long since she'd been made love to this way. As she felt Lane's release, she clasped her arms around his shoulders and savored the last moments of delicious passion.

Then, she wondered how long she'd have to wait before they could come together again.

****

It pleased him that Gertie didn't behave like a

virgin in the bedroom. She had been free with her loving in the clearing during the storm, but now that they had come to an understanding after their discussion on the front porch, she acted even more uninhibited.

The passionate nature of the woman excited him. It came as just one more part of her character to fall in love with. And damn, but he loved her.

Which made his mind swirl as hard and fast as a dust devil on the plains. He held her in his arms, yet he hardly knew which way was up, his mind spun so. The thought of telling her his full reason for coming to Wylder weighed heavy on him.

She would be angry. He'd tried to talk about Grant once already, and she'd thrown her kin into the dust, crushed him beneath her heel, and told him in no uncertain terms not to mention the man again. He got all that, but he'd promised her brother to deliver news and discuss it with her.

It might get him tossed out on his ear, but he aimed to do what he'd said he would.

She nestled so sweetly against his side, a loving woman whose fiery moans still echoed in his mind. Maybe their lovemaking would soften her up a bit. At least, that's what he hoped.

He cleared his throat. No time like the present.

"Gertie, honey, you must know my coming out to find you in Wylder…well, it wasn't an accident. Belle and I rode a lot of miles to see you."

The fingertips that had been stroking circles on his chest stilled. When she didn't speak, he went on.

"Now, I know this might make you, um, well it might get you momentarily unhappy, but I must tell you why I'm here. I can't forget what made me come all this way. It wouldn't be fair to either of us." He took a deep breath. "Or to Grant."

The temperature in the room dropped by ten degrees. She turned to stone beside him, and for an instant, he didn't feel her breathing. When she exhaled, it came with a low growl that raised gooseflesh on his arms.

Gertie sat and clutched the top of the sheet, covering her breasts.

It wasn't her bosom that caught his attention, though.

Her eyes flashed thunder. Above them, her brows pulled into one straight, angry line.

And her pretty, bow-shaped lips were set in a hard pucker, as if she'd sucked on a lemon.

Oh, he was in for it.

"I told you not to mention that man's name again." Her words dripped ice.

He nodded. "You did. But you know he's the one who sent me to talk with you."

One of her eyebrows shot up her forehead, as if yanked by an invisible string. "Talk with me? Is that what you're calling this—" She waved a hand through the air between them, over his half-covered, naked body and her own. "—this thing we're doing now? Talking? And is that why you're here, in my bed?"

His blood ran cold when he realized she believed he'd seduced her to further Grant's interests. Good God, but did she really think so little of him?

"You can't imagine that I'd—"

"That you'd wriggle your way into my bed like one of Grant's well-trained snakes?" She tugged on the sheet and jumped from the bed. Instinct made him drop a hand to cover his privates, but he needn't have bothered. She didn't have the faintest interest in them—or him—any longer, and it showed clearly on her face.

"Gertie, listen—"

"Get out." She turned for the bedroom door and pulled it open. A hand rose, and a finger pointed to the hallway. "Get the hell out of my house."

He stood and grabbed his pants from where they lay on the floor. While he stepped into them, he wracked his mind for something to pacify the woman. He dared a look at her face and wished he hadn't. Red cheeks, hard lines where sensual ones had been, and eyes that practically spit fire.

He'd rather have tussled with Old Scratch himself than dive into it with an angry woman. No way out of this, so he buttoned his fly and moved to stand in front of her. The walls of the large bedroom closed in on him, as if her anger shrunk the space.

"Listen, I understand you're upset. I know you and Grant had a falling out, but I swear to you, I didn't seduce you so I could…what did you call it? Wriggle in like one of his snakes?"

"Last night's love talk? Was it all so you could get me to listen to this message from Grant?" He opened his mouth to reply, but she cut him off. "No, don't answer. It doesn't matter. I should have known anyone in cahoots with my brother would do anything to do his dirty work."

"I meant every word I said last night. I would never—"

"You need to leave."

Her gaze burned a hole in him, but he didn't look

away. "I came to discuss some business, a lot of money that Grant insists belongs to you. It's your share of family assets he's put in an account under your name. I have the paperwork so you can transfer the funds. I promised I'd help you."

He stood firm as she glared at him. Shirtless and barefoot, he would've liked to cover up but knew better than to move. Perhaps if he stood nearly naked in front of her, she would see he had nothing to hide.

The feud between her and Grant ran deep, he realized that. Yet shouldn't she be grateful for a windfall? After all, everyone could use money. And it's not as if her brother tried to foist something upon her that wasn't rightfully hers. The financial benefit belonged to her, and it came from her family.

Surely, she had to see that he'd only agreed to deliver the news as a favor to her brother.

"I don't want his money." Her voice came low and even, almost without any feeling at all.

As if he were dead to her.

"It's not his money." He held out a hand but didn't touch her. A good thing, because although she didn't step back, her gaze shot to his palm with a clear burst of animosity. "It's from your parents' holdings. It's your share, is all."

She went on as if he hadn't uttered a word. Again, in a cold, lifeless voice. "And I don't want your help." Gertie tipped her head toward the hallway. "Now get out of my house."

He wanted to reach out and grab her, but the ice in her eyes kept him from doing it. Instead, he gathered his boots, shirt, vest, gun belt, and hat and stepped into the hallway. He turned to meet her eyes, and hopefully make her see reason, but she dropped her gaze to the floorboards.

"Gertie, honey…please…can't we talk about this?"

She shook her head, sending the hair that fell in loose waves around her shoulders dancing. "We don't have anything left to talk about." She lifted her face and looked him in the eyes. "And if you come back here, I won't be alone. Will's six-shooter will be in my pocket, and I won't hesitate to use it. I've worked too hard for this life. No one's going to disrupt it." She paused for a breath. "Now, get out. And stay away."

What could he do? Lane turned and walked down the hallway. His bare feet on the stairs made no noise, but the sound of his shattering heart filled his head. At the bottom, he took a minute to dress, then opened the front door and walked out onto the porch.

As he lifted his face to the sun, he wondered how on earth the best part of his life had been snatched from him this way. He'd finally found happiness, only to have it torn to shreds in a heartbeat.

Over money. Damn it all, that was the worst of it. No one should argue over money, ever. Money came and went like the scent of roses on a breeze, something that made life better when it swept in but didn't steal breath when it left.

Damn it all, but he wished he'd never agreed to come to Wylder. At least before he'd been a lonely, but reasonably happy, man. Now he would never be content again, and it came down to other people's bank accounts. Of all the stupid reasons to ruin a life!

****

The best thing she could do, to keep busy, would not be a difficult burden. With Founder's Day just days away, this time when she would've rather holed up in her house until Lane rode out of town wouldn't allow that. Too much to do to wallow. And she reminded herself that she did not take kindly to those who rolled around in self-pity.

Her morning ablutions were swift. The sooner she got out and began her day, the less time she had to think of Lane's deception. And it had been deceitful, no doubt of it in her mind. He and that horrid brother of hers had transpired to send him here, to offer her monetary compensation for the bad treatment that had come her way when she decided to move west. Well, she wouldn't be told what to do then and she couldn't be bought now.

She'd defied Grant and despite his anger at his widowed sister refusing to sit home and weep for the rest of her life, she'd done what he said couldn't be done. She'd found a new life, on her own, out of the protective, suffocating, secure enclosure Richmond and their family money offered.

Her brother had threatened that if she went against him and set off for the frontier on her own, he'd have nothing further to do with her. Whatever happened, she'd be on her own, at the mercy of the world and unable to turn to him for anything. He'd wiped his hands of her in no uncertain terms.

And now he thought he'd wiggle back into her good graces? Or worse, that she'd accept his generosity and be in some way indebted to him? Well, she wouldn't ever be beholden to anyone again. She sat at the reins and directed the course of her life. Not Grant. Not a bank full of money. And certainly not Lane Hutchins.

"Forget about him." Her voice echoed in the empty house.

Brave words. Too bad they didn't soothe the pain in the center of her chest.

No need to dwell on that. The day would give her enough diversions that maybe she'd be able to push the truth of the man to the back of her mind.

A pounding came on her front door, so she hurried down the hallway. A fast check to see who stood beyond, then she pulled the door open.

Alexia fell forward, her arms spread as if she were a small child running to her mama. Instinct made Gertie grab her. The young woman trembled so she pulled her close.

Brenda Milligan ran up the porch steps and skidded to a stop in the open doorway. She, too, looked shaken.

"Whatever is going on? Why aren't you two at the schoolhouse?"

The girl in her arms pulled back, and she saw the tears streaming down her cheeks. "The bunting is ruined! Someone pulled it down during the night and ripped it up!"

She looked at Brenda, who nodded in agreement. "It's true, Miss Gertie. When we got to school, the pretty garland we hung last night…oh, I can't even bring myself to say it." She took a step back and waved her hand. "Best if you come see it for yourself. Miss Bloom sent us to fetch you."

She hurried out, holding Alexia in a side hug. The girl still shook, and she wasn't about to let her go until it subsided. Brenda pulled the door closed behind them as they set off for the school.

"Don't fret, girls. We'll fix whatever's been done

to the bunting."

Who could have done such a thing? Well, anyone tall enough to reach the fabric could have pulled it down.

But who would have any reason to do it?

She couldn't think of one person in Wylder who would stoop so low. No one who had a grudge against her or the Founder's Day celebrations.

Her heart stuttered in her chest as her mind ran through the possibilities. Only one person held any animosity toward her this morning.

Lane. She hated to believe it, but who else would try to undermine her contribution to the celebrations? He knew how important the festivities were to her and how diligently she worked to make the event a success.

That low-down, horrible man.

Her mother had a saying when they were young, that if you played with dogs you were liable to get fleas. Apparently, Lane had been in cahoots with her brother long enough that he'd become just as flea-bitten as his companion.

Well, she'd put an end to his interference in her life. She'd been fooled by the man's charm, but he'd killed that interest the minute he tried to make her see her brother as anything other than a self-serving weasel.

****

The girls hadn't exaggerated. The bunting they'd hung with so much optimism, pride, and joy just hours before lay in pieces on the ground and hanging from the trees in front of the schoolhouse. One end draped from a corner above the door low enough to hit anyone passing through in the head.

Violet Bloom and her pupils stood in a cluster near

the wishing well. As she walked up with Brenda and Alexia, Gertie heard the schoolteacher speaking with the children.

"Now, there's nothing to fear." The teacher raised her voice to be heard above the buzzing whispers of her pupils. "Whoever did this is long gone and won't be back."

One boy toward the front of the group, one of the smaller ones, raised a hand. "But why would someone do that?" He pointed toward the mess. "They broke the school!"

An older girl spoke up. "They didn't break the school."

Miss Bloom nodded. "Kate is right. No one damaged our schoolhouse. Their vandalism tore apart the garland, but the school is intact."

"But why?" The little boy persisted, a frown creasing his small face. "Why would someone be so mean?"

Brenda reached a hand out to the child, and he took it. Their teacher smiled her approval over the girl's attempt to comfort her unsettled charge and nodded toward the girl. "Brenda, would you like to explain what you think happened? After all, you and Alexia worked very hard on that bunting with Miss Gertie. You must be very upset to see what's happened here."

The teacher looked to Brenda, then back to her student.

A wise woman. It gave Gertie a minute to compose herself. The shock of seeing their hard work in such a state made her both livid and sad all at once. She feared that if she were to speak now, some of the anger would tumble out, and it wouldn't do to show that to the pupils.

But the young woman rose to the challenge and spoke in a calm voice. Her demeanor gave no indication she had been so unnerved by the scene that a few minutes ago she could barely speak. Now, it showed clearly that the girl would make an excellent teacher. She took control and calmed the children.

"It's unfortunate that someone would be mean enough to try to destroy something as special as the schoolhouse bunting we made for the Founder's Day celebration." She looked over at Gertie and Alexia before turning to face the pupils again. The girl had a presence that came as both reassuring and authoritative. "We worked many long hours to make it pretty and hung it last night to surprise all of you this morning."

A boy in the back, one of the older pupils, shook his head. "Well, we got a surprise all right."

Brenda nodded. "We did, but this isn't anything that can't be fixed. When folks would bring us down, which is what whoever did this meant to do, we need to show them that they can't pull us low." A murmur among the children. Heads nodded their agreement. "We're stronger than whoever did this. Our founders braved harder circumstances to settle in Wylder. I don't think Naomi or Ralph would have been brought down by a broken bunting, do you?"

A chorus of agreements came from the group.

Miss Bloom spoke up. "Well said, Brenda. Now, children, let's all pick up the pieces of the garland. I'll go inside and grab my sewing box. Maybe some of the younger children can hold the pieces while the older ones stitch them all together again. Then, we'll hang the bunting back in place." She looked from face to face.

They'd all calmed in the last minutes. "And then we'll show whoever did this that they can't disrupt us—or Founder's Day."

Out of the corner of her eye, Gertie noticed the sheriff striding down the center of the street. A few men followed him, but she didn't chance to notice who they were. Her interest lay in the one charged with upholding the law.

Branch Wylder stopped beside them. While the children had begun to collect bunting pieces, she and Violet remained near the wishing well.

The man surveyed the scene for a long moment. He'd been sheriff for a while and had shown himself to be an intelligent man. While she had no doubt he could take the wings off a housefly with a single shot, she appreciated a man who used his brain before resorting to his revolvers. Since he'd become sheriff, he made a habit of walking the streets of Wylder, checking in on its residents and making his presence known.

Now, children smiled up at him. He pushed his hat back on his head an inch, so his eyes were unshaded and directed his question to the teacher. "Was it like this when you got here this morning?"

"It was. I waited for you to see it." She gestured to the students gathering the torn fabric. "They've just begun picking the pieces up from the ground and around the steps. Would you like me to have them stop?"

"That won't be necessary. I can see what happened, and the ground's too dusty for there to be footprints, anyhow." He shot them a tiny grin. "Besides, I'll bet your students' feet would have covered footprints had there been any." He pulled a watch from his vest pocket, checked the time, then rubbed a thoughtful thumb over its glass face. His gaze rose, then rested on Gertie. "Miss Gertie, I know you and the girls hung this last night. Do you know of anyone who'd want to tear it down?"

She met his gaze and shook her head.

The lawman didn't settle for her reply. He lowered his voice and pressed her. "Miss Gertie, is there anyone in Wylder who would want to see you hurt? We all know how important the Founder's Day celebrations are to you, how you take the planning to heart." He tucked his watch back into his vest pocket. "Think about it. Would anyone want to upset you? I'm sure this isn't a random act. Someone is saying something with this mess. Do you have any ideas?"

She sucked in a deep breath and pulled her gaze from his. A turn to look over her shoulder. A small crowd had gathered behind them. Some familiar faces and a few she didn't recognize.

Town began to come alive for the day. She heard wagon wheels rumbling over rutted streets. From a distance, the sound of metal hammering at the blacksmith's forge. A horse whinnied, and a door slapped shut.

Who would try to undermine her hard work? Her mind spun but still yielded no good answers. Wylder's tussles usually involved too much whiskey and the Five Star, not widow women living respectable lives.

Her gaze raked the crowd. The expressions on faces were startled and concerned. A few looked annoyed by the mess, but no one seemed satisfied with the destruction.

A familiar figure strode toward the scene. He

crossed the street without bothering to look and had to sidestep a buggy, but that didn't slow him down. Long legs covered the distance quickly.

A flash in her mind, of those legs twined with hers.

She pushed it aside as Lane moved to stand near her. Their gazes met, and her heart hardened.

The sheriff pressed her yet again. "Any idea, Miss Gertie? Who would want your Founder's Day preparations to fail?"

Her mama would have a conniption fit if she could see her daughter now. She'd been raised to act like a lady, but her arm raised of its own accord, and she pointed—without thinking of her poor mother rolling over in her grave—a finger at the man.

"Him." The word fell like a stone and caused the crowd's chatter to still. She didn't care that everyone listened. If they figured out how she knew the man, so be it.

Branch Wylder pushed his hat back another tiny bit as he addressed Lane. "You've been staying at the boardinghouse, haven't you?"

No one could say the sheriff didn't have his finger on the pulse of his town. How he kept track of everyone, newcomers and passersby included, amazed her. She didn't think she'd be able to keep everyone straight but was grateful Branch could.

"I have." He put his hands on his hips and gave a nod. "Along with a bunch of others, I'd reckon."

"What's your business in Wylder?"

"I came to see Missus Jackson."

He glanced over, but she kept her eyes focused on the sheriff. The man sashayed into town acting as if they were long-lost friends, and had managed to turn her nice, calm world upside down. She didn't cotton to behavior like his and wouldn't grace him with a kind look now.

Let him dig himself out of the mess he created. He should have stayed back east, in her past, where he belonged. If Branch Wylder threw him in a jail cell and let him rot, it would be his own doing.

Lord help her but she was furious. Not only at him, but at herself, too. She had given him her trust, let him back in her life, and allowed the man into her bed. Welcomed him there, if she came clean about it. What a fool she'd been!

And not just then, but now, too. Even as she stood seething in the street faced with the evidence of his anger, parts of her ached for him. They recalled the feel of his skin on hers and tingled. Warmed by memories of the passion they'd so recently shared, there were bits of her that still felt molten. And despite being furious over his deception and betrayal, some of her wished she could fall right back into his arms and that he'd tell her that it had all been a mistake. He had only come to see her and nothing more.

She gave herself a mental shake.

The man was a snake, the same as her brother— only worse. He'd seduced her to gain her trust.

Branch cleared his throat. "Miss Gertie, is that true? Is this man in Wylder to spend time with you?"

She shook her head. "I don't believe a word he says." A hard swallow around the lump in her throat. "All I know is he's the only person in town who would benefit from seeing my plans fail. He'd like that, if Founder's Day, well, if it fell flat and folks blamed me for its being a disaster."

"That's not true, and you know it. Why I—"

The sheriff held out a hand and cut Lane off. "Now why would anyone want the celebration to not go well?"

Time to swallow her pride. Too bad most of Wylder stood witness to her admission. Well, it couldn't be helped. "He wants to humiliate me, so I'll agree to go back east with him." The words gave her courage. "The man is trying to make me fail in front of the townspeople, so I'll look like I shouldn't be in charge of this important event." She waved her finger at him a second time. "Well, I won't stand for it. I think he tore the bunting down this morning when I chased him from my house!"

And there, in that instant, as the words flew from her lips on a cloud of anger and self-righteous indignation, she realized her mistake. All the time she'd been in town, an upstanding widow woman who never besmirched her reputation, didn't matter.

She'd admitted she chased a man from her home. And she'd done so in the light of day in front of nearly every woman in town.

Within the hour, everyone would know she'd entertained this stranger overnight.

Before the sun hit its zenith, she'd hear scandalous murmurs behind her as she walked down Wylder Street.

By tomorrow, the others on the Founder's Day committee would surely decide that next year's planning honor would go to another.

She knew all of that, deep in her heart where it hurt the most, yet she did not regret what she'd said. It was the truth, all of it, and let those who would shun her be damned.

A widow's life didn't come easy, but she sure as hell wasn't going to let those who did her wrong get away with it. Not her kin. And not the man who had stolen a piece of her heart.

"Well, then, it seems you and I need to have a talk, Mister…" The sheriff raised an eyebrow.

"Hutchins." The word came through gritted teeth. Lane's eyes narrowed as he stared at her, but she didn't look away. "Lane Hutchins."

Branch nodded. His hands had gone to his hips, where they tucked into his blue jean trousers above the pair of Colt pistols he wore. "Well, Mister Hutchins, why don't you have a seat right over there on the edge of that wishing well while I take a closer look at the damage?" He swept his gaze over to Addison Merriweather, the attorney with biceps so large they strained the fabric covering them. "I'm sure Mister Merriweather won't mind keeping you company for a few minutes."

Addison crossed his arms over his chest. "Don't mind a bit, Branch. You just take your time with your investigation."

Chapter 15

Lane didn't suppose he could blame Gertie for being angry with him.

Sure, he should've shot straight with her from the beginning. Before getting close to her, he should have come clear about his whole reason for being in town and delivered Grant's message, as well as the transfer of funds, to her. He'd intended to do that, but seeing her again set his mind in other directions. His heart, too.

And now that lapse in judgment had him headed to the Wylder Jail with the town's sheriff and an attorney. Neither seemed in the mood to speak. In fact, when he tried to explain, the sheriff had told him they'd talk at the jailhouse.

As they covered the distance between the schoolhouse and jail, he considered his options. Another man might've made a break for it, but he'd done nothing wrong so that wouldn't do. Nothing, that is, that would land him behind bars. No sheriff would jail a man for dallying with a woman's affections, which is what he supposed he'd done.

Damn, but he hated himself right now. A whole lifetime of wandering on his own, of having no one to share his life and love, to finally have all of that in his grasp...and lose it. What a fool he'd been!

The door to the jail stood open so the sheriff motioned him inside. He went in first, followed by the sheriff and then the attorney. Opposite the jail cell, a desk and two chairs. The lawman dropped into the seat behind the desk and nodded toward the one facing him.

"Sorry, Addison. Things're kind of tight in here."

The attorney leaned against the bars of the unoccupied cell. "No worries. I'm fine like this."

Wylder scrubbed a hand over his face. "Early in the day for this, isn't it?" He gave a half smile. "Haven't had my Arbuckles yet. So, why don't you tell me how you know Miss Gertie?"

"We were acquainted in Richmond. Our families know each other."

A nod. "You've known each other for how long, exactly?"

He did a mental calculation. The first time he'd met Gertie she wasn't even married.

"Maybe twenty years?" Close enough, he figured.

"So, a long time?" The lawman took his hat off and placed it on the edge of his desk. "And you've always been on friendly terms, all those twenty years?"

He'd never had a quarrel with the woman until this morning. Not one bad word or a cross look.

"We have been."

The sheriff sat back in his chair and reached for his pocket watch. It slid from his vest and into his hand, and he didn't even glance down at it. Instead, he turned it over and over in his palm.

Nervous gesture or habit? No way of knowing.

"Well then why, out of all the people in Wylder, did she name you as the one person who might be behind the mischief at the schoolhouse?"

"No idea."

A snort from the attorney beside him and the

sheriff raised an eyebrow.

They weren't buying it.

Lane sighed. "Fine. She's annoyed with me, because I brought a message from her brother." He ran a hand through his hair and tried to figure out how much of the story he could reasonably leave out. The tiny jailhouse grew warmer by the minute, and he couldn't wait to escape this interrogation, as well as the hot little building. "He sent me here to talk with her and to deliver something, but the two don't get along so she's angry that I'm doing this favor for him."

Addison Merriweather spoke up. "And that's the reason she thinks you would have torn the bunting down?"

He swung around in his chair and met the man's gaze. "It is. She found out this morning why I'm here and…well, I don't think she's gotten over it yet, that I said I'd do this favor for her brother, Grant."

The cell behind the attorney didn't offer much room for a grown man. The cot didn't look none too comfy, either.

The lawman spoke so he gave him his attention. "That does make sense. Women can be funny about things like that." He reached into his pocket and pulled out a scrap of black fabric with several long, blonde hairs spread over it and placed it on the scarred wooden desk. "Any of this look familiar to you?"

Lane leaned in and studied the pile. The hairs were longer than one would typically find on a man's head, so he assumed they were from a woman.

He shook his head. "Nope. Can't say that it does. Where'd you find it?"

The lawyer took a step forward and peered down at

the desk. "At the schoolhouse?"

Wylder nodded. "Yep. That scraggly bush near the front corner of the schoolhouse, right there, tangled in the upper branches. Alongside a blue-and-white triangle. I reached for the triangle and saw this." He took a deep breath, then let it out slowly.

Merriweather tipped his head to the desk. "Thinking it might belong to whoever ripped the bunting?"

"That's exactly what I'm thinking."

Lane looked from one man to the other. He motioned toward his own head. "Well, seein' as I've got brown hair, that lets me off the hook."

A slow smile spread across Branch Wylder's face. "You were never on the hook, Mister Hutchins."

"Lane."

The lawman gave a thoughtful nod. "Lane, then. And just to satisfy my curiosity, since you are such a long-standing friend of Miss Gertie's, do you have any idea who would set out to undermine her hard work?"

"No, I don't." He rose to his feet and clapped his hat back on his head. His gaze shifted from one man to the other, then back to the sheriff. "But I aim to find out."

****

Gertie had too much to do to waste time fretting over things in the past that couldn't be changed. After losing Will and living so long without him, she should have known that by now, but she guessed this incident with Lane came as a reminder.

In no time at all, a handful of eager schoolgirls and Miss Bloom helped repair the bunting. A cheer went up when they rehung it. A number of pupils assured her it would not come to further harm. She imagined there would be several sets of eyes focused on it for the remainder of its decoration duty.

She hurried down Wylder Street toward the cluster of men standing beneath a newly hung banner. Grateful they hadn't waited for her arrival but had taken its hanging onto their own shoulders, she didn't stop until she stood right beside them.

All offered greetings, but her attention went straight to the banner. It hung from one corner of the mercantile building to a pole in front of the building opposite. They'd pulled it nice and tight, and the words were clearly visible.

Founder's Day Celebration!
Tomorrow in the Schoolyard!
Contests! Dancing! Music! Food! Prizes!
Everyone Welcome!

Gus Wright, the undertaker, stood to her right. She turned and met the soft-spoken man's gaze. His eyes were gentle, and she saw why he came as such a comfort to grief-stricken families. He had a way about him, a compassion that came through when he looked at a person.

"What do you think, Mister Wright?" She didn't know him that well, which given his profession came as a blessing since it meant she hadn't had to bury any kin in the Wylder Cemetery, but she offered a friendly smile. "Are you looking forward to the celebration?"

A slow, careful nod. "I am." He tipped his head toward the words above them. "Lots to grab a man's attention. Who doesn't like food? And music…and dancing…"

He looked as if he wanted to say something but

thought better of it. She couldn't tell for certain, but he sure gave off the impression of being a man with thoughts on his mind.

"You partial to dancing?"

The corners of his lips tugged upward, ever-so slightly. A little nod. "I am."

Had she hours to spare, she would've dug deeper, but time ran short, so she looked to the three other men standing beside them and tipped her chin to her chest. "Well, there'll be enough music and dancing to make everyone happy, I expect. Thank you, kind sirs, for hanging this banner. The whole town thanks you."

A wave before she turned and headed for the door to the mercantile. Finn Wylder had one of the flyers about the fruit pies right in his front window. Good. She didn't need any of the town's ladies complaining that they didn't know the judging had opened up to all kinds of fruit fillings.

Lily Harvey, her son on one hip and a basket slung over the other arm, met her in the doorway. A hair escaped the woman's updo, a telling indication that she'd already had a busy morning. No secret that the homesteading wife knew how to wield a hairpin, so seeing her with a dangling lock beside her temple said a lot.

The toddler scowled, evidence of tears in the reddened eyes.

Gertie gave the little one an extra-large smile. If she had someone to hold her while she cried, she might be tempted to shed a few tears, too. Not in her nature to do so, but this day tested her resolve.

She glanced at Lily but spoke to the woman's child in a friendly voice. "Why, good morning. I'm happy to see you again." A quick wink which had the toddler blinking as he tried to imitate her action. "And you can wink, too! Oh, I just love a good winker."

The boy giggled as he buried his face in his mother's shoulder. Lily heaved a sigh, snuggling him closer while the exasperation fell from her expression.

"Why you're just a magician, Gertie. How on earth you got my grumbly little man to giggle, and so quickly, too, is beyond me." She jostled the boy on her hip and shook her head when she saw how he tried to wink. So far he hadn't mastered the task but was giving it his best effort. "You have a way with children. I've seen it before, when you've stopped by the schoolhouse to speak with my sister, and I've happened to be there, too."

Her heartstrings tugged when the boy successfully winked at her. "Well, there's a lot to love about children." She swallowed around the tightness in her throat. "So nice to run into you, but if you'll excuse me, I've got to check in with Finn about tomorrow's celebration."

Lily took a step forward but paused in the doorway. "I'm sure Finn will be glad to see you. Poor man got his head screeched off by my fellow here. I don't expect he'll be sorry we're leaving." She smiled. "I'll see you tomorrow. And thanks for being so kind."

She waved at the child and turned to go into the mercantile.

Kindness. If the mother only knew how her heart ached to hold a child in her own arms, she'd see how finding a smile for a wee one was a blessing rather than a chore.

****

Lane had no idea how he'd get Gertie to forgive him. All he knew was that he wouldn't give up trying until she did. Sure, she held him in very little—if any—regard right now, but that would change when she cooled off. It had to. He'd never once wronged her, aside from this instance, and that had to count for something.

His life after the war had taken a bad turn. A lot of things lingered in his mind from his past, bad smells that no matter how hard he tried to clear his head of them hung on. Most days he went about his business without a whiff of any haunting him.

Other things he'd done...well, they were more difficult to push into the deep recesses of his mind, but he worked at it and managed pretty well. He'd been a hired gunslinger for a while, but when the toll of hunting down men who would do just about anything to evade the consequences of their actions began to wear on him, he walked away from the life. Let others bring those to stand for their sins. He had enough of his own reckoning to do.

But this, his deception to the woman he loved, hit harder than any other act he'd committed. It tore at him more than killing on the battlefield, and that had ripped at his soul. But those men he killed, they'd chosen to stand in those fields and fight. Gertie hadn't done any such thing, and yet he'd managed to wound her.

There had to be a way out of this mess.

If only he could figure out what kind of shenanigans were going on with regard to the celebration she held so dear. Someone wanted to undermine her, no secret in that. But who?

The attorney, Addison Merriweather, walked

beside him. When he left the jailhouse, the lawyer had followed him out, and now they traveled down Wylder Street, each lost in his own musing.

They passed the man's office. Lane had seen it before, right next to Thomas Harvey, the mining financier's place of business. The two shared a building, and he imagined it must be convenient for both. More than likely they shared clients, too.

When it became clear that Merriweather wasn't going to stop anywhere soon, but rather continue to walk with him, he decided to use the man's Wylder information to his advantage. Tagging along came with a price. Didn't everything?

"You've been living in Wylder for a while, is that right?"

Merriweather didn't try to deny it, and he didn't seem to take offense at being asked. "I have. A good while." A shrug sent the man's shirt tight on his shoulders. Lane decided that if he ever needed an ally in a barroom brawl, he'd want the man and his muscles on his side. "And before you ask, yes, I've had my business open since I came to town. I figured a frontier settlement would be filled with characters needin' a good defense attorney."

"How'd you know what I planned to ask next?"

The man gave him a sideways grin. "It's my profession, to know what people are thinking and try to figure out why they're acting the way they are." He slowed his steps, so Lane did, too. A lot of folks were already out and about, despite the early hour, but they were all too caught up in their own business to pay much attention to the two men talking. "That's what's got me stumped about this whole Founder's Day business. Gertie Jackson is highly thought of in Wylder. Why, the woman doesn't have a single, solitary enemy. So who's doing this? And why?"

"Maybe one drunken ranch hand who left the Five Star with a mind to having a last bit of giddyup before hitting the hay?"

"I thought of that. But the schoolhouse doesn't usually attract that sort of attention." He shook his head. "No, they usually go hoot and holler in the street a while. Go blast a couple of shots into the air before finding somewhere to sleep it off."

"Not random, then?" He had hoped it hadn't been an intentional act of vandalism. "You're sure?"

"As sure as I can be, seeing as I didn't witness the decoration being torn down." He folded his arms across his broad chest and took a deep breath. The man must be formidable in the courtroom, because he commanded attention on the dusty street. "We can't forget the other incidents. They show a pattern."

"Incidents?" His pulse quickened. Had someone been harassing Gertie without his knowing about it? If that were the case, the culprit had best be on his way out of Wylder. His fists clenched thinking about how it would feel to grab the one who threatened his woman.

His woman.

She wouldn't give him the time of day, and he had the wherewithal to call her his woman? Damn, but he'd been struck hard with the stupid paddle. Right in the head, too, where it addled his brains.

A mental shove to clear the chatter from his mind.

"What incidents?" He stopped, and so did Merriweather. They hugged the wall of the closest building, looking for a bit of shade against the

217

unforgiving morning sun. "I wasn't aware there were other problems."

The attorney sucked in a deep breath, then let it out in a long, slow stream. "Well, there's the bundle of bunting pieces that went missing from her front porch. We have to assume they didn't walk away on their own, so someone took them."

Fabric scraps. He knew about those. They were the reason they'd made the trip to Theo Harvey's place.

"I forgot about that." He wanted to be supportive of the other's train of thought, but so far he couldn't see the connection. "But a pile of cut-up material isn't the same as tearing something down off a building."

Merriweather leaned against the weathered wood siding behind him. He lifted one polished black boot off the ground and planted it against the wall. "You're right. But then there's the issue with the cemetery."

He should've known the man had more to his case. "What about the cemetery? I know Gertie said there's a short part of the festivities that takes place over there, but that doesn't happen until tomorrow."

"You're right." He tipped his hat to an older woman who nodded when she passed. "But you see, Gertie makes sure that the founding gravesite is prettied up for the ceremony. She's been up there a couple times already. When she leaves, the place is nice and tidy, just the way we know our Miss Gertie would leave it." He turned to meet Lane's gaze. The man's eyes were dark, and a double row of furrows appeared on the bronzed forehead. "But within a day, that gravesite is a mess. Desecrated, I tell you." He paused, as if to let it sink in.

For his part, Lane appreciated the long moment.

The very idea that someone would willfully defile a final resting place sent his mind spinning. A despicable act, and cowardly, too.

"Who the hell would do such a thing?"

The attorney tipped his hat brim back in place, so it shaded his eyes. "Don't rightly know. But I do aim to find out." He nodded to another passerby, this time a young woman holding a cooing baby. When she had gone a few feet from them, he added, "How do you feel about sitting in a graveyard after dark? That type of thing give you the willies?"

He learned long ago that the dead can't hurt the living. Only the living could do that, so he shook his head. "Nope. I figure we've got more to fear from a man standing on his feet than lying on his back in a pine box. You lookin' for someone to keep watch with you tonight?"

"I am."

"You got yourself a partner, then."

****

Gertie didn't see Lane for the rest of the morning and that sat just fine with her. If she never saw the man again, it'd be okay in her book. After he'd lied to her, then seduced her, he should count his blessings that she didn't go after him with her six-shooter.

She hated feeling foolish. She'd allowed that man to drag her self-esteem so low she'd have to tilt her head back to see eye to eye with one of the fattened pigs kept out at the Harvey homestead. A damn shame that she'd been so ridiculous, but she had to put it—and him—behind her. No sense crying over the last slice of cake after you've dropped it on the barn floor. And he was, by everything she held holy and dear to her heart, the last slice of man cake she'd ever taste. No man, no matter how tantalizing he might be, warranted a nibble if this was how she'd feel afterward. She'd sworn off men years ago, and her only mistake came in forgetting that vow. Well, never again.

A flurry of activity turned the area behind and beyond the schoolhouse into a human beehive. Wagons filled with tables were being unloaded and their cargo set in place. A pile of pine boards had a half dozen men busy building a dance floor. Displays were being hung from low tree branches. Everywhere she looked, townspeople worked to bring the festivities to fruition.

She never would've been able to pull this off without such conscientious committee members. Everyday duties went undone in a few businesses while shopkeepers sent their helpers over to assist in the setting up. Women left homes, toted babies and toddlers, and came to help. Surely their household chores waited on them, but for the founding celebrations, all that got pushed aside. A wave of gratitude swept over her as she paused to watch the activity.

Violet Bloom declared the founding of their town to be part of the school's history lessons. She spent the weeks leading up to the celebration teaching about how the frontier settled, where families came from, and how they'd gotten to Wylder, as well as some facts about the town's founders. Now when the festivities were nearly upon them, she pressed her pupils into service.

Older boys hung more banners while other children directed them on pinning them higher or lower. A small group of younger students helped the eldest girls sort a box of dishware for the refreshment table. Another bunch tacked signs on trees near the game area.

"Everything's lookin' good, isn't it?" Minnie Milligan walked up to stand beside her. Today she had a baby on each hip, and Gertie couldn't help but wonder how the woman did all she did. She reached for the Miller infant who came without fuss. "Thanks. Jacob's a small one, but even the littlest bundles do get heavy, don't they?"

Kate's son settled against Gertie's shoulder. He smelled clean and sweet, the way a baby should. She inhaled the scent of him, smiling when his wispy hair tickled her nose.

"They do, at that. Is Kate at the doctor's again?"

Minnie glanced around to see if they could be overheard. No one in earshot so she shook her head. "She is. I keep tellin' her she's going to lose that baby unless she stops the heavy liftin' and such, but she's determined to keep going on with her day-to-day, as if she weren't expecting." She lowered her voice and leaned in. "That's all fine when you're first married, but Kate wasn't a young bride when she had Jacob here. Now she's another year and some older, and I worry."

Most women in town knew the Millers had nearly lost Jacob early on in the pregnancy. A shame that she had difficulties with this second one, too.

But holding the babe brought heaps of joy to Gertie's heart. The way he nestled in, so small and trusting, pulled a satisfied exhale from deep within her.

As if on cue, the baby sighed in his sleep.

Minnie smiled. "Looks like he's happy with you." She glanced down at her youngest. She'd set him on the ground, and the toddler held both her hands and danced around her feet. "And mine is happy to have his mama's attention all to himself, aren't you?" The boy grinned, showing his few teeth and nodding his head so hard his whole body jumped.

"Well, if this isn't a pretty sight." They both turned at the sound of Branch Wylder's voice. The lawman sauntered across the schoolyard from the street. Behind him, both Addison Merriweather and the one man Gertie did not want to see. She refused to look at Lane and kept her gaze on the sheriff.

Minnie didn't waste a moment. "Sheriff, have you figured out who pulled down the bunting? My Brenda is awful upset over it."

He tucked his thumbs in his gun belt and shook his head. "I'm sorry, but no. I've got a bit of evidence to go on, but so far I haven't been able to cipher it out." His dark-eyed gaze met and held Gertie's. "And anyone who might've looked, ah, suspicious this morning has been cleared of any mischief."

Her eyes narrowed. So, he didn't think Lane Hutchins capable of wrongdoing? Well, she knew better.

"Mischief? Is that what you're calling the mess we found this morning?" She struggled for control. Branch had replaced the old sheriff, Earl Hanson. Earl had never treated trouble in town this lightly. She had half a mind to inform Branch of such but bit her tongue.

"No, ma'am. I'm only trying to tell you that I'm working on the situation but have no idea yet who's responsible." He glanced over his shoulder toward the two men who had paused a short distance behind him. When he turned back to face her, he shrugged. "I only know who it isn't, is what I'm saying."

They both looked up at the sound of a shout from

the street.

"Branch!" Thomas Harvey jumped from the back of a black horse, wound the reins around a hitching post, then strode toward them. He slapped a hand against his thigh, as if trying to wipe it clean. "Just the man I'm looking for. Was going for the jailhouse but I spotted you here." He looked around at the activity. "Seems like half the town's here."

"What's up, Thomas? You and your horse look bothered."

"Well, you could say that. I went up and checked the cemetery the way you asked." He shot a glance at the women and babies, but the sheriff nodded for him to go on. "The grave isn't as it should be. Someone's, ah…"

Branch scowled. "Vandalized it again?"

"That's right." Thomas' expression could have scared the devil himself. The amiable man looked ready to wring a neck without provocation. "And just the one grave. None of the others have been touched."

Gertie looked from one man to the other. Behind them, she saw Lane and Addison exchange head shakes. It hit her in the gut, that whatever was going on had to do with the celebration. If not, the men wouldn't be searching the crowd as if they were ministers looking for sinners in the pews at the rear of their church.

"Whatever are you talking about, Thomas? Who would vandalize a grave? Why, that's sacrilege!" She tightened her grip on the sleeping baby, wanting to hold him closer to protect him from the unpleasantness. "Whose grave is it?"

The men all looked down at their boots. None

would meet her gaze, so she pressed.

"Thomas? Branch?" She turned from one to the other. "Whose grave was vandalized? I want to know this very instant!"

The sheriff heaved a sigh as he lifted his head. "One of my kin, actually." He met her gaze and she saw sadness in his eyes. "Naomi Wylder. You go over there to check on it and leave it looking fine for the celebration, but when I go to the cemetery afterward, it's always a mess. I've been fixing it up, so you won't know."

One of the founders, the woman more responsible than any other for the place they all enjoyed. The safe homes they'd built on the frontier were because of her and her husband. It made no sense that anyone would do such a thing. "But why didn't you tell me?"

The lawman shrugged. "You're working so hard to get Founder's Day perfect. I didn't want you to know someone else's going at it just as hard to cause trouble."

Her mind reeled. Why would anyone want to ruin the celebration? Along with the Christmas Eve party, the Founder's Day celebration brought the town and surrounding homesteads together.

She turned to Minnie and handed the baby boy back to her friend. "I'm going to the cemetery. To Naomi's grave." She patted the over-under pistol in her skirt pocket and met Branch's gaze. "This won't be tolerated!"

****

Lane hated the look of disbelief etched onto Gertie's lovely features. Her eyes rounded, and her lips parted, but not in the way they'd done when they'd been alone together. Now shock arranged her expression, and he wished he could soothe the frown lines from her forehead.

Naomi Wylder's resting place had been vandalized, no doubt about it. Shredded flowers, with drying petals lying like confetti across the gravesite made an obscene picture, as if drunken revelry had taken place in the not-too-distant past. The glass jar that held the blooms had been smashed against the stone marker showing her death date. Shards of glass sparkled in the grass.

He watched the woman take it in.

She'd insisted on seeing the evidence of what she termed hatred despite Branch and Thomas' attempts to keep her away. They'd all walked the distance with her when she refused the sheriff's offer to drive her in a buggy from the livery.

She'd not uttered a word of objection when he fell into step with the others, although the stiffness in her spine and her stubborn refusal to look his way showed exactly how she felt about his presence.

Her prerogative, he figured, to despise him for however long it took for her to get past their current misunderstanding. And he did intend to stick around until they were on good terms again. Longer, if she would have him.

Not the time for thinking about that now.

"Why?" She spoke so quietly that had he not seen her lips move he might have thought a breeze rustled the leaves of a nearby cottonwood tree. She stood at the foot of the grave and waved her hands over the ruined flowers. Her voice rose. "Why, Branch? Why would someone be so cruel?" She pushed a lock of hair off her temple with the back of one hand. "How can someone have so much grief inside?"

Gertie had always been one for getting straight to the heart of a matter. While they'd seen an act of vandalism, she saw cruelty. One came from dishonoring society and the other as a result of emotional turmoil. It hit him yet again that she saw past what most people witnessed, himself included. He'd never considered how the person suffered.

Thomas reached down and picked up a handful of petals. He stood, then let them fall through his fingers. "Why, I wouldn't have looked at this that way if you hadn't pointed it out. You're right, whoever did this put a lot of emotion behind it."

"Well, I'm looking to find the responsible party and make sure they show their emotions in other ways." Branch crouched and ran a hand over the cross at the top of the grave. He tossed a few glass shards into a pile. "Feelings aside, I don't take kindly to someone disrespecting my kin or our town."

Lane kept his mouth shut and his opinions to himself. He agreed with all that had been said, and more. To his way of thinking, this came as a personal attack on Gertie Johnson, an attempt like the bunting incident to undermine her perfect celebration. And that, disrespecting the woman he loved, was something he wasn't about to stand for.

Chapter 16

Lane watched from the shadows of Thomas' house. It came as a fortunate coincidence that he lived right next door to Gertie. He had a clear view of her front porch.

Afternoon had given way to evening. Gloom surrounded him, making his hiding spot even more inconspicuous.

Every twenty minutes or so, he crept toward the back of the house just to make sure no one tried to enter from that direction. Gertie had no idea, but he'd tied a string with a bell across the back porch pillars leading to the door, so he'd hear if it tinkled while he watched the front of her building. An old trick that he'd learned while soldiering, to never allow the enemy to sneak up unnoticed.

Damn, but he wished the person responsible for messing with the Founder's Day celebrations would show himself. He'd love nothing more than to grab the good-for-nothin' by the shoulders and shake the truth from him.

And it wouldn't hurt none if Gertie thought more kindly of him than she did at the present moment. God, but the woman could scowl! She'd damn near burned a hole between his eyes when he followed her to see Naomi Wylder's grave.

Nearly time for him to meet up with Addison and

Branch in the cemetery. He'd rather stay near the house in case the miscreant showed up at her place, but he'd given his word to help the others so that's what he'd do. They'd already worked out hiding places for each of them, so that they could cover the grave from more than one spot. They hoped it would give them an edge on catching the person desecrating the site.

Thomas promised to keep an eye on Gertie's home after he had to leave, so he tapped a knuckle against the window above his head. The financier said he'd wait in his study beside the window for the knock, then take up a position outdoors beneath the window until Lane returned.

The other man gave an answering tap. A minute later, he appeared in the shadows.

When they crouched side by side, Lane spoke out the side of his mouth. "Thanks for this. I'll be back as soon as I'm able."

The other answered in a whisper. "Do what needs to be done. I'll be here, watching. Alexia is over to the Milligan place, so I've got nothing better to do."

One last glance up to where a light burned in Gertie's bedroom window.

A silent prayer that no harm would come to her in his absence.

Then, he forced himself to move. Belle waited at a hitching post across the street and would carry him closer to the cemetery. He'd leave her beneath a tree and walk in—where they'd hopefully put an end to the trouble casting a dark cloud over what should be one of the happiest weekends in Wylder.

****

Gertie stood in front of her bedroom window and

stared out into the darkness. Had her mama been alive she would have said her daughter had more troubles on her shoulders than a horse has flies on its behind. She would've been right, too. The weight of so many difficulties weighed her down, and she would've loved nothing more than to share her thoughts with her dear departed mother.

Departed. A reminder of the damage that had been perpetrated at poor Naomi's gravesite sent a bolt of anger flashing through her. No matter what your feelings were for the Wylder family, no one had cause enough to desecrate a resting place. They were sacred, to be respected, not trampled. She could only imagine how this weighed on poor Branch's heart. She wondered if the rest of the descendants knew.

Oh, if she found out who did such a thing, there'd be hell to pay. Surely the sheriff could put such a person in his jailhouse, couldn't he? It didn't seem right to give someone intent on destroying sacred ground the freedom to walk their streets.

Well, one thing at a time. First to find out who did it. Then, on to punishment. And that penalty should be stern. No slap on the wrist for someone so despicable. No, the crime deserved retribution to be paid, and paid well.

She shivered. The warm Epsom salt bath and worn flannel nightdress took care of her physical body, but the chill from the inside, near her heart, couldn't be bundled up and put to rest. Even her skin, the bit surrounding her wounded heart, held traces of the man's touch.

Her eyelids fluttered closed, and she remembered how his fingertips traced a slow, tender trail across her shoulders. Down her collarbone. Over her breasts, to dance upon her nipples one after the other before heading toward her midsection. Her nipples pebbled at the memory and heat pooled within. His fingers had fallen lower. Touched her in the spot only ever loved by one other man.

A sob rose in her throat as her eyes flew open. How could she have been so stupid, thinking the man cared for her? Good heavens, but she acted like a lovesick schoolgirl with less brains than sass. That, too, weighed on her. Lane lied but she wasn't without fault. Practically throwing herself at the man like some common soiled dove. Writhing beneath him on the hard ground, rutting like animals. Then, bringing him into her bedroom. Good Lord, her mama's being gone came as a blessing. If she were here to see her daughter now, she surely wouldn't approve.

Mama raised me better than this.

Gertie brushed away the tear that slid down her cheek with a fierce knuckle. No more crying. Not another moment of regret. What's done is done.

She'd been telling herself that. Now, to find a way to believe it. *What's done is done.*

As she turned from the window, she caught a glimpse of something moving in the shadows of Thomas and Alexia's house. A cat, maybe. She squinted, hoping to see it again. There, headed toward the back of the house, creeping in the darkness.

A man? But why on earth would a man skulk beneath the windows at the Harvey place? A look at the windows showed the residents were home. Lights burned in rooms, a sign that the house wasn't unoccupied.

Maybe her eyes deceived her. She had been crying, after all.

With a sigh, she walked across the floor to her writing desk. The chair cushion welcomed her when she folded her legs and sat. Too many emotions tumbling through her to keep anything straight. So much had happened, and in such a short time period, that she shouldn't be surprised she imagined seeing things that weren't there.

Like fancying herself in love and feeling passion that wasn't real.

Concentrate on what you can control, she reminded herself. That had always seen her through tough moments in the past and it would carry her again now. All she had to do was get through the Founder's Day celebrations without incident. Then, she could hunker down in her tidy home and rest. Forget what happened between her and Lane. Let her shattered heart repair.

And then, never, ever lose that heart to any man again.

She pulled the drawer open with enough force that writing paper fluttered. The top sheet landed on her desktop, so she closed the drawer and reached for her pen and ink bottle. Time to write a last-minute preparation list for the morning.

After that, she'd slip into bed. Hopefully she'd get some rest...although she feared sleep would be an elusive bedfellow.

****

Damn soldier's knees.

Lane crouched so long behind a boulder near the edge of the cemetery that he could barely feel his toes. And his knees protested more strenuously with each passing minute. They'd spent too many hours in battlefield trenches to appreciate another stretch of punishment and showed their displeasure by sending shooting stabs down to his calves.

A soldier's body. Never returned in the same condition as the one that marched off to war.

And he'd been younger then. The years sat heavy on him, almost as weighty as the regret turning his heart over and over in his chest. A fish floundering on the shore, desperate for a return to the water and a chance at life. He'd concluded that without Gertie's forgiveness he had no reason to go on. The woman made him feel whole, and now that he'd finally felt that, he refused to live the rest of his life yearning to experience it again.

He had to convince that beautiful woman to give him another chance. He'd spend every breath trying to make that come true.

That is, if his knees didn't kill him first. Damn, but they ached!

He peered into the darkness but couldn't see anything but vague outlines of monuments and wooden crosses. Too bad the moon wasn't full. It would make such a difference.

Merriweather took a post at the far side, near the most distant graves. Those who were buried by the kindness of strangers, without family in a simple wooden box donated by the undertaker. A ring of trees stood on one edge and another on the other. The man hid in one of the stands. They hoped the troublemaker wouldn't expect someone to linger out that way.

Branch, Merriweather, and Lane agreed the person responsible for the destruction at Naomi's grave would want to be sure it remained defiled for the big day. A speech at the gravesite, with just about every town resident in attendance began the festivities. What better time to show disrespect than during the speech?

The person would want to see there were no flowers on the site. And with just a few hours before morning, they had to make a move soon.

He hoped his knees would hold out long enough to catch the troublemaker.

A shift of position in the hope of finding relief in his screaming joints. Instead, the right knee cracked so loudly it could have been a pistol shot. Pain radiated from the point, a spear up into the tender thigh muscles. A bite on the inside of his mouth to hold back the groan that rose in his throat.

"Hey! Hold up—stop right there!" The shout sounded like the lawman.

He stood and took a step forward. The sound of a scuffle cut the night air. He headed toward the gravesite where he assumed the noises originated but only got two steps before his boot went low into the ground. He fell, his arms windmilling, but between his bad knees and one boot buried in the earth up to his shinbone, he didn't have a chance.

"Stop—dammit! I said stop!" Wylder's voice came in strangled gasps. "Aw, hell."

The weight of his body slamming into the ground pushed the air from Lane's lungs in a great whoosh. He pushed up with his palms, doing his best to ignore the shooting pain traveling up his leg, and struggled to stand. But with one foot buried and the other knee screaming, the best he could manage, turning onto his side, didn't get him back on his feet.

The ground vibrated beneath him. Someone ran his way, growing closer by the feel of things. He stared into the darkness and tried to rise again.

Just as he made it to one knee, a figure appeared. "Hey! You—stop!"

He threw himself forward and reached, sending his arms wide to grab the form. He wrapped his arms around the person and brought them both down to the earth. The trespasser struggled to get free, but Lane held on.

Muffled grunts accompanied the scuffle. He'd gotten lucky and pinned the other's arms, so there was little chance of getting punched. Still, with one leg in a hole, his position didn't leave room to take the upper hand.

"Stop it, damnit!" He tightened his hold. The figure pressed solidly up against him, and for an instant, he thought he felt... But no, it couldn't be. It didn't make sense. But no time to consider as the person flailed in his arms. "I've got you, just stop already."

Where the hell was Wylder? Or Merriweather, for that matter?

They rolled over which put him at a disadvantage. One foot stuck in a hole and a body on top of him thrashing around. An elbow caught him in the gut. Bootheels to the shins and knees. He managed to hold the bear hug that kept arms and fists from being useful.

He hissed as the elbow jabbed a second time. "Dammit—"

Losing his breath hurt.

Getting kicked smarted.

But when a bootheel landed squarely against his crotch, his vision exploded.

"Ahh!" His grip released as his body curled to cradle itself against the wall of pain. His eyes clenched as he gasped. "Son of a…ahh…"

A fight for air. He held tight to his nuts, certain in that instant that the bastard had cracked them right in half.

Son of a bitch, but he'd never felt a pain so intense. Not even a gunshot wound came close to this.

Footsteps thundered on the ground. He opened his eyes. Wylder stood over him, holding his head with one hand. "Got past you, too?"

Lane nodded. He pulled a hand from his groin and held it out. "This." God, it hurt to breathe! He pulled in a steadying breath and handed the fabric scrap to the sheriff. "Tore when we rolled around." He released his grip and returned his hand to his crotch. Oh, hell, he'd be throbbing down there for longer than he wanted to consider. "Bastard kicked me in the balls. Damn, but no man should do that to another."

Wylder reached down and offered his hand. He took it, and together they managed to get his boot out of the gopher hole. When he stood, still bent from the waist as he waited for his testicles to stop screaming, he wiped his hand down his pants leg.

"What is that? Blood?" He glanced at the lawman. The hand he'd offered had felt slick.

A nod. "Sure is. Sonofabitch hit me with the stone marker on Naomi's grave." He wiped his hand over the gash that now showed on his temple. "Can't believe a man would play so dirty. Never had anyone wallop me that way."

He sucked in a breath and tried to straighten up. He made it, mostly. A little bent at the waist, but at least he wasn't staring at his boots anymore.

"Don't think it's a man."

He considered the way their scuffle had felt. The figure didn't have a lot of meat on its bones, and while the person fought hard, the wrestling lacked strength. Except for the crotch shot. That one had a lot behind it. And at one point, he'd been certain his palms swept over breasts.

Female breasts.

The more he thought about it, the more convinced he became that they weren't dealing with a man.

He met Branch's gaze in the darkness. "It's a woman. I'm sure of it."

The lawman's brows rose, but he didn't dispute the statement. He held one hand against his temple but reached into his jacket pocket with the other. When it emerged, several long yellow strands dangled from his fingers.

"A woman with blonde hair, looks like." He scowled when he pulled his hand from his head and looked at the smeared blood. "And one who plays dirty."

Lane looked toward the far end of the cemetery before he met Branch's stormy gaze again. "We'd best go lookin' for Merriweather. Makes me nervous, that he's so quiet."

The sheriff nodded. "You're right. Could be she clocked him, too."

"Or crushed his damn nuts." He rubbed the spot once more before he leaned down and picked up his hat. As he slapped it back onto his head and took a step, it hit him that he hardly noticed his knees anymore.

And there you go. The cure for bad knees is a boot

to the nuts.

He shook his head, hoping that the attorney fared better than he and Wylder had.

****

Gertie tossed and turned. Bedclothes tangled about her legs, so she kicked at the covers. The rest she needed eluded her, but at least if she didn't sleep, she couldn't have nightmares. That was something, anyway.

Her gaze focused on the dark ceiling. No answers to the questions swirling through her mind were written above her head, but that didn't matter. She'd done a good bit of thinking before blowing out the bedside candle. Her options were few, but the path remained clear. She intended to follow it with no reservations and hope to someday find her way back to the contented woman she had been before the last few weeks upended her world.

Easier said than done.

Ridding herself of the love that made her heart ache seemed impossible. Perhaps she wouldn't even try. Maybe she'd learn to live with it, the way she had with the heartbreak of losing Will. They were similar, weren't they? Holding a man close in her heart while he couldn't be held in her arms?

Her first response to Lane's treachery had been to rail against him and vow to cut him from her heart. But that wasn't realistic. Slicing bits from a beating organ? Not going to happen, no matter how much that piece of her hurt.

She sighed, the sound getting lost to the space around her.

Space.

She had come to Wylder seeking peace. Room to grow into a new life, one without the shadow of her loss hanging over her head. She had gotten that, and more, and refused to lose it now.

She turned on her side and closed her eyes.

Even if sleep wouldn't come, she would rest. Tomorrow the evidence of weeks of hard work would be revealed, and she didn't want to miss any of it.

Chapter 17

Lane rose with the sun, the way he'd done for years. The first fingers of light falling through the dusty boardinghouse window were enough to send his legs over the edge of the rope-strung bed and onto the floor.

Long days were best started without fuss, so he washed up at the basin, dressed, and fastened his gun belt in place. When he passed his hat, he grabbed it and dropped it onto his head. Then out the door and down the stairs.

He'd stayed in the place long enough to know better than to step in the center of the third tread from the top. Its creak would give his presence away, and the last thing he wanted was to be cornered by the woman who ran the establishment. She'd done that once, and it left an impression. Not a good one, either.

He made it to the front door and out onto the porch without being detected. A sad state of affairs when a man spent his days running from women. He recalled the advances of the female in charge of the public baths. She'd been anxious to lay claim to his body, even if only for a few minutes. And the woman he'd woken up beside after drinking too much at the Five Star. Another one eager to sell herself for some tenderness.

Is that what living in the frontier did to a woman? He wondered, as he took off down the street toward the diner. And in his case, did a lifetime of loving one elusive woman spoil him for finding happiness with any other?

He had no answers for the questions plaguing his mind, but it didn't matter none. Today he planned to set things right with Gertie. One way or another, he would convince her to listen to him.

The door to the small eatery stood open. This early in the day, the sun hadn't had the chance to turn Wylder into a red-hot skillet, so any cool morning breeze was welcome. He removed his hat when he crossed the threshold. Easy to spot Branch Wylder since most tables were vacant. He'd chosen one near a window and already had a mug of coffee on the table in front of him.

He walked over and sat on the chair opposite. As he did, his jewels reminded him that they'd been recently mistreated. He shifted, seeking comfort, then placed his hat on the table near the sheriff's Stetson.

A woman walked over and placed a mug of rich dark coffee in front of him. She tipped her head toward the lawman. "Sheriff here ordered two specials, eggs over easy with big helpings of fried potatoes. That sound about right to you?"

He nodded. "Sounds great, thank you."

With a small smile, she hurried to the doorway leading to the kitchen. He watched her until she disappeared into the other room before turning his attention on his breakfast companion.

Branch looked rough. The area around the gash had gone purple, and the stitches appeared tight enough to be painful. He sure didn't envy the man having been hit on the head with a stone. Getting a toe to the nuts had been bad enough, but at least the doc hadn't taken a needle and thread to him.

"Do you feel as ornery as you look?" He raised a brow and took a swallow of coffee. Good and strong, the way he liked best. "Or is that scowl just for me for letting her get away?"

Branch shook his head, then winced. "Nah, it's not you. If I'm angry at anyone, it's me." He scrubbed a hand over his chin. "I should've known better than to let her get the jump on me. We were both down on the ground, in the dark, and she just brought her hand out from behind her back with that damn grave marker in it. Smacked me before I even saw it coming."

He imagined how he'd feel if he stood in Branch's boots. He'd want some kindness, especially since he'd certainly already given himself a dressing down. "Ah, in the darkness like that everything looks different. Besides, she was pulling the flowers apart. Who would expect to be hit with anything heavier than a daisy?"

Branch chuckled. "Damn, that stone must be the hardest thing on the planet because it nearly cracked my skull. Coyote looked at me when he stitched me up. Checked my eyes and all. Said it's a miracle she didn't do more damage." He ran a finger over the stitches. "For what it's worth, I think she did plenty of damage, thank you."

"My nuts would agree with you."

The woman served their breakfasts. The plates were heaped with food, the scent of peppers and onions mingling with toast and eggs. Lane's mouth watered as he picked up his fork and began to eat.

Neither spoke for a few minutes. Their coffee mugs were refilled as they tackled the meal.

Finally, the other man put his fork down. He picked up his mug, took a swallow, and met Lane's gaze. "What do you want to bet she shows up today?"

"I'd say it's a sure thing. For the past week she's tried to ruin the celebration, so I'm thinking that she'll go all out today to do whatever's on her mind." He took a last bite of toast and washed it down with the hot coffee. "Trick is keeping her from beaning anyone else." He thought of his testicles. "Or worse."

The lawman nodded. "Or worse is right. You and I are at least standing. Merriweather might not be for a few days, at least. According to Doc Sullivan, that bump on his head might prove to be serious. Only time will tell." He dropped some silver on the table, enough for both meals, and tipped his head to the door. "Figured we'd stop by to see him before heading to the schoolyard. You game?"

They rose and put their hats on. As they stepped out into the sunshine, Lane shot the other man a look. "Well, seeing as you've just bought my breakfast, it'd be mighty mean of me to let you go face Missus Merriweather on your own."

A chuckle escaped Branch's lips. "I appreciate that. Daisy was madder than a herd of angry bulls last night when she got a look at her husband. What I wouldn't give for a woman to care for me the way she does him."

They set off down Wylder Street, headed for the attorney's home. Lane hoped the man had improved by this morning. The last thing he wanted to see so early in the day, an angry female. He figured he'd have to face one later, when he and Gertie had a come-to-Jesus talk about what'd been going on between them, and one riled up woman a day was enough for any man to endure.

"I hear you on that one, Wylder. I've damn near

spent my whole life waiting for just that very same thing."

****

Gertie looked out over the faces in the cemetery and felt her heart swell in her chest. This outpouring of pride in and love for their town, this one day when neighbors put their differences aside and they all came together to celebrate Wylder made all the weeks of hard work worthwhile.

Neighbors stood shoulder to shoulder. Fathers held small hands, and little ones snugged up against blue-jean-clad legs, as well as mothers' skirts. Every age looked on, from the newborn babe in a homestead wife's arms to old Mister Hugh Fennel. Depending on the day and his mood, the man professed to be either seventy-three or eighty-one. Either way, he claimed to be their eldest resident.

She cleared her throat. This honor, delivering the short speech that would begin their day of festivities, always brought a lump to her throat. She swallowed hard and willed the prickles behind her eyes away. For a few minutes, she could keep her composure. After that, well who would blame her for shedding a few happy tears?

Orange, red, and yellow blooms filled two large glass jars at the top of Naomi Wylder's gravesite. The granite block testifying to her being so well-loved sat polished at the base of the cross marker.

Gertie inhaled, then let the air out slowly. She tipped her face to the sky to gauge the sun. A bit of time before it rose high enough to make them sweat.

She gave the townsfolk a small smile.

"Welcome to our annual Founder's Day

celebration. As you all know, every year we start the day here, with one of the founders of our dear town. Naomi Wylder braved endless miles of uncharted territory to arrive here with her family. A courageous woman, she rose to every challenge along the way so that her children would live in an exciting new world." She paused, searching for Finn Wylder's face in the crowd. When she found it, she dipped her chin and smiled at the man. Because of his family, they all stood here, and she acknowledged that before she went on. "Naomi Wylder's adventurous spirit helped bring this town into being, and this morning before we all go about having fun and celebrating, we should spend a quiet moment of thanks right here, with her."

A nod to Father Sebastian, a priest at the small Catholic church. The crowd parted so he could stand at the foot of the grave. He turned his back on the markers and addressed the townspeople.

Thankfully, his short prayers were legendary in town, and he didn't disappoint on this auspicious morning. He said a few words, made the sign of the cross over those assembled, then stepped away. Gertie nodded her appreciation for his blessing, and then turned to the folks gathered on the grass.

"I want to thank everyone who's worked so hard to make this year's celebration a success. You'll see a few things have changed, but most are the same as they've been every year. We've got some new games, beautiful buntings, and even a twist on the apple pie competition, so please enjoy the day." Her throat tightened at the sight of so many happy faces. The prickly feeling began again behind her eyes, so she hurried to add, "We all know Wylder is the best town in the Wyoming

Territory. Now, let's go have some fun!"

The crowd thinned as some folks visited relations' graves while others started for the schoolyard. She stepped aside so the Wylder family could pay their respects to Naomi if they wanted.

Alexia and Brenda came up with glowing faces. Both girls wore navy-blue dresses and matching hair ribbons. The Milligan girl's dress showed signs of being washed and pressed, but the fabric had grown thin in spots. Its hem had been let down, too, leaving a line no amount of pressing could erase.

A shame the family struggled so. And with Brenda being the eldest and wanting to go to school to become a teacher...well, she didn't know how they could ever afford such an undertaking.

But no time to dwell on sad facts. This day called for laughter, and lots of it.

"Miss Gertie, thank you for mentioning our buntings." Alexia beamed. She'd worked so hard on the project. Now she would hopefully hear some accolades from admirers of her handiwork to boost her a bit. The girl needed every scrap of uplifting she could get to make up for not having a mother. Today, with its recognition for her hard work, would be a good day for her. "I'm so happy we were able to work on the decorations for the celebration but...well, I need to ask you something."

The girl turned suddenly shy. Her toe scraped the grass, and she looked over at Brenda, as if searching for support.

She reached out a loving hand and placed it on Alexia's shoulder. When the girl met her gaze, she asked, "What is it, honey? You can ask me anything, remember?"

The minute she said the words, she recalled the last time she'd offered that same sentiment. It had opened an hour-long conversation about breasts and other feminine topics.

Please, not today. Don't let her ask any more breast questions...

"I just wonder if we can continue with my sewing lessons." Alexia gave her a hopeful smile. "That is, if you're not too busy." She waved toward Brenda. "You see, Brenda could work with me, but her mama is awful busy with her sisters and brothers. She needs all the help she can get. And Brenda's studying to be a teacher, too, so she doesn't have a lot of time to sew."

She could only imagine how busy life in the Milligan household might be. Compared to Alexia and Thomas' life, where just the two of them rattled around in their large home, it must seem as different as night from day.

It lifted Gertie's spirits to be that point between those two realities for this sweet young woman.

"I would love to give you more sewing lessons. Why, I'd been thinking of asking you if you're interested in that very same thing myself." The fib rolled off her tongue, and when it brought a joyful smile to the young woman's face, she went on. "I've had a mind to piece together some baby blankets and would appreciate the help. It seems we've got a lot of babies arriving in Wylder. And I've got lots of scrap fabric, so why not do some good with it? Would you like to help me do that?"

The girl grabbed her in a fast hug. When she stepped back, her eyes shimmered. "I would love that,

Miss Gertie. Thank you!"

"Aw, you're welcome, honey." She waved a hand toward the schoolyard. "Now why don't you two head on over to the celebration? I'll be along shortly."

She needed a moment to catch her breath so when they dashed off, she folded her hands at her waist and looked at the sky. A blue, cloudless expanse, the ideal backdrop for their celebration. A long sigh, then she dropped her chin and took a step forward.

That's when she spotted the very man she hoped to avoid.

Lane stepped closer, touched a hand to the brim of his hat, and offered a tiny smile.

"Morning, Gertie." He widened his smile. "That was some touching speech you gave. A fine testament to how this town came to be."

His gaze raked her body, and while he didn't linger on any particular spot, she heated beneath his gaze. The man touched her without even coming near, something that both excited and unsettled her.

Her job today, to be kind to all who attended the celebration, nudged her to politeness.

"Thank you." She paused to gather her thoughts. "It's not difficult to tell the truth, and the fact is Wylder is a wonderful place to live." She raised an eyebrow. "As I said, telling the truth isn't hard, not if you're accustomed to doing so. Now, if you'll excuse me."

She stepped to the left with the intention of putting a lot of space between them, but he moved, too. He closed the gap so when she passed she came so close that the spicy male scent of him filled her head.

"We need to talk." He kept his voice low. Nearly everyone had gone from the graveyard, but she appreciated that he didn't give stragglers reason to look their way. "I know you're angry with me, but we really do need to talk."

She paused. Met his gaze. Tried not to allow herself to melt into the penetrating stare he used to hold her.

A fast head shake. "We don't have anything to say to each other anymore. We're done talking."

"That's where you're wrong." He reached out a hand, but she took a step back, so he let it drop to his side. "I have a lot to say, and I plan to say it all. And I'm going to do it again and again, until you realize how sorry I am for hurting you."

The words grabbed her heart, but she refused to let him see how he affected her.

Another quick shake of her head as she took a step. "You don't understand. I don't care how sorry you are. And I don't plan to forgive you, so save your breath." She looked up at him. "It's time for you to leave Wylder, Lane. Maybe you'd best go today, while it's still early."

****

Lane refused to be put off by Gertie's words. He'd known her for decades and saw through the hard façade. Her mouth said one thing but those eyes...they spoke differently.

He'd respect her wishes and not badger her for an audience, not today. But he wouldn't leave without trying to sort things out between them. Even if she wouldn't forgive him right away, he planned to stick around town for a while. The place had grown on him in the short time since he'd arrived. And the truth of it was that he had nowhere else to hang his hat, no one who expected to see him again, and nothing to keep him from staying.

In his heart, he knew they were meant to be together. He'd known it for so long it was one of the only truths of his life.

He'd screwed up, certainly. But a man shouldn't lose the love of his life because he'd been too frightened to offer details he knew would upset her. Damn Grant and his damned money! Had it not been for that, he and Gertie would be strolling hand in hand, instead of her ignoring him while he watched her from a distance.

Not the best way to spend his first Founder's Day in Wylder, but hopefully it wouldn't be his last time at the celebrations. He'd look for next year being better, after taking this one to atone and set things to rights with her.

She had to forgive him. He couldn't stand the thought of her hating him forever.

****

Gertie gazed at the festivities with a satisfied smile on her face. Her heart filled with joy and, as in years past, this moment made every sleepless night of the last few weeks well worth it.

Everyone at the celebration looked like they were having a good day. When the crowd wandered in after the cemetery speech, there were tables set up with assorted buns and breads and pots of coffee for folks to enjoy. After eating, they dispersed to stroll the area or sit in the shade of cottonwoods. Lawn games and rope swings provided entertainment for the younger crowd. Men gathered in groups to compare harvests and talk cattle.

Inside the schoolhouse, displays of home goods filled tables set up around the perimeter of the large room. Homespun yarn, quilts, decorative table runners, and much more were laid out for admiration. Most women scrambled to get their daily chores and the essential sewing and baking done. Anything fancy, like some of the runners and quilts, showed commitment to do a bit extra for family and home. Every woman who traced a fingertip over another's stitches knew how they may have come long after a family slept, in a dark corner of a cold room during a woman's only hours of solitude.

In the center of the room, the benches that usually held children were occupied by folks visiting with one another. Some of the town's eldest sat side by side, their bottoms and backs cushioned by blankets brought from home. They leaned forward on walking sticks to speak around each other, their words creating a din like the kind created by children at recess. Exuberance and near-deafness were nearly one and the same, it seemed.

She walked from one table to the next, stopping to admire the assortment of textiles on display. She hadn't seen them before now, as Violet and Lily collected entries and set them out. They'd done a good job, too, using straight pins to affix tags to each item to identify who had contributed the work. The two women would choose which entries would receive blue ribbons, as well. By the afternoon, the crowd would see whose work stood out.

She stopped near a baby quilt. A flip of the edge identified it as the handiwork of Daisy Merriweather. The green-and-white, nine-patch pattern would have been simple had it not been for the intricately embroidered scenes on the patches themselves. Lambs and ducks strutted across the green fields she'd created using colored thread and imagination. On the white patches, cardinals and geese flew among clouds.

The piece set her mind wandering. Addison and Daisy probably hoped for a houseful of children. Why else would a woman spend so much time on a baby blanket? Addison's status as an attorney afforded the couple a lifestyle grander than most, although they never acted better than anyone else. But the truth, that Daisy most likely didn't need to work at homemaking as hard as a lot of other women did showed. She had time to sit and stitch.

"Quite a piece of work, isn't it?"

The smoothness in his voice sent shivers up her spine.

She should have known better than to think Lane would steer clear of her. When she turned to face him, she scanned the room. As she suspected, he was the only man in the schoolhouse, aside from those seated at the tables in the center of the room. No other Wylder male perused the textile offerings the way he did.

A smile brought the edges of his lips high. She considered them for a moment, remembering how they felt against hers. Her mouth went dry, so she ran her tongue over her lower lip. His gaze flicked down to her mouth, then rose to meet her eyes again.

"Why are you in here?" Her voice sounded shaky, so she swallowed before she went on. "Most of the men are outdoors talking about, well, whatever it is that menfolk talk about when women aren't around. Don't you think you should be out there, talking man talk?"

When he chuckled, amusement flashed in his eyes.

251

"You think men shouldn't be interested in what their babies are wrapped in or how much work goes into making any of these things?" He waved a hand to the display tables. "Shouldn't it matter to them, too?"

She pressed her hands to her temples. The man did ask some unusual questions. Her mind raced, searching for a reply that wouldn't lead the conversation deeper into territory that left her tongue-tied.

"I'm just saying it doesn't usually interest men, the sewing that women do." She glanced at Daisy's baby quilt. So much love in those stitches. She spoke without considering her words. "And most men are more interested in making babies than swaddling them."

Lane's eyebrows rose so high they hit the lower edge of his hat. He smiled so broadly that she couldn't help herself. She smiled back.

"Why, Missus Gertrude Johnson, did you really just mention that topic out here in public? Whatever would your sainted mother have to say about that?"

They both knew exactly what she would've said, so Gertie's cheeks heated.

She refused to rise to the question, so she kept her lips closed and stared at him.

And, as it had before, the world around them slipped away. All she saw, all that mattered, stood before her. A tug from her heart to reach out and touch him, so strong and real she leaned forward a few inches before she remembered where they were—and that she still held a grudge for what he'd done.

She straightened. Shook her head to clear it. Patted a hand over her hair pins, confirming that while she felt a tad scandalous her outward appearance hid that well.

"I need to go outdoors and check on the pie table."

His hand shot out and touched her wrist. She looked down at it, so large against her frame.

"Gertie, we need to talk. You know I won't give up on it until I've had my say." He paused and ran his hand lower, toward her fingertips. He touched them, a slow caress, before he stepped back and tucked his hand in his trouser pocket. "Please, talk with me. We've known each other for so long, don't we deserve a few minutes to clear the air?"

She hadn't forgotten what he'd done or how it made her feel, but her temper had died down. The moments she'd stood in the graveyard earlier had affected her. Life wasn't endless, and being annoyed forever wasn't anything she planned to do.

"Fair enough. But I'm still angry."

"I expect you would be." He glanced around at the activity that surrounded them. "Is there someplace quiet where we could go?"

She nodded. This certainly wasn't a good spot for a serious discussion. "Yes, outdoors. There are tables set up beneath the trees. Why don't you see if there's one that's empty? I need to go check the pie table, then I'll meet you."

"I'll be waiting."

She watched him walk away. He stood taller than every woman gathered, so his head and shoulders were visible despite the crowd. The man did something to her, muddled up her insides, and sent her mind in five directions at once. She hardly knew which way was up, but when Lane came near none of that mattered.

Good Lord, how had she fallen in love with the man?

And what would she do about it? The decisions

she'd made in the dark of night vanished on the warm breeze. So, too, did the anger that she felt earlier in the cemetery. She'd spent so much time on her own that trying to deny the opportunity to be with another—one who made her heart so happy—seemed foolish.

Still, she couldn't forget why he'd arrived in Wylder.

She'd listen to what Lane had to say. Then, she'd consider her future. With him, or without.

****

Lane drummed his fingertips on the scarred wooden tabletop. A glass jar filled with pink cosmos sat in the center. Evidence that this day caught everyone's heart, that they went this far to make everything beautiful.

He stood when he saw Gertie walking toward him. It took a few minutes, as she must know everyone because she was stopped several times. People looked to be thanking her, and that made him smile. She certainly had made a name for herself in Wylder.

Now if she would only allow him the same kind of grace she showed others, he might be able to convince her to give him a second attempt to make things right. When she drew close, he held out a hand to the empty chair beside his while he held the crossed fingers of the other one behind his back.

"I'm glad you're here with me." He took a deep breath. This conversation would affect the rest of their lives. It wasn't like a roundup gone wrong, where there were more chances to get the job done. This one shot was all he had. He prayed for the wisdom to touch her heart with his. "I know you're upset, and I don't blame you. Not one bit. I should have told you the whole truth of why I'm here when I saw you the very first day I came to town."

"Why didn't you?"

He'd asked himself that question a hundred times, at least. Now all he could offer, the humble truth. "I got scared."

Gertie snorted. Unladylike, but coming from her it warmed his heart. "Scared? You expect me to believe that?"

"It's the truth."

"But you fought in the battlefield. Will told tales before the war of the two of you tussling with other local boys and sending them away with blackened eyes." She paused, then added, "And I know you haven't been a choirboy since the war, Lane Hutchins. I don't know what all you've done, but I'm no fool."

She looked at him with such gumption that he had to smile. He might have been frightened when he first saw her, but Lord knew it would take more than a first meeting to scare her. An indomitable presence, she faced him down now, and challenged him to come up with something better than his excuse.

But he stuck with it. The truth deserved to be told.

"I'm not going to ask how you know, or even what you think you know. I'll trust that a woman's instincts are at work." He dropped the smile and pinned her gaze with his. Time to put joking aside. "But it's true, I got nervous when I saw you. It hit me hard that the feelings I've had for you all these years have grown. They overwhelmed me. I wanted to pull you into my arms and hold you tight, and all the while I feared you'd send me away, that you wouldn't want a reminder of the past here in Wylder. And that all hit me so fast that I couldn't even begin to bring myself to talk about why I'd come."

She took a minute to consider his words, and while he didn't need his pocket watch to show the pause didn't last long, it felt like a lifetime to him. His breath didn't flow as he waited, but when she lifted her gaze and smiled, he exhaled in one long whoosh.

"I believe you, Lane. I can tell by the look in your eyes that you're not lying." She ran a hand down the front of her light-rose-colored skirt. "But I don't understand why you got so worked up."

Had they not been surrounded by people he would have dropped to his knee in front of her and proposed. But they were, and besides he wasn't sure she'd give him a favorable answer. She mightn't ever be ready to wed again, and he'd have to accept that if he wanted to be with her.

Which he did. Very much.

"It's like this…I have loved you forever." Her eyes rounded, but he didn't back down. "Maybe it was wrong to have those feelings when you were married to Will, but I never let on, did I? I never let how I feel come between our friendship or my allegiance to Will. He was like a brother to me, and he always will be. But that didn't keep my heart from feeling how it did toward you."

She murmured, "The heart knows what it wants."

His heart swelled, hope filling in the bits that had been broken by their misunderstanding. "It does. And mine wants you if you'll have me. I love you, Gertie. Please, give me another chance to show you that I'm not a scoundrel."

Her laughter cut the warm air like music. "I never

believed you a scoundrel."

"Well, I acted like a fool." He took a deep breath and plunged on. "And I'm not going to do it again, so I have to mention the reason I came to Wylder. Grant sent me, you know that now. I have paperwork that makes you a very wealthy woman. The money is yours and even if you don't want to have anything to do with your brother, you should at least consider what you'll do with the funds."

A stubborn set to her mouth turned her lips into one straight line. He resisted the urge to lean over and kiss them until they softened.

"I don't want to talk about Grant. I won't forgive him for how he acted after Will was killed."

"Fair enough. He knows he behaved badly, but he also sees you've moved on. There's no way he can change what he did or said, and we don't need to mention his name again, but the money is yours."

"I don't want anything from him."

Lord, but the woman could be stubborn.

"It's not from him. It's family money, and it belongs to you." He ran a hand through his hair and leaned closer. "Look, you've said some families in Wylder are financially challenged. Why not use the funds to help them out? Didn't you mention a young girl who wants to go to school to become a teacher, but she's from a family that's barely making a go of it? And a small child named Beattie. You said she needs some specialized medical attention. Seizures, wasn't it? You could use the money for good, Gertie."

She sat back and looked at the activity around them, and he didn't interrupt. Let her see that she could put the funds to work helping the town she loved so much, and she might forget where it came from.

She loved this place. These people.

He looked around while he let her ponder. He'd only been in Wylder a short time, but he'd already met a lot of folks.

On the dance floor, Gus Wright and Rosemary Fortune swayed. The woman at the piano, Sarah, filled the air with a sweet melody, but he suspected her first two dancers shared their own music.

Miss Addie, the owner of the Social Club, bustled by. The woman had impeccable taste. She and the two young women who followed her, also laden with food baskets, looked respectable enough to be preachers' daughters.

Others milled about, laughing, talking, and visiting. Widows, seamstresses, shopkeepers, couples, children, the elderly...they were what kept the town from being any other stagecoach stop along the dusty westward trail.

They were her family. This was her home. How could she not help when she had the means?

Finally, a nod. "I like that idea."

"And us?"

Gertie glanced over her shoulder, then to the people nearby, before she leaned close and brushed her lips over his cheek. A butterfly touch, over almost before it began, but enough to show his heart what it needed to know.

"I like that idea, too." When she met his gaze, the expression in her eyes had softened. "I can't promise that I'll ever forget the life I lived with Will."

"I don't want you to forget." He risked talk and took one of her hands in his. "I only hope that there's room for me in this new life you lead. Here, in Wylder, a promise of a happy future for us."

She nodded. "There's room. And I promise, we've got a future together here—"

A commotion came from behind the schoolhouse. Lane stood, turning his head toward the noise.

"I'll be right back." He dropped her hand and headed toward the disturbance. He wasn't sure, but it sounded like Addison Merriweather and a woman yelling. He couldn't make out their words but whatever it was, it didn't sound good.

****

Gertie nudged her way through the crowd behind the schoolhouse until she reached the front of the tangle of onlookers. In a small circle, Addison and his wife, Daisy, along with the sheriff and Lane, stood with an unfamiliar woman. It hit her that the attorney should be in bed, but her attention fell onto the woman standing in their midst.

Dressed in shabby men's clothing, the newcomer scowled. A hat lay in the dirt, and a mass of blonde curls fell down her back. Young, maybe in her early twenties, and pretty, even with a streak of dirt across one cheek.

Daisy pointed a finger at the woman. "I caught her knocking the legs out from under the tables set up to hold the dinner dishes. She made them so the tables will buckle as soon as any weight hits their tops." Daisy's long curls swept over her right shoulder. Somehow, she'd lost a few hairpins, and the woman's strikingly beautiful hair danced around her head with every word. "She's trying to ruin dinner, sending all the platters crashing to the ground."

The stranger's scowl deepened.

Branch shot the blonde woman a look that was not at all amused. "I'm not going to ask whether that's true or not. All we need to do is take a peek at those tables to see whether the legs have been tampered with. What do you have to say for yourself?"

A foot stamp came as the only reply.

Branch pulled two scraps of fabric from his vest pocket. They were the same shade of washed-out black as the jacket she wore. "I expect that if we examine your jacket we'll find the spots where you lost these bits. One showed up here the morning the bunting was destroyed and the other I tore off your jacket last night in the cemetery." He touched a fingertip to his head wound. "Unless you want me to march you right over to the jail and lock you up, you'd best start talking."

Addison moved closer to Daisy when the newcomer glared at her. He draped an arm around his wife's shoulders and glared back at the woman.

"Okay, you want to do this the hard way, then." The sheriff stepped forward and reached for her arm, but she smacked his hand away. Another foot stamp as she lifted her chin to shoot him a hard stare.

Gertie gasped. She'd never seen anyone do that to the sheriff!

"Don't you dare put a hand on me." The stranger stamped once more. "My mama will reach right down from Heaven and slap you hard." She waved her hand in the air between them. Then she pointed her finger to the sky. "Don't think your kin are the only Wylders up there."

Her words brought stunned silence from the crowd. No one moved, not even the smallest child. It struck her that even Branch looked tongue-tied.

Finn Wylder stepped out of the crowd. An intelligent, considerate man, he looked like a cool breeze beside the simmering tempers. The man stopped beside Branch and stared down at the blonde.

"Are you saying you're a Wylder?" Finn's voice wasn't nearly as brusque as his cousin's, but then he hadn't been knocked on the head with a hunk of granite a few hours ago. Anyone could see how a bashing like that could put a fellow in a bad mood. "Is that what I'm hearing?"

"Don't look so shocked." The woman sniffed. She swiped a palm over her hair, pushing it off her face. "It's not as if your side of the family are the only ones with a right to the name. Not everyone gets a fancy town, the way you all have. But some of us, we have the same blood in our veins as you do. And in the end, that's what matters, really."

Lane spoke. "I saw you in an alley, didn't I? A man ran out, and I ducked in to see if anyone needed help." He paused and turned to Branch and Finn. "I found this young woman in the alley. She looked like someone upset her, but she refused my help and ran off." He gestured to her and added, "She wore the same clothes she has on now. Dressed like a man, with a hat covering her hair."

For a long moment, no one spoke. Then Branch turned to her. "Is all this true?"

She nodded.

The lawman pressed her. "But why were you trying to disrupt the Founder's Day celebration?"

A shrug sent the slight shoulders high. "Angry, I guess. The man in the alley came part way to Wylder with me. Said he'd protect me on the trail. And he did, but when we got here, he took my money and ran. Haven't heard from him since, which is fine. Except it's hard to eat when you have empty pockets."

Gertie went to stand beside Lane. She met the woman's gaze. Her eyes were the color of larkspur, clear and pretty. "You're the one who took the bunting pieces, aren't you?" When she got a nod in reply, she asked, "Why?"

"Because it eats at me that you all have such a good life here. Wylder is like one big, happy family. Why, I even saw you all feed a starving man, take him in, give him a job working for you." She nodded at a man at the edge of the gathered crowd, then to Addison.

Gertie sighed. The man who had tried to rob them on their way to the Harvey homestead hardly looked the same as when she'd shot him. The doctor tended him, the diner fed him, and the Harveys employed him. No longer a bandit, but a respectable part of their community. They'd taken him in, made him one of their own.

"And all of that eats at you? Why?" She gentled her tone and took a step nearer the woman. She saw Daisy do the same. They insulated her from the crowd and circle of men. "Why do you hate us enough to wreak havoc during what is obviously a very important time for everyone? It doesn't make sense."

The woman's shoulders sagged. "All I have is standing right in front of you. No home, no family, no roots. Martin Wylder took his pleasure with my mother but never gave her his name. So, I'm no one, going nowhere, with nothing." She met Gertie's gaze. A sheen covered the gorgeous eyes, unshed tears threatening to fall. "Wouldn't that make you angry?"

She didn't have a chance to answer. Finn and Branch both stepped closer.

Finn put a hand on the woman's shoulder. "You are someone. And you do have a family."

Branch cleared his throat. "And a place to stay."

Gertie watched the two fold their newly arrived kin into their arms and heard the soft sounds of reassurance.

She looked over to where Lane stood. She, too, had all she'd ever need. Right here, in Wylder, with the man who held her heart in his hand.

What more could a woman want?

Nothing, that's what.

Epilogue
May 1881

A fire crackled in the hearth and the rocking chair creaked on the wide wooden floorboards as she stitched. The front parlor had never been this cozy, or she so content. Amazing how life could change in a heartbeat.

A tiny, unexpected, miraculous heartbeat.

She looked up when she heard Lane's bootheels cross the front hall. He'd taken to spending mornings at his desk in the study, writing for hours. The work held a place in his heart, a story borne of pride and heartache, so she didn't disturb him. When he'd reached a stopping point for the day, he would come to find her, the way he did now.

Her heart jumped when he came through the door and over to her. He perched on the side table near her chair, leaned down to brush a kiss over her lips, and gave her a smile that lit up her world.

"I missed you."

She jabbed her embroidery needle into a spot near the edge of the fabric and raised one eyebrow. "But you've only been in the other room. Surely there couldn't be that much missing between here and there."

They teased each other like this every day, and it never grew old. She didn't expect it ever would.

He ran a slow hand over her shoulder, massaging near the base of her skull and sending tingles across her skin. "A lot of missing, believe me. Whenever I can't see you, I feel lonely, Missus Hutchins."

Missus Hutchins. The words still thrilled her.

"Well, that's good to know." She raised the baby quilt so he could see her progress. "Do you like it?"

Across the top edge, scenes from Richmond. Shops. Houses. Cobblestone streets.

In the center, the journey westward. Stagecoaches. Mountains. Dusty trails. Tumbleweed.

And at the bottom edge, the spot she worked now. Wylder, in all its glory. Their home and the Harvey home beside it. The schoolhouse with a Founder's Day banner flying from one tree to another. The cat they'd taken in and named Harry. A horse that looked like Lane's beloved Belle.

The baby's story because it was their story. Their gift to pass on, the way the book was meant to be.

Lane's book covered his and Will's part in the war. The south they left and the one they returned to. The battles, with triumphs and heartaches. Struggles on the home front with loved ones left behind. Broken men returning to shattered lives and devastated families.

All of it, because every life had a story, and every story, he'd decided, deserved to be told.

"It's nearly done, isn't it?" He ran a thumb across the little cat she'd placed beside their front porch.

"It is. By the end of the week, I'll be sewing this front to the backing of the quilt."

"A good thing. Coyote seems to think our little one will be here any time now."

She smiled and ran a hand over her belly. "Yes, I'm aware. This little surprise baby is making herself known. Kicking all morning, with no sign of stopping."

"Herself, hmm? You're so sure it's a girl?"

She knew Lane didn't care what sex their baby

was. Both just prayed for a healthy child. Nothing else mattered, but she did like to tease him a bit when she got the chance.

Now she placed his hand beneath hers so he could feel the babe, too. As if on cue, a foot or elbow, hard to tell which, struck out and made their hands jump.

Lane kissed her, tender and with so much happiness behind it she felt as if she might burst. Not from being so pregnant, but from sheer joy.

They let their foreheads come together and shared the baby's movement. Such a miracle, this child. After losing the first following Will's death, she never imagined she would be blessed this way. But life has a funny way of working out, as she and Lane had seen.

"I guess we'll find out soon enough what the sweet baby is." She rubbed his hand over her belly. "Coyote's right. I think it'll be any day now."

Lane kissed her temple. "Well, whatever it is, I love it already. And I love its mama and will spend the rest of my life showing you both how much you mean to me." He lifted his gaze to hers. In his eyes, she saw all she ever dreamed of, all she'd ever need or want. "And that's a promise, honey. A Wylder promise from me to you."

"That's the only promise I'll ever need, Lane."

A word about the author...

Sarita Leone loves happy endings—in life and on the page.

When she's not busy writing her next novel, this adventure-loving yoga teacher likes to hike, travel, and dance beneath the stars. She studies languages, enjoys making a mess in the kitchen, and never says "no" to fun.

Finding pockets of peace everywhere she goes, this author plans to make every moment of this journey count.

Thank you for purchasing
this publication of The Wild Rose Press, Inc.

For questions or more information
contact us at
info@thewildrosepress.com.

The Wild Rose Press, Inc.
www.thewildrosepress.com